The Birthday Book

The Birthday Book

In aid of

The Prince's Foundation for Children & the Arts

With a foreword by

HRH The Prince of Wales

Edited by

Michael Morpurgo & Quentin Blake

JONATHAN CAPE • LONDON

THE BIRTHDAY BOOK
A JONATHAN CAPE BOOK 978 0 224 08360 7

Published in Great Britain by Jonathan Cape,
an imprint of Random House Children's Books
A Random House Group Company

This edition published 2008

1 3 5 7 9 10 8 6 4 2

RANDOM HOUSE CHILDREN'S BOOKS
61–63 Uxbridge Road, London W5 5SA

www.kidsatrandomhouse.co.uk
www.rbooks.co.uk

Addresses for companies within The Random House Group Limited can be found at:
www.randomhouse.co.uk/offices.htm

THE RANDOM HOUSE GROUP Limited Reg. No. 954009

A CIP catalogue record for this book is available from the British Library.

Printed and bound in Italy

Contents

I would like to thank all those who have contributed to this book, which has been published to support my Foundation for Children & the Arts. In particular, I would like to thank Michael Morpurgo and Quentin Blake, the book's co-editors, Eleanor Updale and Patrick Janson-Smith, who encouraged us to go ahead with the project, and Random House Children's Books who so kindly agreed to publish it.

I thought that as you have started to read the book, you might also like to learn a little about the reason why I created my Foundation for Children & the Arts and why I am so pleased at how, by buying this book, you are supporting its work in schools around the UK.

It all started when I visited a school for excluded pupils in Birmingham a few years ago. In one class I came across an inspirational teacher who was teaching Shakespeare's Romeo and Juliet to some of the children whose interest and attention had clearly been aroused by the content of the play. On the way home I remembered that Romeo and Juliet was then playing at Stratford-upon-Avon, not far from the school. In my capacity as President of the Royal Shakespeare Company, I got in touch and arranged that the teacher and her class could go together and see it. Sometime later I received some wonderful letters from the teenagers saying that it was the best thing that had ever happened to them and that they had been entertained on stage after the performance by the cast.

This was the seed from which my Foundation for Children & the Arts was born. We are now working with 34,000 children in schools across the UK, giving children a chance to develop confidence, self-esteem and new skills.

The ambition that I have for my Foundation for Children & the Arts is that it should give children, who might never otherwise have this chance, a high quality and sustained introduction to the magical world of the arts. The arts really are a fundamental part of our humanity and I believe that the inspiration, understanding and sheer fun of the arts should be easily available and accessible to every child and, indeed, to everyone in our Country.

Humpty Dumpty

From *Through the Looking-Glass*

Written by LEWIS CARROLL
Illustrated by NICOLA BAYLEY

In this sequel to *Alice's Adventures in Wonderland*, Alice finds herself in a world where her favourite nursery rhymes are come to life – Tweedledum and Tweedledee, the Walrus and the Carpenter, and of course good old Humpty Dumpty! Alice discovers she is a pawn in a gigantic game of chess. Everything in the story is about games and mirrors and tricks of the light. Nothing is what it seems.

Through the Looking-Glass was written more than a hundred years ago but is just as brilliant today as ever it was. Best of all is Humpty Dumpty's invention of the un-birthday present, to celebrate all those days in the year that are not our birthday! When I was little, my mother did this on extra-special occasions. After I grew up and had children of my own, I did the same . . . So, thank you, Humpty Dumpty, and thank you, Alice!

Kate Mosse

Humpty Dumpty

'This conversation is going on a little too fast: let's go back to the last remark but one.'

'I'm afraid I can't quite remember it,' Alice said very politely.

'In that case we may start fresh,' said Humpty Dumpty, 'and it's my turn to choose a subject—' ('He talks about it just as if it was a game!' thought Alice.) 'So here's a question for you. How old did you say you were?'

Alice made a short calculation, and said 'Seven years and six months.'

'Wrong!' Humpty Dumpty exclaimed triumphantly. 'You never said a word like it.'

'I thought you meant "How old *are* you?"' Alice explained.

'If I'd meant that, I'd have said it,' said Humpty Dumpty.

Alice didn't want to begin another argument, so she said nothing.

'Seven years and six months!' Humpty Dumpty repeated thoughtfully. 'An uncomfortable sort of age. Now if you'd asked *my* advice, I'd have said "Leave off at seven" – but it's too late now.'

'I never ask advice about growing,' Alice said indignantly.

'Too proud?' the other enquired.

Alice felt even more indignant at this suggestion. 'I mean,' she said, 'that one ca'n't help growing older.'

'*One* ca'n't, perhaps,' said Humpty Dumpty, 'but *two* can. With proper assistance, you might have left off at seven.'

'What a beautiful belt you've got on!' Alice suddenly remarked. (They had had quite enough of the subject of age, she thought: and if they were really to take turns in choosing subjects, it was her turn

now.) 'At least,' she corrected herself on second thoughts, 'a beautiful cravat, I should have said – no, a belt, I mean – oh, I *beg* your pardon!' she added in dismay, for Humpty Dumpty looked thoroughly offended, and she began to wish she hadn't chosen that subject. 'If only I knew,' she thought to herself, 'which was neck and which was waist!'

Evidently Humpty Dumpty was very angry, though he said nothing for a minute or two. When he *did* speak again, it was in a deep growl.

'It is a – *most* – *provoking* – thing,' he said at last, 'when a person doesn't know a cravat from a belt!'

'I know it's very ignorant of me,' Alice replied, in so humble a tone that Humpty Dumpty relented.

'It's a cravat, child, and a beautiful one, as you say. It's a present from the White King and Queen. There now!'

'Is it really?' said Alice, quite pleased to find she *had* chosen a good subject, after all.

'They gave it me,' Humpty Dumpty continued thoughtfully, as he crossed one knee over the other and clasped his hands round it, '– for an un-birthday present.'

'I beg your pardon?' Alice said with a puzzled air.

'I'm not offended,' said Humpty Dumpty.

'I mean, what *is* an un-birthday present?'

'A present given when it isn't your birthday, of course.'

Alice considered a little. 'I like birthday presents best,' she said at last.

'You don't know what you're talking about!' cried Humpty Dumpty. 'How many days are there in a year?'

'Three hundred and sixty-five,' said Alice.

'And how many birthdays have you?'

'One.'

'And if you take one from three hundred and sixty-five, what remains?'

'Three hundred and sixty-four, of course.'

Humpty Dumpty looked doubtful. 'I'd rather see that done on paper,' he said.

Alice couldn't help smiling as she took out her memorandum-book, and worked the sum for him:

$$
\begin{array}{r}
365 \\
-\ 1 \\
\hline
364
\end{array}
$$

Humpty Dumpty took the book, and looked at it very carefully. 'That *seems* to be done right—' he began.

'You're holding it upside down!' Alice interrupted.

'To be sure I was!' Humpty Dumpty said gaily, as she turned it round for him. 'I thought it looked a little queer. As I was saying, that *seems* to be done right – though I haven't time to look it over thoroughly just now – and that shows that there are three hundred and sixty-four days when you might get un-birthday presents—'

'Certainly,' said Alice.

'And only *one* for birthday presents, you know. There's glory for you!'

'I don't know what you mean by "glory",' Alice said.

Humpty Dumpty smiled contemptuously. 'Of course you don't – till I tell you. I meant "there's a nice knock-down argument for you!"'

'But "glory" doesn't mean "a nice knock-down argument",' Alice objected.

'When *I* use a word,' Humpty Dumpty said in rather a scornful tone, 'it means just what I choose it to mean – neither more nor less.'

'The question is,' said Alice, 'whether you *can* make words mean different things.'

'The question is,' said Humpty Dumpty, 'which is to be master – that's all.'

Alice was too much puzzled to say anything, so after a minute Humpty Dumpty began again. 'They've a temper, some of them – particularly verbs, they're the proudest – adjectives you can do anything with, but not verbs – however, *I* can manage the whole lot! Impenetrability! That's what *I* say!'

'Would you tell me, please,' said Alice, 'what that means?'

'Now you talk like a reasonable child,' said Humpty Dumpty, looking very much pleased. 'I meant by "impenetrability" that we've had enough of that subject, and it would be just as well if you'd mention what you mean to do next, as I suppose you don't intend to stop here all the rest of your life.'

'That's a great deal to make one word mean,' Alice said in a thoughtful tone.

'When I make a word do a lot of work like that,' said Humpty Dumpty, 'I always pay it extra.'

'Oh!' said Alice. She was too much puzzled to make any other remark.

'Ah, you should see 'em come round me of a Saturday night,' Humpty Dumpty went on, wagging his head gravely from side to side: 'for to get their wages, you know.'

(Alice didn't venture to ask what he paid them with; and so you see I can't tell *you*.)

In the Land of the Flibbertigibbets

Written by JOHN FOSTER
Illustrated by EMMA CHICHESTER CLARK

Like Prince Charles, I was a fan of *The Goon Show*, and Spike Milligan's poetry has appealed to me ever since I discovered his *Silly Verse for Kids*. I like both his quirky sense of humour and the way he plays with words in his nonsense poems. So for *The Birthday Book*, I've chosen my poem 'In the Land of the Flibbertigibbets', which was inspired by one of Spike Milligan's nonsense poems, 'In the Land of the Bumbley Boo'.

John Foster

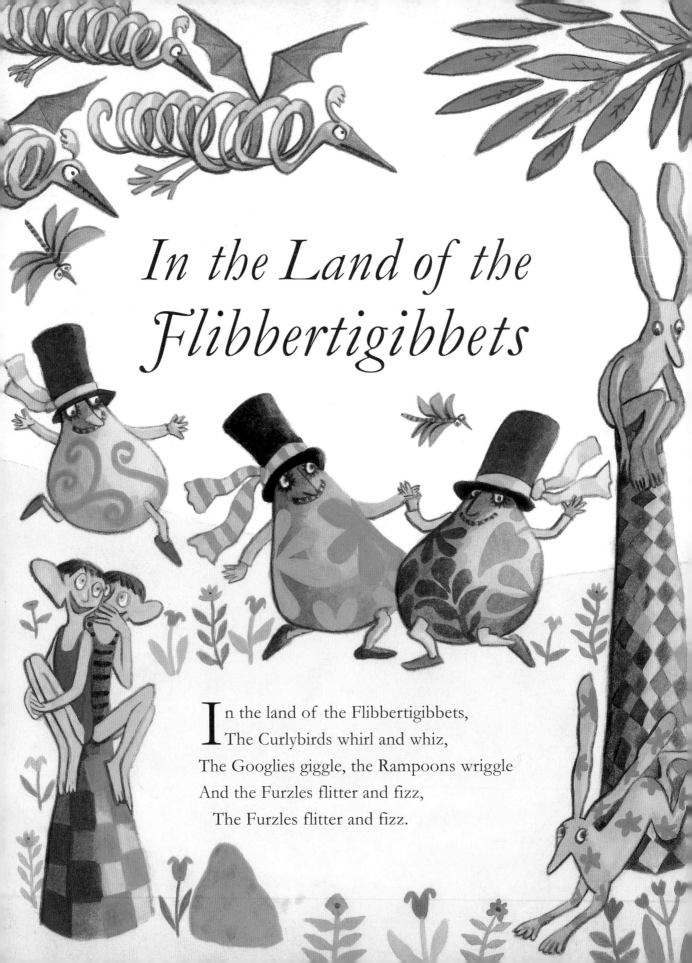

In the Land of the Flibbertigibbets

In the land of the Flibbertigibbets,
The Curlybirds whirl and whiz,
The Googlies giggle, the Rampoons wriggle
And the Furzles flitter and fizz,
The Furzles flitter and fizz.

In the land of the Flibbertigibbets,
The Humdrums simper and sing,
The Bamboozles bump, the Jamborees jump
And the Plimpets zip and ping,
  The Plimpets zip and ping.

In the land of the Flibbertigibbets,
The Dobblers dibble and dive,
The Clutters clatter, the Chitters chatter,
And the Junkets jiggle and jive,
The Junkets jiggle and jive.

Blame the Mouse!

From *Jack Sweettooth*

Written by Malorie Blackman
Illustrated by Emily Gravett

Don't you just love birthdays? I do. Of course, as you get older, time seems to move that much faster so that one birthday appears to rapidly follow another. But when you're a child, a whole year between birthdays seems like an awfully long time. Maybe that's part of the reason why children seem to appreciate birthdays more than adults. With *Jack Sweettooth*, I wanted to write a story about a birthday that affects the whole family, including Jack, the pet mouse. Now, I have to admit, I'm not a great lover of mice, so I'm afraid I would probably behave rather like Shani and Matthew's mum. But I hope that, like her, I'd have the grace to admit when I'd been wrong – even to a mouse!

Malorie Blackman

13

Blame the Mouse!

EIGHT O'CLOCK

Hi! I'm Jackson Winstanley Sweettooth the seventy-third – or Jack for short – at your service!

I live with Mr Bailey, Mrs Bailey, Matthew and Shani, in this house.

Mr Bailey likes me. 'As long as he doesn't run over my feet!'

Shani is very fond of me. 'Jack is great fun!'

Matthew loves me. 'Jack is my best friend.'

Mrs Bailey . . . isn't too keen! 'Keep that smelly, horrible creature away from me!'

Never mind! It's Shani's birthday today and I intend to be extra-super-duper helpful. I shall prove to Mrs Bailey that she's all wrong about me!

EIGHT FIFTEEN

'AARRGH! No one move. No one *breathe*! The ruby has fallen out of my eternity ring. AARRGH!' shrieked Mrs Bailey.

'I've been telling you for ages to go and get your ring fixed, dear,' sighed Mr Bailey.

Mrs Bailey fell to her knees and started sweeping her hands back and forth over the grey carpet. 'Come on, you lot! No breakfast until my ruby is found!'

'But that could take ages,' said Matthew, his stomach rumbling.

'Then the sooner you start helping, the sooner we can all eat,' said Mrs Bailey.

Matthew walked over to me. 'Come on, Jack,' he whispered. 'If anyone can find Mum's ruby, you can.'

He let me out of my cage and put me on the carpet. Here was my chance to shine! This was my chance to show Mrs Bailey that I, Jackson Winstanley Sweettooth the seventy-third, could be *useful*!

I was soon on the job! Sniffing here and searching there and keeping my eyes peeled. I ran everywhere – over the videos and under the sofa and between the books on the floor, until . . .

'EEEK! Who let that nasty, disgusting creature out of its cage?' screamed Mrs Bailey.

'I thought Jack could help us,' said Matthew.

'Help us! HELP US! I bet that . . . that . . . mouse has *swallowed* my ruby by now!' said Mrs Bailey.

'But, Mum . . .' Shani protested.

'Jack wouldn't do that,' said Matthew.

'Dear, I really think . . .' began Mr Bailey.

But Mrs Bailey wasn't having any of it.

'Matthew, put that animal back in its cage. We're all going round to the vet's,' said Mrs Bailey. 'I just know that rodent has eaten my ruby!'

15

So we all left the house and got into the car and off we went to the vet's.

NINE FORTY-FIVE

EIGHT FORTY-FIVE

'Has Jack had any breakfast this morning?' The vet scratched her head.

'None of us has had any breakfast this morning,' muttered Mr Bailey.

Mrs Bailey elbowed her husband in the ribs.

'No,' said Matthew, 'Jack hasn't eaten anything since yesterday evening.'

'Good. That makes it easier. If Jack has swallowed the ruby from your mum's eternity ring it will show up nicely on the X-rays,' said the vet.

I was put under a huge machine which clanged and rumbled and whirled. There was a sudden loud buzzing sound, but it didn't hurt at all – and then it was all over.

Five minutes later, the vet came out into the waiting room, where we were all sitting. Guess what?

'Sorry, Mrs Bailey,' said the vet. 'I don't know where your ruby is, but it's *not* in Jack's stomach.'

Huh! I could've told you that! I thought.

So we all drove home again.

NINE FIFTEEN

'I guess my ruby has gone for good,' Mrs Bailey sighed unhappily once we were home.

'Never mind, dear,' said Mr Bailey, giving her a hug. 'I'm sure it will turn up.'

'Mum, what about my birthday party?' said Shani. 'All my friends will be here at three.'

'Never mind your birthday party! What about breakfast?' said Matthew.

'OK! OK!' said Mr Bailey. 'I'll make breakfast. You two go and make your beds and tidy your rooms until I call you.'

Off went Matthew, huffing and puffing and mumbling about his breakfast. I was pretty hungry myself!

Mr Bailey made bacon and beans on toast for breakfast and Matthew sneaked me some. It was most excellently tasty!

After breakfast, Mrs Bailey started making Shani's birthday cake.

Meanwhile Shani and Matthew made all kinds of sandwiches: banana and bacon, ham and mustard, cheese and raspberry jam, strawberries and sugar, egg and pickle. Then they put lots of different kinds of cakes and mini Swiss rolls and pizza slices on lots of different-sized plates.

And I watched the whole thing from Matthew's shirt pocket. It all looked yumptious! Matthew even managed to slip me a bit of a strawberry and sugar sandwich. Scrumptious!

ELEVEN O'CLOCK

'Come on then, Shani, Matthew. Time to go to the hairdresser's,' said Mrs Bailey. She turned to her husband. 'Paul, can you keep an eye on the birthday cake and take it out of the oven when it's cooked?'

'Of course, dear,' smiled Mr Bailey. He hates going to the hairdresser's!

'Shani, you can have your hair styled, and, Matthew, you can have yours cut,' said Mrs Bailey.

So off we went.

When we reached the hairdressing salon, it was jam-packed solid full of people. Almost every sink had someone's head leaned backwards over it. Each hairdryer had someone sitting under it. We had to wait a while, but then Shani was taken off by one hairdresser and Matthew was led away by another. It wasn't too bad, until . . .

A woman under a hairdryer started the commotion.

'EEEK! A MOUSE!' she screamed. 'AARRGH! HELP!'

The man beside her flung his newspaper in the air and leaped out of his chair. But he forgot that the hairdryer was still over his head. His head hit the inside of the hairdryer with a loud THWACK!

Then the man slid back down into his seat. I think he knocked himself out.

Meanwhile a man wearing perm rods leaped onto his chair, yelling,

'A MOUSE! A MOUSE!'

By this time, all the other grown-ups were joining in. They were dashing here, there and everywhere. They fell over each other, yelling and screaming. Some leaped over chairs in their hurry to get out of the salon. One woman fainted and dropped to the floor like a stone.

It was worse than sports day at Shani and Matthew's school! Another woman ran into the loo and locked the door, screaming,

'Call the police! Call an ambulance! Call my husband! AARRGH! A MOUSE!'

Shani came rushing over. 'Matthew, you idiot! You didn't let Jack go, did you?'

But before Matthew could answer, Mrs Bailey appeared to stand in front of Shani and Matthew, her hands folded across her chest. Lightning bolts flashed from her eyes.

'I want a few words with you, Matthew!' she said stonily.

TWELVE O'CLOCK

'I didn't do it, Mum,' Matthew said immediately. 'Honest I didn't.'

'Why did you let that dreadful mouse loose?' Mrs Bailey asked. 'That wasn't very funny.'

'Mum, I didn't—' Matthew started.

'Of all the daft, pea-brained—' began Mrs Bailey.

'But, Mum, it couldn't have been Jack,' Matthew said. 'Jack's in—'

'Not another word,' Mrs Bailey interrupted.

'Oh dear! I'm so sorry, Mrs Bailey. I really must apologize.' One of the hairdressers came running up.

Mrs Bailey looked surprised. 'Apologize? For what, Sam?'

Sam hopped from foot to foot, looking very embarrassed. 'Er . . . it's just that . . . all week they've been knocking down that old cinema a few doors down. And the place was infested with hundreds of mice. They've been running through all the shops in the high street. I'm sorry if they scared you. We are trying our best to get rid of them.'

'Mice! You mean this salon is full of mice?' Mrs Bailey stared.

'That's what I was trying to tell you, Mum,' said Matthew. 'It couldn't have been Jack. Jack is still in my pocket.

See!'

'Oh!' said Mrs Bailey. 'Matthew, I'm sorry, I didn't let you explain.'

And then Mrs Bailey gave me a really strange look.

We stayed in the hairdresser's until Shani had had her hair styled and Matthew had got his hair cut.

Then Mrs Bailey drove us home. And I didn't see a single mouse the entire time. What a shame! I would've liked to say hello to some of my cousins!

ONE FIFTEEN

There it sat, on the kitchen table. It was perfect! It was stupendous! It was the best, the most wonderful, the most rumptious, the most delectably delicious birthday cake Mrs Bailey had ever made.

'I'm brilliant!' smiled Mrs Bailey.

'I was the one who took it out of the oven,' said Mr Bailey. 'That's where all the skill was needed!'

When the cake had cooled, Mrs Bailey poured *tons* of chocolate icing all over it.

'Oh, Jack! Look at that!' Matthew breathed. 'I bet . . . I bet, if I had a teeny-tiny, itsy-bitsy little bit, no one would ever know!'

Uh-oh! I thought. Uh-oh! And my whiskers started to quiver – a sure sign of TROUBLE!

TWO O'CLOCK

'Mum! MUM! Look at this!' Shani yelled from the kitchen.

We all came running.

'Look!' Shani pointed to her birthday cake. And there, in the side of it, was a hole . . .

'Matthew, have you been letting that repulsive, revolting rodent nibble at your sister's cake?' Mrs Bailey glared at me with beady eyes.

I went hot – from the end of my tail to the tips of my whiskers.

'I'm waiting, Matthew,' said Mrs Bailey.

'I . . . I . . .' Matthew spluttered.

And as Mrs Bailey continued to scowl at me, I could feel myself getting hotter and hotter.

'Wait a minute, Mum,' said Shani. She prodded at the hole in the cake with her fork. 'There's a whole lot more missing from this cake than just a hole! And someone's tried to disguise it by smearing over the chocolate icing to cover it up!'

Shani prodded the cake from the top, as well as the side. 'There's a whole slice gone!' she said.

Mrs Bailey turned to Matthew. 'As far as I know, mice can't cut *slices* out of birthday cakes!' she said.

'I . . . I . . .' Matthew stammered.

'You greedy, toad-faced gannet!' Shani pouted. 'It was *you* who cut a slice out of my birthday cake. And there was Mum blaming poor Jack!'

'Matthew? Did you take some of your sister's cake?' asked Mrs Bailey.

'Yes, Mum.' Matthew hung his head.

I glanced up at Mrs Bailey. There! You see! I didn't do it! I thought.

And Mrs Bailey watched me, a strange expression on her face.

TWO THIRTY

Matthew's mum and dad discussed whether or not Matthew should be allowed at his sister's party.

'It's up to you, Shani,' they decided.

'Oh, all right then. You can come, Matthew.

But if you take so much as a crumb off this table before my party starts . . .'

'Thanks, Shani!' Matthew grinned gratefully.

'I mean it, Matthew!'

'I won't. I promise,' Matthew said quickly.

'Hmm!' said Mr Bailey.

'Hmm!' said Mrs Bailey.

'Hmm!' said Shani. 'You'd better not!'

Still in disgrace, Matthew was sent to wash his hands and face before the party.

'Oh dear!' Matthew sighed to me. 'I shouldn't have done it, but I couldn't resist it! That cake looked so tempting!'

I burrowed down into Matthew's shirt pocket. I'd had enough of being blamed for everything for one day!

Matthew closed the bathroom door. He fished me out of his pocket and let me run over the bathroom floor, the way he always does.

'It wasn't my fault,' Matthew muttered. 'That cake was calling to me, *teasing* me.'

I ran back and forth and up and down, stretching my legs.

And then I saw a strange thing. A gleaming, glinting, strange thing, winking at me from the tiny space between the bath tub and the bathroom cupboard. I nudged my nose closer to it and there it was! Mrs Bailey's ruby!

I squeezed myself into the teeny-tiny space and started to nose out the ruby.

'What are you up to, Jack?' asked Matthew.

'Squeeek!' I said. 'Squeeeek!'

And I carried on pushing at the ruby with my nose until it was out in the open.

'SQUEEEEEK!' I said.

Matthew picked me up and put me back in his shirt pocket. He bent over to see what I'd been doing. Then he saw it. His mum's gleaming, glinting ruby. He snatched it up.

'Mum! MUM!' Matthew shouted.

Mrs Bailey came running. So did Shani and Mr Bailey.

'What is it? What's the matter?' asked Mrs Bailey.

'Here it is! Your ruby! Here it is!' Matthew jumped up and down.

'Well done, Matthew!' Mrs Bailey kissed Matthew's cheek.

Matthew looked at his mum. Then he took me out of his pocket. 'I . . . I didn't do it, Mum,' said Matthew. 'Jack found it. He pushed it out from between the cupboard and the bath tub.'

Mrs Bailey gave me another strange look. A long, slow, very strange look. Then she did something she'd *never* done before. Very slowly, very carefully, she picked me up and sat me in the palm of her hand.

'Thank you, Jack,' smiled Mrs Bailey, using my proper name for the first time ever. 'I've blamed you for everything that went wrong today. I think I've always been too hard on you and I'm really sorry. I'll try to make it up to you.'

And she did!

THREE O'CLOCK
I got some of *everything* from
Shani's birthday party – and Mrs Bailey
made me my very own birthday cake, even
though it wasn't my birthday.

Double rumptious-yumptious-scrumptious!
It's so nice to be appreciated!

Bobby Bailey's Brown Bread Birthday

Written by ELEANOR UPDALE
Illustrated by POSY SIMMONDS

How can this be? A story for the Prince of Wales that makes fun of the simple life? What's 'Bobby Bailey's Brown Bread Birthday' doing in this book? Well, I'm trusting that Prince Charles's sense of humour is as strong as his love of organic farming, and that he'll understand that I'm really teasing people who are slaves to fashion. I hope this story will make him smile on his own special day. Bobby Bailey loves his mother, but she does sometimes go over the top, and Bobby is worried that she will embarrass him at his birthday party. I can't imagine that the Prince of Wales has ever suffered from, or been, an embarrassing parent. I wonder whether he will ever tell us . . .

Eleanor Updale

Bobby Bailey's Brown Bread Birthday

Bobby Bailey's mother had always been at the height of fashion. Over the years Bobby had suffered many embarrassments. His mother had turned up to collect him from school with red spiky hair and a purple leather jacket saying BABE in silver glitter on the back. She had gone to a parents' evening with her tummy sticking out of a tiny T-shirt, showing off a jewel in her belly button and the word BOBBY tattooed up her spine. When she came to support the football team, Bobby had looked the other way as the high heels on her shiny red shoes sank into the mud at the side of the pitch; and he had hidden out of earshot when she joined in the karaoke competition at the summer fair.

But her latest craze was different. Now she was into health food, recycling and the Simple Life. All the carpets in their house had been torn up to expose the splintery floorboards. The bright curtains were gone, and dark wooden shutters had been specially made to cover the windows. The expensive kitchen, with its steel surfaces and electric machines, had been replaced with one that looked old and cheap – though it was actually new, and had cost just as much. These days, Bobby's mother wouldn't dream of buying the ready-made microwave meals Bobby had grown up on. She cooked everything herself. She walked round food shops complaining loudly about chemicals, peering through the thick glasses that had replaced her contact lenses to read the small print on every label. At home, now that she had got rid of the telly, she spent the evenings in a rocking chair knitting clothes for Bobby.

Bobby's mother was very proud of herself. But she couldn't knit very well, and Bobby cringed as he set off to walk to school in a lumpy jumper with one sleeve longer than the other (and both of them too long for him). She had made him a balaclava which was very warm – but the spaces for the eyes were too far apart, so he had to choose one hole to look through and hook the other over his ear to keep it in place. He ended up with one blind eye and one cold ear, while his breath made the inside of the hat slimy and wet. And everything was very, very itchy.

His mother's cooking wasn't any better. She tried hard, but did it all with just a little too much enthusiasm. She had started making her own bread – solid brown wholemeal lumps the shape and weight of bricks. The loaves smelled nice when they first came out of the new rustic oven. But once they cooled down you had to saw away with a very sharp knife to cut them into slices, and then chew for ages before the bread was soft enough to swallow.

But Bobby knew it wasn't worth complaining. His mother simply wouldn't take any notice. She was in love with her new way of life.

There was one compensation. Hardly any of Bobby's friends knew what was going on. To combat Global Warming, his mother had stopped driving him to school. Even if she had walked with him (which she didn't, because she was too busy doing the washing by hand), they wouldn't have recognized her. His rock-chick mum was now a dowdy woman in spectacles, with mousy hair scragged back into a ponytail. She dressed in baggy skirts run up on an old sewing machine, with droopy woollen tights and sensible shoes.

So most of the time Bobby could carry on as if nothing had changed, and in the company of his friends he led his old life. Lots of them had turned ten recently, and he had gone to their parties – fighting with lasers and paintballs, bowling, swimming, eating hamburgers and glugging fizzy drinks. But now humiliation loomed. His own birthday was coming up, and to his horror his mother wanted him to have a party too. Bobby couldn't bear the idea of his classmates seeing the inside of his house and eating his mother's terrible food.

'There's no need, Mum,' he said, trying to put her off. 'Maybe we could just give a donation to charity or something. I'm sure everyone would understand.'

'That's really thoughtful of you, darling,' said Bobby's mother. 'But I can't let you suffer because of my principles. And we must return all the hospitality you have had from your friends. Besides, I see a party as a great opportunity.'

Bobby was worried. 'An opportunity for what?' he asked.

'An opportunity to show them the good sense of living simply,' said Bobby's mother. 'When they go home and tell their families what a lovely time they've had here, everyone will want to be like us.'

So Bobby's mother started making invitations – hand written on recycled cardboard, and hand delivered on a weary trudge round the cold winter streets. She might have ignored Bobby's plea to go without a party, but she did take up his other idea. The invitations said, in big letters, NO PRESENTS, PLEASE, and suggested a few charities that might welcome donations. Bobby's heart sank even further.

When his birthday finally came, Bobby gloomily helped with the party preparations. He chopped carrots and celery into little strips. He weighed out brown flour and brown sugar, and sliced brown bread for brown sandwiches. Most of the pictures in his mother's health-food cookbooks were pretty appetizing. There were some lovely glossy spiced buns he was really looking forward to trying. But when they came out of his mother's oven, they were unrecognizable – hard brown lumps with black burned raisins sticking out across the tops. The home-made lemon drink made Bobby shudder, and the big birthday cake included some sort of healthy chocolate-substitute that seemed to have gone a bit wrong. It wasn't the right shade at all. Layers of light-brown sponge were stuck together with sludge-coloured butter cream in a sloping construction topped with greyish icing. There were nuts on the top, but for once Bobby didn't feel tempted to steal one.

Instead of buying packets of crisps Bobby's mother was frying

slices of parsnip, turnip and swede. In the book they looked golden and tasty. In the kitchen they were soggy and brown. Bobby's mother's glasses were fogging up as she leaned over the hot stove making batch after batch of them.

'These will do everyone a power of good,' she said, heaping them onto a plate. 'Who needs all that artificially flavoured, mass-produced muck, anyway?'

The doorbell rang. *Oh no*, thought Bobby. *They're early. I'm doomed.* In just a few minutes he would become a laughing stock. The others would tease him for months to come. Perhaps for ever.

'Get that, darling,' said his mother, taking off her apron hurriedly.

Bobby felt sick as he opened the door – and not just because he had eaten one of the turnip 'crisps'.

But it wasn't one of his friends. It was worse than that. It was his Auntie Jo, his mother's younger sister.

'Happy birthday, Bobby,' she said as she stumbled into the house

under the weight of a very big bag and her small fluffy white dog. 'Don't look so miserable. You're having a party.' Then she bent down to kiss him and whispered, 'I've come to help.'

Bobby's mother had always criticized Auntie Jo. She thought her sister wasn't cool enough – never up with the latest trends. But in some ways that was useful. It gave Bobby's mother someone to dump her old clothes on every time she lurched into a new fad. So today Auntie Jo was dressed in tight jeans, a sequinned top and a fake-fur jacket. She was as loud and gushing as her sister had once been. Some of her bright red lipstick came off on Bobby's cheek as she kissed him. It was the same colour as her shoes – the very high heels that had disappeared into the soft sports field only a year before. *Oh no*, thought Bobby, seeing this reminder of his mother's last trend. *Two of them. Everyone's going to see Mum and Auntie Jo.* He didn't know which was more embarrassing.

Auntie Jo tottered towards her sister, who was frantically fiddling with the food. 'Why don't you slip upstairs and get yourself ready?' she said. 'I can finish here.' She guided Bobby's mother to the stairs. 'Just straighten your clothes and brush your hair, love,' she added, knowing that her sister wouldn't be putting on make-up this year. 'You go too, Bobby. You need to get that lipstick off your face. I'll lay the table. Take your time. I'll call you if anyone comes.'

She went into the kitchen and locked the door. When Bobby and his mother came back downstairs, they could hear her banging about inside. Eventually she let them in. Bobby was amazed. Auntie Jo had managed to make the table look good. The plates of brown food were artistically arranged with bright carrots, tomatoes and pieces of fruit in between. And instead of the dull woven placemats Bobby's mother had put out, the table was covered with huge white sheets, hanging right down to the floor.

'I was going to bring a plastic tablecloth,' said Auntie Jo, 'but I thought these would be more eco-friendly.' Bobby's mother looked pleased.

There was another ring at the door. This time it really was the first of the guests. They hadn't read the invitation properly, and had brought a gift. As Bobby said a heartfelt 'thank you' for the construction kit, his mother embarrassed him with some sharp words about plastic. Then she made it worse by talking about wasted resources as she stuffed the wrapping paper in the recycling.

More children arrived. Bobby's mother took them all down one end of the room. 'We're going to have some good old-fashioned party games,' she said. 'Jo, you organize everyone. I'll play the piano.'

And so Bobby's mother sat with her back to the children thumping out some tunes as Auntie Jo led everyone in Musical Chairs and

Musical Bumps. The visitors weren't impressed. They played Pass the Parcel with a package wrapped entirely in old newspaper. When Bobby's mother stopped playing as each layer was torn off, she nagged them to make sure that the paper went into the recycling box. At the end of the long game the poor winner was disappointed to find that the prize was an apple. Auntie Jo's little dog got in the way, bobbing about among the children and jumping up on them with too much affection, especially when they were playing Musical Statues and trying to keep still. No one was happy, even though Bobby's mother kept shouting out things like, 'This is better than that disco rubbish!' and 'Hooray for the good old ways!'

Bobby was crushed. And while he was worrying about what they all thought of his mother, he glimpsed two of his best friends giggling at Auntie Jo prancing around in her tarty clothes. Then he saw Auntie Jo pick up his mother's glasses from the top of the piano. She put them in her pocket. He wondered why she'd done that, but before he could say anything, his mother stood up, closed the piano and declared: 'Right! It's time for a good healthy tea!'

Bobby's friends were polite, well-behaved children, but even so he caught some of them rolling their eyes to the ceiling or nudging each other as they settled down at the table. His mother was distracted, looking for her glasses. Auntie Jo pretended to help her, which Bobby thought was a bit funny, since he knew they were in her pocket.

Eventually, Auntie Jo gave up. 'You can see well enough to play the piano, can't you, dear?' she asked Bobby's mother.

'Oh yes, I don't need to read music,' she said smugly. 'I could play blindfold if I had to. I know all those old tunes by heart.'

'Then let me look after the table while you play some more for us,' said Auntie Jo. 'It will make the party go with a swing.'

Bobby heard one of his guests stifle a giggle, and he put his head in his hands. When he looked up, he saw Auntie Jo cradling her little dog in her arms and feeding him one of the hard brown buns. The dog seemed to like it. Auntie Jo was nodding in a funny way, as if she was trying to signal something to Bobby. Then he worked out what she meant. She wanted him to look under the table. He thought she must have dropped something, so he got down on his hands and knees and lifted up the sheet.

It took a moment for his eyes to adjust to the dark, but then he began to take in what was under there. Something was stuck to the underside of the table. Lots of things. All sorts of strange shapes. He remembered when the big farm-style table had been delivered, only a few weeks before. The men had carried it in sideways to get it through the door, and Bobby had seen what it looked like underneath. It was smooth then. There weren't any lumps and bumps. This was very strange.

A string had been tied round one of the table legs, and dangling from it was a torch. Bobby turned it on and shone the beam of light around him. Auntie Jo had certainly been busy. As he looked up, he could see packets of crisps, sausages, popcorn, bars of chocolate, sweets, lollipops and cartons of juice. And in the middle, strapped on with thicker tape, was a small metal box. Bobby examined it by the light of the torch. It was a DVD player. He pulled at the lid and the screen opened out. He looked around guiltily. No one could see him. The flaps of the sheets made the space under the table into a perfect little den. He could see feet, in pairs, poking beneath the edge of the cloth. He recognized the shoes of his best friend, Sam, and tapped on them until he had his attention. Sam's face appeared under the sheet.

'Wow!' he shouted before Bobby had time to shush him quiet.

'Come down,' said Bobby. 'Bring Harry.'

Sam pressed a button on the DVD player, and it lit up. A silent film started running. It was an old black-and-white comedy about two men trying to decorate a room. The boys lay on the floor watching the film and stuffing their mouths with goodies. By chance, Bobby's mother's piano music fitted the film perfectly. As she played *London Bridge Is*

Falling Down, the fat man knocked over a ladder, and when paint dripped from a can, she started *There's a Hole in My Bucket*. Under the table, the children couldn't stop laughing, and the others, still sitting up with the brown food, realized that something interesting was happening down on the floor.

One by one they all joined Bobby, and devoured the secret sweets. Jade, who was the last to brave it, brought the news that Auntie Jo was still giving some of the official birthday food to her dog, and putting the rest into a big black plastic bag. The children could see her red high heels dancing round the table. They all laughed and laughed.

Then, suddenly, the music stopped.

They heard Bobby's mother's voice. 'Jo, have you found my glasses yet?'

Bobby saw the thick straps of his mother's sturdy sandals approaching, and he switched off the DVD. Children were still giggling. His mother was bound to discover them.

Just in time, Auntie Jo shouted back, 'Sorry. No sign of them. But everybody's having such a wonderful time. Don't stop playing. They're loving it.'

The sandals stopped, turned and moved back towards the piano.

'It's lovely to hear them all having such fun,' said Bobby's mother. 'You see? The simple things are best. I told you so. Just one more song, and then we'll have the cake.'

As Bobby's mother struck up with *Oranges and Lemons*, Auntie Jo lifted one side of the sheet, and the children climbed out: hot, glowing and buzzing with sugar. They rearranged themselves in their seats just in time. Bobby's mother played *Happy Birthday* and Auntie Jo carried the cake to the table. It looked even less appealing than before. 'Only one candle, I see,' she said, winking at the children. 'Best not to be wasteful.'

Bobby blew out the flame with a single puff. He looked round at his friends. Some of them seemed rather ill. Auntie Jo's junk food was beginning to take effect in their bloodstreams. He feared that Sam might be about to be sick. He knew that no one would be able to face the concrete cake.

'Mummy,' he said, in his best little good-boy voice. 'Mummy, we've all had so much already. Perhaps with so many starving people in the world it would be wrong to have cake as well.'

Sam realized that Bobby was trying to save them all from a horrible experience, so he chimed in, 'Oh, yes. I'm full, and my little brother was really jealous of me coming to a party. Do you think I could possibly take my piece home to him, instead?'

There was a catch of emotion in Bobby's mother's voice as she replied. 'Oh, Sam,' she said. 'I can't tell you what it means to me to hear you say that. Normally after a party everyone is too hyper to think at all, let alone to consider others. You see what good food and wholesome, old-fashioned fun can do?'

Auntie Jo interrupted. 'I'll cut up the cake and wrap it in newspaper for them to take home, dear. Why don't you play some more music while I tidy up?'

So there was one more game at the far end of the room while Auntie Jo packed the evidence of what had really been going on into her bin bag. When she was quite sure that she had cleared everything away, she took the spectacles out of her pocket.

'Here they are!' she cried, as if she had just found them in the debris of the party. Bobby's mother put them on, and was pleased to see the children properly at last, especially as they all looked so happy.

Parents began to arrive to collect their children. Bobby's mother couldn't resist the chance to give each of them a little lecture about using their cars unnecessarily, and to offer the recipe for the cake the children were clutching as they left. She praised them all for their good behaviour, and told the parents that it was all because of the plain, healthy food she had given them to eat.

As if to prove her point, the children each said a charming 'thank you'. And they really meant it when they said it had been one of the best parties ever. They had indeed had lots of fun hiding under the table, watching the film and eating sweets – even if they were beginning to realize that they would have tummy aches later.

As the door closed behind the last guest, Auntie Jo whispered to Bobby, 'The DVD player is still taped to the table. The charger is hidden behind the dustbins. It's up to you to find a new hiding place. It's your birthday present from me.'

'Thank you, Auntie Jo,' said Bobby, giving her a hug. 'I can't bear to think what the party would have been like if you hadn't come.'

'Well, I know that your mum can go over the top sometimes,' said Auntie Jo. 'She's always a bit too dedicated in the early days of one of her fads, and she's never been much of a cook. And I also know how cruel children can be if you're a bit different. That's why I stepped in to help today. But she does have a point, you know. You shouldn't eat junk food all the time.'

'Right now I wouldn't mind if I never saw a bag of sweets again,' said Bobby.

'Well, remember how that feels,' said Auntie Jo, 'and next week I'll take you to a wholefood café where everything tastes good. Maybe between the two of us your mother and I can find a middle way.'

Auntie Jo picked up her bin bag and called her dog, who lumbered up sleepily after his health-food feast. 'I'd better be getting home,' she said. 'I'll drop this lot off at the recycling centre on my way.'

'Thank you, Jo,' said Bobby's mother. 'I'm glad to see you taking an interest in the environment at last. You're always that little bit behind me, but you usually get there in the end.'

'That's right,' said Jo, winking at Bobby again. 'You never know — this time next year I may be baking my own bread.'

'Oh good,' said Bobby. 'I'll look forward to tasting it.' Then he kissed Auntie Jo on the cheek and whispered with a smile, 'But who can say what Mum will be doing by then?'

'All Right'

From *Crummy Mummy and Me*

Written by ANNE FINE
Illustrated by MICK MANNING & BRITA GRANSTRÖM

My heroine, Minna, comes from a somewhat mixed-up family. There is her hippy mother, whom she teases as 'Crummy Mummy'; Mum's easy-going boyfriend, 'Crusher Maggot'; and her baby half-sister, 'Crummy Dummy'. Seven short stories make up the book *Crummy Mummy and Me*, and in them we learn a very great deal about what happens when you're only ten years old but still by far the most sensible and foresighted person in your house.

Birthdays so often bring the past to mind. If you're no longer living with both of the parents you started with, then it can easily set you thinking. And that's exactly what is happening here . . .

Anne Fine

'All Right'

Meeting Crusher's old father that day set me off wondering about my own dad. It's not as if I've ever seen that much of him. In fact, there were times I could barely recall what he looked like. I knew he worked in a big garage about a hundred and fifty miles down the motorway, but whenever I asked Mum anything more about him, she only said:

'Oh, he's all right.'

It isn't much to build on, is it?

'Well, is he *good-looking*?'

'He looks all right.'

'Is he *intelligent*?'

'His brain works all right.'

'Is he *amusing*?'

'He made me laugh all right, I suppose.'

'Is he *kind*?'

'He was always all right with me and the cats.'

I lost my temper then.

'If he was never any better than *all right*,' I snapped, 'why did you bother to have *me*?'

Mum laughed, and stretched out her hand to stroke my hair.

'Oh, *you*,' she said. 'You're all right, too, you are.'

You see? Hopeless. Absolutely hopeless. So I gave up.

But then, a few days later in school, we started something new: a project on Families. Mr Russell told everyone to be quiet, and then he tossed up to see whether we were to start with mothers or fathers. And fathers won, so fathers it was.

'I haven't got one,' Andrew said.

'Neither have I.'

'Mine's in Australia.'

'Lucky you!'

Then Mr Russell told everyone to be quiet again.

'If you haven't got your own, real, original, biological father,' he said, 'pick out the person who comes closest. Pick someone . . .' He paused, and waved his hands around in the air, searching for an example. 'Pick someone you would ask to fix your bike.'

'I haven't got a bike,' said Joel.

'My mum always fixes my bike,' said Sarah.

'I *asked* my dad to fix my bike,' grumbled Arif. 'Six weeks ago! He hasn't even *looked* at it yet.' He scowled, and added with real bitterness: '*And* he's my own, real, original, biological dad.'

'My uncle fixes my bike. He's got a bike shop.'

'Nothing has ever gone wrong with my bike.'

'I've never even had a bike,' Joel said sadly.

'At least you've got a father,' said Andrew.

Joel was just telling us he thought he'd much prefer a bike, when Mr Russell told everyone to be quiet again.

'Father,' he said. 'Or someone like it. I want a picture or a photograph, and two whole sides of writing, by Friday.'

We all groaned loudly. And by the time Mr Russell had told everyone to be quiet again, the bell had rung.

I ran off home.

Mum was leaning against the draining-board. She was wearing her plum-coloured plastic boots and her fishnet stockings. She was fiddling with her tarantula earrings. Crusher Maggot was slouching at the kitchen table, wearing funny dark glasses and playing a tune on his skull with his knuckles.

What do they *do* all day long when I'm away at school, that's what I'd like to know.

I asked Mum:

'Do you have a photo of my real dad?'

'Yes,' she said. 'No. I don't know. No. Yes.'

I do try to be very patient.

'Which?' I said. 'Yes or no?'

'Both, really,' she replied. 'I do have a photo of him, yes. But I'm afraid that my left elbow got in front of most of his face, and what little of him shows is terribly blurry. You'd never know that it was him.'

'Weren't there any other photos?'

Mum tipped her head on one side to think. One of the tarantula earrings crawled over her cheek, and the other got tangled in her hair.

It was very off-putting.

'There were some others,' she recalled. 'But you were in them, too, so he took those with him.'

I thought that was a little daft, myself. One of them might have realized I would grow up, and want to see them. But, still as patient as could be, I asked:

'Where is this famous photo of part of his blurred face and your left elbow?'

'I'm not sure,' Mum said. 'I think I've lost it.'

(I simply can't *think* why they call it 'home' work. I'd stand a better chance of getting it done on the *moon*.)

'I need a photo,' I told her, 'to take to school.'

'Take that nice one of Crusher,' she told me.

I'm too kind and polite to point out there is no such thing. In the only one I've seen, his hair is in flaming red and orange spikes, his teeth ferociously bared, and his tattoo is showing.

'No, thank you,' I answered as politely as possible. 'I'd like one of my own, real, original, biological father.'

'All right,' said Crusher. 'Suit yourself. I'll ask him for one next time I see him.'

I turned and stared.

'*See* him?' I said. 'Do you get to see him?'

'Quite often,' Crusher said. 'I always fill up with petrol at his garage. Why, I stopped in and had a couple of words with him only a week ago.'

I was amazed. Simply amazed.

'How is he?' I asked. 'How is my very own, real, original, biological father?'

Crusher wasn't at all irritated by this display of crippling sarcasm.

'All right,' he said. 'He was all right.'

But Mum was a little put out by my rudeness.

'Original and biological he may be,' she said. 'But who fixes your bike?'

(I'd really like to know where they pick up all this fix-your-bike business.)

I was still angry.

'Next time,' I said, as cold as ice, 'next time that someone drops in to have a few words with my own, real, original, biological father, do you think they might possibly bother to mention it to me?'

'I'll do better than that,' Crusher offered. 'I have to go down there anyway so I'll take you with me.'

'When?'

'Whenever you like.'

I thought about it.

'I need the photo before Friday,' I told him.

'Tomorrow, then.'

'*All right*,' I said. 'Tomorrow. *All right*.'

So that's how it came about that the very next day I borrowed next door's fancy new camera, and Crusher borrowed the other side's car since his own wasn't going, and I travelled with him all the way down the motorway. It meant I had to take the whole afternoon off school. Mum said it didn't matter since I'd be doing school work in taking the photo, but I didn't dare tell that one to Mr Russell. That sort of thinking really annoys him. He calls it 'slack'. I did consider trying to explain, but he was in one of his terribly busy moods, and in the end I just did what everyone else in the class does, and told him that I had to go to the dentist.

It took Crusher and me exactly two hours and forty minutes to drive down the motorway as far as the garage.

It was a big one, set back a little from the road. There were several lines of pumps, and every one of them was busy with people filling cars and motorbikes.

Crusher pulled up beside the air and water.

'Tell you what,' he suggested, picking next door's fancy new camera off the back seat and thrusting it into my hands. 'I'll give you over to your own, real, original, biological dad, and then I'll nip off for a while and do what I was going to do.'

'What *were* you going to do?' I asked, suddenly suspicious.

First Crusher looked blank, then a little bit shifty.

'I really haven't the time to stop and explain,' he told me.

I gave him a look – one of my *searching* looks.

'You drove all the way down here just to bring me to see my dad, didn't you?' I accused him.

'No, I didn't,' said Crusher.

'Oh yes you did.'

'No, I didn't.'

'You did. I can tell.'

'All right,' said Crusher, embarrassed. '*All right*. Maybe I did, but I certainly didn't drive all this way just to sit in the front seat of the car arguing with you.'

And he got out.

I followed. Crusher was looking round the garage forecourt.

Suddenly he nudged my elbow.

'There,' he said, nodding towards a man in overalls who was bending over a pile of cut-price tyres. 'There he is.'

'Really?'

'Yes. That's him.'

And Crusher bellowed across the crowded forecourt:

'Hey, Bill! *Bill!* Here's your young Minna come to see you!'

The man in overalls lifted his head and stared in our direction. I say 'our' direction, but it was only 'my' direction by then, because Crusher Maggot had disappeared in a flash after making his announcement, and I was left standing alone on the petrol-station forecourt, clutching a camera, and ten yards from my own, real, original, biological father I hadn't seen for ages.

It was all right. In fact, he was jolly nice, really. He gave me tons of comics and free bars of chocolate from the garage shop, and a bunch of flowers for the people next door to make up for my borrowing their camera. He helped me take a lot of photos, and even showed me how to set the time-release button so we could get some of us standing together with his arm round my shoulders. He made me promise to send him copies of all the ones that came out properly, and he laughed like a drain when I told him about the only photo of him that Mum has left.

He asked me quite a lot of questions about our family, and he seemed pretty interested when I told him all about Crummy Dummy. He said he was glad to hear I had company now, and he made me promise to send a photo of her, too. And a good one of Mum.

He asked me about school, and my friends, and the house. He said that he was very pleased to hear I could swim, and he sounded interested in my roller-skating. Then he left someone else looking after the forecourt, and took me for a spin up the motorway in one of the open sports cars parked round the back of the garage.

That was fantastic. The wind blew my hair till it stuck out like Mum's. (He said I looked a bit like Mum, anyway.) He drove miles faster than Crusher Maggot does, and when I told him so, he grinned, and said that he was glad to hear it.

I didn't know quite what to call him. I tried to say the word 'Dad' once or twice, but it sort of got stuck because I didn't know him well enough yet. Then he said: 'Why don't you just call me Bill? Everyone else does.' And that was easier.

When we drove back towards the garage, I could see Crusher standing waiting on the forecourt.

Bill slowed the car right down. And just before we came close enough for Crusher to overhear, he asked me privately:

'Do you get on with him? Is he all right?'

I looked at Crusher, who was watching me anxiously to see how I was getting on with my own, real, original, biological father.

'Yes,' I said. 'He's all right.'

'Good,' Bill said. 'Good.'

So that was that, really. The three of us shared a quick cup of tea out of the machine, and I ate one more chocolate bar, and took one more for the journey. Bill insisted on filling the car up for nothing. 'It's not every day my daughter comes down to visit me,' he said. Then Crusher and I got in and drove off.

I waved, and Bill waved and shouted that he'd pop in next time he came up our way, and I was to give his best wishes to Mum. Then we were out of sight.

Crusher settled himself more comfortably in the seat, then:

'Well?'

'All right,' I told him. 'He was all right.'

When we got home, it was dark. Mum was really pleased to see us. All of the photos came out fine. Some were really good. (I've got the best ones pinned on my bedroom wall now.)

I even managed the two whole pages of

writing about my own, real, original, biological father – though I could tell that Mr Russell was really disappointed that I'd chosen to do him instead of Crusher Maggot, whom he's seen hanging around for me at the school gates.

And now, as you can see, I'm in the habit too. Yesterday, when Arif and I were sitting on the kerbside watching poor Crusher trying to fix our bikes, Arif asked me what my real father was like. And, without even thinking, I answered:

'Oh, he's all right.'

Sometimes I worry that I'm getting just like all the rest of them, honestly I do.

Cross

From *The Illustrated Mum*

Written by JACQUELINE WILSON
Illustrated by NICK SHARRATT

I often write about birthdays in my books. Tracy Beaker is furious that she has the same birthday as little Peter in the Children's Home and has to share a birthday cake! The five girls in *Sleepovers* all have very special birthday parties with different themes and very elaborate cakes. It's great fun writing about birthdays. It's even better celebrating them yourself! I'm still a big baby about birthdays and I love to get lots of presents. My sixtieth birthday was wonderful and I was given the best presents ever: a beautiful rocking horse and a first edition of Katherine Mansfield's short stories. I hope HRH the Prince of Wales has equally imaginative gifts on his birthday. However, I've chosen to include a rather sad birthday story for this very special book. It's an extract from my favourite out of the ninety or so books I've written, *The Illustrated Mum*. Dolphin is telling the story – and it starts on the day of her mum's birthday . . .

Jacqueline Wilson

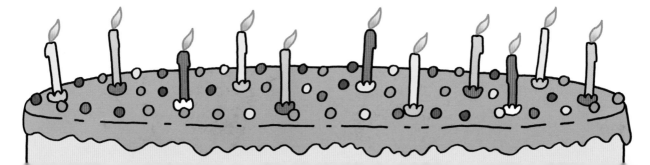

Cross

Marigold started going weird again on her birthday. Star remembered that birthdays were often bad times so we'd tried really hard. Star made her a beautiful big card cut into the shape of a marigold. She used up all the ink in the orange felt-tip colouring it in. Then she did two sparkly silver threes with her special glitter pen and added *Happy Birthday* in her best italic writing. They do Calligraphy in Year Eight and she's very good at it.

I'm still in the Juniors and I'm useless at any kind of writing so I just drew on my card. As it was Marigold's thirty-third birthday I decided I'd draw her thirty-three most favourite things. I drew Micky (I'd never seen him but Marigold had described him enough times) and Star and me. Then I drew the Rainbow Tattoo Studio and the Victoria Arms and the Nightbirds club. I did them in the middle, all clumped together, and then round the edges I drew London and the seaside and the stars at night. My piece of paper was getting seriously crowded by this time but I managed to cram in

56

a CD player with lots of Emerald City CDs and some high heels and a bikini and jeans and different-coloured tight tops and lots of rings and bangles and earrings.

I was getting a bit stuck for ideas by this time and I'd rubbed out so often that the page was getting furry so I gave up and coloured it in. I wanted to do a pattern of marigolds as a border but Star had used up all the orange already, so I turned the marigolds into roses and coloured them crimson. Red roses signify love. Marigold was very into symbols so I hoped she'd understand. Then on the back I did a great garland of red roses to signify a whole bunch of love and signed my name.

We gave her presents too. Star found a remixed version of Emerald City's greatest hits for only £2 at the Saturday morning market. I bought her a sparkly hair clasp, green to match her eyes. We even bought a special sheet of green tissue paper and a green satin ribbon to wrap up the presents.

'Do you think she'll like them?' I asked Star.

'You bet,' said Star. She took the hair clasp and opened it up so its plastic claws looked like teeth. 'I am a *great* present,' she made it say, and then it bit the tip of my nose.

Marigold gave us both big hugs and said we were darlings but her great green eyes filled with tears.

'So why are you crying?' I said.

'She's crying because she's happy,' said Star. 'Aren't you, Marigold?'

'Mm,' said Marigold. She sniffed hard and wiped her eyes with the back of her hand. She was shaking but she managed a smile. 'There. I've stopped crying now, Dol, OK?'

It wasn't OK. She cried on and off all day. She cried when she listened to the Emerald City CD because she said it reminded her of old times. She cried when I combed her hair out specially and twisted it up into a chic pleat with her new green clasp.

'God, look at my neck! It's getting all wrinkly,' she said. She touched the taut white skin worriedly while we did our best to reassure her. 'I look so *old*.'

'You're not old at all. You're young,' said Star.

'Thirty-three,' Marigold said gloomily. 'I wish you hadn't written that right slap bang in the middle of your card, darling. I can't believe thirty-three. That was the age Jesus was when he died, did you know that?'

Marigold knew lots about the Bible because she was once in a Church Home.

'Thirty-three,' she kept murmuring. 'He tried so hard too. He liked kids, he liked bad women, he stuck up for all the alternative people. He'd have been so cool. And what did they do? They stuck him up on a cross and tortured him to death.'

'Marigold,' Star said sharply. 'Look at Dol's card.'

'Oh yes, darling, it's lovely,' Marigold said.

58

She blinked at it. 'What's it meant to be?'

'Oh, it's stupid. It's all a mess,' I said.

'It's all the things you like most,' said Star.

'That's beautiful,' said Marigold, looking and looking at it. Then she started crying again.

'Marigold!'

'I'm sorry. It's just it makes me feel so awful. Look at the pub and the high heels and the sexy tops. These aren't mumsie things. Dol should have drawn . . . I don't know, a kitten and a pretty frock and . . . and Marks and Spencer's. That's what mums like.'

'It's not what you like and you're my mum,' I said.

'Dol spent ages making you that card,' said Star. She was starting to get red in the face.

'I know, I know. It's lovely. I *said. I'm* the hopeless case. Don't you get what I'm saying?' Marigold sniffed again. 'Anyway, let's have breakfast. Hey, can I have my cake now? Birthday cake for breakfast! Great idea, eh, girls?'

We stared at her.

'We didn't get you a cake,' said Star. 'You *know* we didn't. We asked and you said a cake was the very last thing you wanted, remember?'

'No,' said Marigold, looking blank.

She'd gone on and on that we mustn't get her a cake because she was sure she was starting to put on weight and the icing would only give her toothache and anyway she didn't even *like* birthday cake.

'I love birthday cake,' said Marigold. 'I always have a special birthday cake. You know how much it means to me because I never had my own special birthday cake when I was a kid. Or a proper party.

I hate it that you girls don't want proper parties and you just go to stupid places like Laser Quest and McDonald's.'

'They're not stupid,' I said. Star got asked to lots of stuff but I'd never been to a McDonald's party and no one had ever asked me to a Laser Quest either. I hoped I'd maybe make lots of friends when I went to the High School. I wasn't in with the party crowd in my class. Not that I wanted to go to any of their parties. I wouldn't have been friends with any of that lot if you'd paid me. Except maybe Tasha.

'OK, OK, I'll go and get you a birthday cake,' said Star. 'Marks and Sparks opens early on a Saturday. You wait.'

She took the housekeeping purse and rushed out, slamming the door.

'She's cross with me,' said Marigold.

'No, she's not. She's going to get you your cake,' I said.

'Cross, cross, cross,' Marigold muttered, frowning. 'That's what they used to say in the Home. "I'm very cross with you, Marigold." This old bat would bring her face right up close to me so that her eyes got so near they crossed too. "Cross, cross, cross," she'd say, and her spit would spray on my face. She was so mean, that one. She never hit us, she knew she wasn't allowed, but you could tell she really, really wanted to. She just *said* stuff. Cross, cross, cross.'

'Marigold.' I didn't know what else to say. I always got a bit scared when she talked like that, muttering fast, playing around with words. I wished Star would hurry back.

'Just words. Cross words!'

I giggled in case Marigold meant it to be a joke. She looked startled.

'We have crosswords at school,' I said quickly. 'I can't do them. I'm hopeless at spelling and stuff like that.'

'Me too,' said Marigold. 'I hated school. I was always in trouble.'

'Yep. Same here,' I said, hoping that Marigold was better now. I was starving hungry. I took a handful of dry cornflakes to keep me going. Marigold helped herself too.

'Yet Star's clever,' I said. 'And she's got even cleverer since she went to the High School. A real old brainy-box.'

'Well. She obviously takes after her father,' said Marigold. 'Micky was the cleverest guy I ever met. So creative and artistic and yet sharp too. You couldn't ever fool him.'

'I wish he was my dad too,' I said.

Marigold patted me sympathetically.

'Never mind. I've got you for my mum.' I said it to make her happy but it started her off crying again.

'What kind of a useless stupid mum am I?' she said.

'You're the best ever mum. Please don't cry again. You'll make your eyes go all red.'

'Red eyes, ropey neck, maudlin mood. What a mess! What have I got to show for my thirty-three years, eh? Apart from you two lovely girls. What would Micky make of me if he came back now? He always said I had such potential and yet I haven't done anything.'

'You do lots and lots of things. You paint and you make beautiful clothes and you dance and you work at the studio and – and—'

'If I don't do something with my life soon I never will. I'm getting old so quickly. If only Micky would come back. I was a different person when I was with him. He made me feel so . . .' She waved her thin arms in the air, her bangles jangling. 'Can't find the words. Come here, Dol.'

She pulled me close for a cuddle. I nestled against her, breathing in her magical musky smell. Her silky red hair tickled me. I stroked it, letting it fan out through my fingers.

'Your roots need doing soon. And you've got a few split ends. I'll snip them off for you, if you like.'

'You still going to be a hairdresser, Dol?'

'You bet,' I said, turning my fingers into scissors and pretending to chop.

'I remember when you cut all the hair off your Barbie doll,' said Marigold.

'And Star's too. She was so mad at me.'

'You girls. I wish I'd had a sister.'

'Well. You're like our big sister.'

'I feel like I'm at a crossroads in my life, Dol. Cross. Hey, you know what? How about if I got a cross for a tattoo?'

'You haven't got much space left,' I said, rubbing her decorated arms.

Marigold was examining herself, peering this way and that.

'How about right here, across my elbow? Brilliant! The cross could go up and down my arm. I need a bit of paper.' She used the back of my birthday card but I didn't really mind. She sketched rapidly, her teeth nipping her lower lip as she concentrated. I peered over her shoulder.

'You're so good at drawing,' I said wistfully.

Her hand was still shaking but the pen line was smooth and flowing as she drew an elegant long Celtic cross with roses and ivy twining round it.

'Roses,' she said, looking up at me. 'Like the ones on your card, Dol.'

I felt immensely proud. But also worried. I knew what Star was going to say.

'It's a lovely picture,' I said. 'Couldn't you just keep it a picture on paper? We could get a special frame for it and you could hang it over your bed.'

'I want it to be a picture on *me*,' said Marigold, her eyes glittering green. 'I wonder if Steve's got any early appointments? I can't wait! I'll get him to trace it and do it now. Special birthday present.' She leaped up. 'Come on!'

'But Star's getting your birthday cake!'

'Oh!' She screwed up her face in disappointment. 'Oh yes. Well, come *on*, Star. Where's she got to? Why did she have to go out to get this cake?'

This was so unfair of Marigold I couldn't look her in the eyes. She was terrible when she twisted everything about. She always did it when she got worked up. I knew I should tell her she wasn't being fair to Star but I couldn't make myself. It was so special being Marigold and me.

Star was ages. Marigold paced the flat in her high heels, groaning theatrically and watching the clock. When Star came back at last, carefully carrying a plastic bag on upturned hands, Marigold had to make an extreme effort.

'Star! You've been such a long time, sweetie!'

'Sorry. There were heaps of people. And I had to walk back carefully because I didn't want the cake to get bashed. I do hope you like it. I didn't know whether to pick the fruit or the sponge. I got the sponge because it was cheaper – but maybe you like fruit more?'

'Whichever,' said Marigold carelessly. 'Come on then, let's have a slice of cake.'

She was already pulling it out of the box, barely looking at it. She didn't even put it on a proper plate. She rummaged in the drawer for a sharp knife and went to cut the first slice.

'You've got to make a wish!' said Star.

Marigold raised her eyebrows but closed her eyes and wished. We didn't need to ask what she was wishing for. I saw her lips say the word 'Micky'. Then she was hacking away at the cake and gulping her slice so quickly she sprayed crumbs everywhere.

'What's the big hurry?' said Star.

I stopped eating my own slice of cake.

'I'm going to try to catch Steve early, before any clients. I've just designed the most amazing symbolic tattoo,' said Marigold.

'No,' said Star. 'Not another. You *promised*.'

Today

Written by VALERIE BLOOM
Illustrated by AXEL SCHEFFLER

When I was young, we didn't celebrate birthdays much. I guess with nine children it was not easy for my parents to remember them all. (I have problems remembering my own birthday sometimes.) But as soon as I started working, I took pleasure in buying lots of birthday presents for my family.

My children, like most other children, loved birthdays. My youngest daughter especially got very excited as hers approached, and as soon as the party was over she would start counting the days until the next one. It was interesting to see how hard she tried to be good the nearer her birthday came. That was the inspiration for 'Today'. A poem about a birthday seemed a logical choice for the Prince's birthday book. I wonder whether the Prince got up to any tricks when he was young. Or was he a little angel?

Valerie Bloom

Today

Today I will eat my cabbage,
Today I will eat my sprouts,
Today I will swallow my cauliflower
And not spit a single bit out.

Today I will not hit my sister,
Today I will not call her names,
Like toad-face, spotty, walrus rump,
I'll let her join in my games.

Today I'll not argue with Mum,
When she tells me to tidy my room,
I'll not take my sword into her rose bed,
And chop off all the blooms.

Today, no matter how much I long
To sit on my brother, Percy,
And pummel him until he cries
(On his knees) to me for mercy.

However much I want this,
I will restrain myself,
Instead I'll listen to him read,
Help Dad put up a shelf.

I'll let Amy play with my gameboy,
I'll return her tape which I hid,
Today I'll try to put right
All of the wrongs I did.

I will not give cause for complaint,
I'll not act like a twit,
For tomorrow's my birthday. I just hope
The presents will be worth it.

The Birthday Party

From *Swallows and Amazons*

Written by ARTHUR RANSOME
Illustrated by JOHN LAWRENCE

Here is an excerpt from one of my all-time favourite adventure books, *Swallows and Amazons*, describing a birthday celebrated on Wild Cat Island. I have spent many beautiful (and often wet and windy!) months on our own small Welsh island hideaway, and I think celebrating a birthday on a remote island with your family around you has to be the best way I can dream of. If I had to condense it all into the 'perfect' day it would start with an early morning skinny dip, followed by some climbing on our sea cliffs, with maybe a paraglide off the mountain; the afternoon would be spent snoozing in the heather, with my young boys snuggled up, and then returning to the lighthouse cottage for a home-baked thick chocolate birthday cake.

But my most memorable birthday was my twenty-fourth, in 1998, having returned from the summit of Everest after more than ninety days in sub-zero weather, sleep deprived, scared, and lucky to have survived avalanches and crevasse falls (not to mention running out of oxygen above 26,000 feet!) – now that was a birthday to remember!

This is what birthdays are really about to me: a gratitude for life, family and friends, and a moment to stop and give thanks.

Bear Grylls

The Birthday Party

John cheered up, and decided that it was a good day for swimming round the island.

He went down to the camp.

'Susan,' he said, 'it's a lovely day for swimming round the island.'

'Are you sure you can?' said Susan.

'I'm going to try,' said John. 'I can come ashore if I get too tired.'

The others came down to the landing-place to see him start. He swam at first with the side-stroke, fast and splashy. It was easy work to swim to the rocks at the low end of the island. Titty and Roger ran to the harbour, and climbed on a high rock to see him swimming round well outside the rocks that guarded the passage. 'Hurrah,' they shouted as they saw him go by. Then they ran to the western side of the island, where the rock dropped straight down like a wall into deep water. John came swimming along, using breast stroke now for a change, quietly and not hurrying. He began to feel that it was a very long way down that western side.

'Stick to it,' shouted Titty.

'Go it,' shouted Roger.

Susan came up from the camp to the tall pine at the northern end of the island, and looked down from the high rocky wall. John had almost reached the look-out place. He was moving very slowly.

'You can get ashore just here if you're done,' she called, 'then you can rest and go on again.'

John tried to wave his hand, and got a lot of water into his mouth in doing so. He turned on his back and floated, blowing like a whale.

'You're nearly round,' shouted Titty, who had run up to the look-out place and joined Susan.

John began again, kicking with his legs and using his arms only a little. He was round the head of the island. He went on swimming on his back. He turned over and lifted his head. For one moment he saw the landing-place, and *Swallow* lying there pulled up on the beach. His head went down, and he got more water in his mouth. He blew and spluttered. Still the landing-place was really not so very far off. He turned on his side and swam on. Somehow his arms would not pull, and his legs would not gather up and kick as hard as they ought to.

'You've done it,' shouted Titty.

'Come on,' shouted Roger.

Again John caught a glimpse of the landing-place. He must do it now. Suddenly he felt stronger again. He swam in towards the beach. He had started from this side of *Swallow*. Well, he would not touch bottom until he was on the other side. Another two strokes and he gripped *Swallow*'s port gunwale, touched the bottom, and crawled ashore, coughing, spitting, shivering, spluttering, and triumphant. Titty and Roger cheered. John was too much out of breath to speak.

'Here's a towel,' said Susan. 'I've hotted it by the fire.'

He put it round his shoulders. He rubbed first one arm and then the other. He felt much better.

'Well, I thought I could do it,' he said at last. The day was a good day after all, in spite of Captain Flint.

Susan was just thinking of getting dinner ready when there was a shout from Titty, who had taken the telescope up to the look-out place just in case of cormorants, pirates, or anything else worth looking at.

'A native boat,' she shouted. 'It's mother. It's the female native. She's got her little native with her, and the nurse belonging to it.'

The Swallows all ran to the look-out point. The female native herself was rowing. She had already passed Houseboat Bay. Vicky and nurse were sitting in the stern of the rowing boat. The Swallows had one look and then rushed back to tidy their tents and put the camp in order. They spread their blankets neatly over their haybags, and turned down the tops of them. Susan put a lot of fresh wood on the fire. There was not much else to do. Then they ran back to the look-out place. The female native was already quite near. They waved. Nurse and Vicky waved back. The female native couldn't wave, because she was rowing. She passed the head of the island, and a moment later was pulling in

to the landing-place. The Swallows were there before her.

'Sit still, nurse, till I get ashore,' said the female native.

The Swallows had already seized the boat and pulled it up. There was a big hamper in the boat just forward of the rowing thwart. The female native climbed round it.

'Welcome to Wild Cat Island,' said Titty.

'Welcome, welcome,' shouted the others.

There was a general scramble. Mother might be a native, but it was all right to kiss her none the less.

The female native counted the Swallows after she had kissed them. 'One, two, three, four,' she said. 'No one drowned yet. That's a good thing, because it's somebody's birthday.'

'Whose? Whose?' they shouted. 'It can't be John's, because he's just had one.'

'No, it isn't John's.'

'Is it mine?' said Roger.

'No,' said mother.

'Is it mine?' said Titty.

'No.'

'It can't be mine,' said Susan, 'because mine's on New Year's Day, and this is summer.'

'Whose is it?' they asked.

'Vicky's, of course,' said the female native. 'She's two. Rather too young for a birthday, really, so I've brought a present for each of you.'

'What about Vicky?' said Susan.

'Vicky's got a lamb and an elephant. I took her to the shop, and she chose them herself. Now then, help me out with the hamper, so that nurse and Vicky can come ashore.'

'It's a very heavy hamper,' said Titty.

'The presents are not,' said the female native. 'The presents are very small.'

'Then what's in the hamper?' said Roger.

'Birthday feast, of course,' said the female native.

'Hurrah, no cooking,' said Susan.

'Aha,' laughed the female native. 'I thought you'd get tired of that. But I must say you seem to have managed very well. No illness in the camp?'

'None at all,' said Susan, 'and I'm not sick of cooking, but it's jolly not to have to just for once.'

'Of course we've had plague and yellow fever and Black Jack and all the other illnesses belonging to desert islands,' said Titty. 'But we cured them all at once.'

'That's right,' said the female native, 'never let an illness linger about.'

They carried the hamper up to the camp. Nurse brought Vicky ashore, and they all wished her many happy returns. Vicky had the elephant with her. She forgot her lamb in the boat, and it had to be fetched later. Vicky liked the elephant better than the lamb because it was smaller. The lamb was so large it was always being put down and forgotten.

The female native opened the hamper. On the top, well wrapped up in tissue paper, was a birthday cake, a huge one with Victoria written in pink sugar on the white icing and two large cherries in the middle, because Vicky was two years old. Then there was a cold chicken. Then there was a salad in a big pudding-basin. Then there was an enormous gooseberry tart. Then there was a melon. Then there was a really huge bunch of bananas which the female native tied in a tree as if it was growing there. 'You can pick them just as you want them,' she said.

Then there were more ordinary stores, a tin of golden syrup, two big pots of marmalade and a great tin of squashed-fly biscuits. Squashed-fly biscuits are those flat biscuits with currants in them, just the thing for explorers. Then there were three bunloaves and six bottles of ginger beer.

'Hurrah for the grog,' said Titty.

'But where are the presents?' said Roger.

'I told you they were very little ones,' said the female native. 'Here they are.'

She dug down at the bottom of the hamper and brought up four small brown paper parcels, each about as big as an ordinary envelope and as fat as a matchbox.

'The nights are getting very dark now,' she said, 'with no moon, so I thought perhaps you could do with some electric torches. You mustn't keep them lit for long at a time or they'll soon wear out. But for signalling, or looking for something in the dark . . .'

'Mother,' cried Captain John, 'how did you guess we were wanting them? They've come exactly at the right moment.'

The others were flashing their torches at once, but they were not much good in the sunlight. Roger and Titty went into the mate's tent and crawled under the groundsheet to get some darkness.

When they came back, rubbing the mud from their knees, for under the groundsheet it had been very damp and sticky, the female native said, 'I've had a letter from daddy, and he reminded me of something. Can Roger swim yet?'

'He swam on his back for the first time to-day,' said John. 'Three good strokes. Once he can do that he will be able to swim on his front quite easily.'

'Shall I show you?' said Roger, and was for running down to the landing-place at once.

'Before we go home,' said the female native. 'Not this minute. Well, daddy said that Roger was to have a knife of his own as soon as he could swim, and I brought it with me in case he could.'

She dipped into the hamper for the last time and pulled out a knife with a good big blade. Roger was off with it at once, trying it on the trees. 'Now I can make blazes, just like Titty,' he shouted.

'If you can really swim three strokes both on your back and on your front, you can keep it,' said the female native. 'If not, I must take it back to-night and bring it again next time.'

'I'm sure I can do it,' said Roger, wiping the blade on his knickerbockers.

'You'll have to show me,' said the female native. 'No feet on the bottom, you know.'

'Not even one toe,' said Roger.

Then came the birthday feast. There is no need to say anything about that. It was a good one. No one had much time for talking. It ended after Roger had been sent to pick some bananas from the new banana tree.

'I hear you've had some visitors,' said mother.

The Swallows stared at her. It really was astonishing how news flew about among these natives.

'Mrs Blackett called on me yesterday and told me her little girls met you on the island. She seemed very jolly. How did you get on with the girls?'

'Beautifully,' said Susan. 'One is called Nancy and the other is called Peggy.'

'Really,' said mother. 'I thought the elder one was called Ruth.'

'That's only when she is with the natives,' said Titty. 'She is the captain of the Amazon pirates, and when she's a pirate her name is Nancy. We call her Nancy.'

'I see,' said mother. 'Mrs Blackett said they were a couple of tomboys, and she was afraid they might be too wild for you.'

'They aren't any wilder than we are,' said Titty.

'I hope not,' said mother, laughing.

Then she said, 'Their uncle lives during the summer in that houseboat we saw. You haven't been meddling with it, have you?'

'No,' said John, gloomily. 'But he thinks we have.'

'I know,' said mother, 'Mrs Dixon told me. I said I was sure you hadn't.'

'But he thinks we have. He's been here. He came when we

were all away and left this.' John pulled out the note and gave it to mother.

Mother looked at it. 'Who is Captain Flint?' she asked.

'He is,' said Titty.

'Oh,' said mother.

Then John told her of what the charcoal-burners had said, and of how he had gone to give the message himself, because there was no wind and he could not give it to the Amazons.

'You did quite right,' said mother, 'but Mrs Dixon said he was going away for a night or two.'

'He was just going when I saw him this morning,' said John.

'Wasn't he pleased to get the message?' said mother.

'He wouldn't listen to me,' said John. 'He called me a liar.' The whole trouble of the morning loomed up again.

'He wouldn't have called you that if he knew you,' said mother. 'It doesn't matter what people think or say if they don't know you. They may think anything. What did you do?'

'I came away,' said John.

'Mrs Blackett says he is very busy over some writing and wants to be let alone. She says she's afraid her tomboys lead him a terrible life.'

There was silence. It was all right to talk to mother about their own affairs. Mother was a friendly native. But nothing could be said about the affairs of the Amazons. Mother noticed the silence, and at once began to talk of something else. She really was the very best of natives.

The birthday party grew cheerful again. The female native told stories of old days before they had been born. She talked of Malta and Gibraltar, and of sailing in Sydney Harbour when she was a little girl.

Later on in the afternoon they bathed, and mother came down to the landing-place to see Roger swim. He swam three strokes on his front and managed six good kicks on his back.

'If you have got as far as that,' the female native said, 'I think you can keep the knife. All you want now is practice.'

John wanted to swim round the island again to show her that he could do it, but she said that once was quite enough for one day. Titty did some pearl-diving. Susan swam a short race with John and very nearly beat him.

Then there was tea.

At last it was time to take Vicky home.

The empty hamper was carried down to the landing-place.

'How soon are you going to get tired of your island?' asked the female native.

'Never, never,' said the Swallows.

'You've been lucky to have good weather so far,' she said. 'And you seem to be doing yourselves no harm. But there's only another week before we must be going south. You can stay here until nearly the end of it, unless the weather breaks. If the weather breaks, I mean if the rainy season comes on, you'll have to come away. In the rainy season desert islands, even the best of them, are almost uninhabitable.'

The Swallows looked at each other.

'A week's a long time,' said mother.

'But we want to stay for ever,' said Roger.

'I dare say you do,' said the female native.

She kissed them all round. They all kissed fat Vicky. Nurse and Vicky got into the boat and sat down in the stern.

Titty said, 'Mother, you don't mind being a native, do you?'

'Not a bit,' said mother.

'Then just for one minute I'll be a native too. What about rubbing noses? Like the natives you told us about in the Australian bush.'

Titty and the female native rubbed noses, after which, of course, Roger had to do the same.

Then the female native kissed all the Swallows good-bye and took her place in the boat. The empty hamper was lifted in. John and Susan pushed the boat off, and mother rowed away.

'Let's be a convoy,' said Captain John.

In a moment *Swallow* was afloat, her crew was aboard, and Captain John was rowing as hard as he could. The female native waited, resting on her oars. Then they rowed side by side. It was much harder to row *Swallow* than to row the boat from Holly Howe, because *Swallow* was deep in the water and built for sailing, not rowing. But the female native did not hurry. At last, just before they came to Houseboat Bay, Captain John stopped. He did not want to see the houseboat again that day. He turned *Swallow* round.

'Good-bye, natives,' called Titty.

'Good-bye, palefaces,' called the female native. 'Drool is the word, isn't it? Drool. Drool.'

'Let me row,' said Roger.

'Let me,' said Titty.

Captain John gave them each an oar. He and Susan sat in the stern. Roger rowed in the bows. Titty rowed stroke. Susan steered.

Susan pulled out her handkerchief to wave to the boat with the natives, disappearing in the distance. The handkerchief still had a knot in it. She unfastened the knot, but did not say anything.

As they landed once more at Wild Cat Island, John said, 'Titty and Roger had better do some whistling for a wind. We shall have to hurry up about the war.'

Young Again

From *Peter Pan in Scarlet*

Written by GERALDINE MCCAUGHREAN
Illustrated by MICHAEL FOREMAN

I have chosen this extract from *Peter Pan in Scarlet* (the sequel to J. M. Barrie's famous adventures of the boy-who-never-grows-up) to point out that birthdays are not *everybody's* idea of a good thing. Mr Barrie hated them. He believed that each passing year brought closer the dreadful fate of becoming a Grown-Up. That is why there are no birthdays allowed in Neverland.

Peter Pan has no intention of ever growing up – that is why he ran away from home in the first place. If they are to visit him, the Darlings and the Lost Boys (who have grown up into highly respectable adults) must shed twenty birthdays and become young again – as young as their own children.

Geraldine McCaughrean

Young Again

They watched the days go by like trains. Then suddenly the sixth of June arrived, and it was time to climb aboard it and set off for Neverland. Fireflyer had told them how it could be done. A change of clothes was called for.

All over London and as far afield as Fotheringdene and Grimswater, Old Boys got down old suitcases from their attics and took out all the courage they owned. They went to their banks and withdrew all the daring they had saved up over the years. They checked in all the pockets of all their suits and felt down the back of the sofa to muster all the bravery they could.

And still it did not seem quite enough.

They bought flowers for their wives, toys for their children, and washed the windows for their neighbours. They applied for leave from work. They wrote letters to their nearest and dearest but tore them up again, because GOODBYE is much the hardest word to spell.

Bath-time came at First Twin's house and while his twin sons were splashing, he slyly picked up some of their clothes from the bathroom floor and stole out into the night.

Time for prayers came in the house next door, and Second Twin told his identical twin sons, 'Hands together; eyes closed' – then pinched a school uniform and sneaked away on tiptoe.

At the Doctor's house in Fotheringdene, Curly reached out to steal his child's rugby kit . . . but the new puppy beat him to it, grabbing the collar and hanging on grimly. The animal growled and whined, and its claws scraped loudly on the polished floor. The child roused up – '*Who's there?*' – so there was nothing Curly could do but pick up both shirt and puppy and run.

Storytime came in Mr John's house, and Mr John read his little ones to sleep, took one last look, then crept to the door holding a stolen sailor suit. On the landing, he gave a guilty start, for there stood Mrs John. She knew, of course. Mr John had not breathed a word about the Journey, but she knew anyway. Wives do. Now she presented him with a packed lunch, a clean pair of socks, and a toothbrush. She even ironed the sailor suit before he put it on. 'Take care, my love,' she said, kissed him fondly, and led him to the front door. 'Do give my warmest regards to Peter Pan.'

Judge Tootles realized, rather late in the day, that he only had daughters. The thought quite unmanned him. His fingers strayed to his large moustache and he stroked it like some dear pet that he must leave behind because of moving house.

Nibs . . . well, Mr Nibs simply could not do it. Standing beside the bunks in the back bedroom, watching the sleeping faces of his little ones, he simply could not imagine going anywhere without them –

ever. He resigned then and there from the trip to Neverland. In fact he even woke the little ones up to ask, 'What has Neverland got that could *possibly* be better than you?'

And the Honourable Slightly Darling? Well, he sat alone now in his elegant flat, nursing his clarinet. When Fireflyer had told them the secret of growing young again, Slightly had nodded but said nothing. He had watched the day come nearer, and dreamed dreams of Neverland, but said nothing. He had seen the others steeling themselves for the adventure, dusting Fireflyer's lampshade each day for fairy magic, getting ready to go . . . and still said nothing. Now he sat in his elegant flat, his clarinet silent in his lap.

He was not one to spoil another chap's fun. That was why he had not spoken up. And they had all forgotten – his adopted brothers and sister – that Slightly was a widower and had no children – no one whose clothes he could borrow, no one to make him young again.

Because, of course, that's how it is done. Everyone knows that when you put on dressing-up clothes, you become someone else. So it follows that if you put on the clothes of your own children, you become their age again.

In wardrobes and broom cupboards, hopping down lamp-lit streets, squeezing their heads through little neck-holes and their feet into tiny football boots; straining seams and tripping over dressing-gown cords, dropping wallets and fountain pens, and pocketing puppies, the Old Boys struggled into their children's clothes. You may ask how it was possible for Judge Tootles to fit into a smocked party dress and ballet shoes. All I can say is that there was a tambourine moon shining, magic at work, and somehow all the hooks did up and all the buttons fastened.

Their minds filled up with thoughts of Neverland and of running away. Oddly, as they ran, their feet no longer avoided puddles but preferred to splash through them. Their fingers chose to blip metal railings, their lips to whistle, their eyes to shine.

Dr Curly felt good sense trickle out of his head like sand, to be replaced with squibs and sparklers. The Twins suddenly remembered each other's favourite fairy stories. Judge Tootles found she could see without her spectacles and, when she swung from the climbing frame in the park, her teeth did not throb. But her top lip felt oddly bare, since for ever so long she (or rather he) had worn a great curling moustache there and she missed it now as you might miss a pet hamster.

As the Old Boys rubbed fairy dust into the napes of their necks, short, prickly haircuts grew silky beneath their fingers – except for Tootles, of course, who found she had long yellow plaits and knew ballet positions One to Five.

. . . But the Honourable Slightly had no children. So he sat in his elegant flat, feeling every one of his thirty years weigh on his shoulders. Tugging off his evening tie, he went early to bed, hoping at least to *dream* of Neverland.

As for Mrs Wendy, well, she wrote a letter to the household, explaining how she was going to visit a distant friend and would return very soon. Before she put on her daughter Jane's clothes, she darned the girl's slips, rubbed out her day's mistakes with an India rubber, crocheted a happy dream to slide under her pillow, and put her prayers in alphabetical order. Then she packed a few useful things in a wicker basket and wriggled into a small, clean sundress appliquéd with sunflowers and two rabbits.

'It is always so sultry hot in Neverland,' she told her sleeping child. '. . . How extraordinary! A perfect fit.' Surprised by the last sneeze of her cold, she quickly reached for a handkerchief from the pocket of her discarded gown, tucked it up her little puffed sleeve, then crept out on to the balcony.

As she combed her share of fairy dust through her hair, lists and birthdays emptied out of her head, along with politics and typewriting; poems and recipes. Even her husband became a shadowy recollection. Not her daughter Jane, of course. No mother could ever forget her daughter. Not under any circumstances. Not for a minute.

In the sky over Kensington Gardens, a flock of flying children gathered, like birds in autumn getting ready to migrate. They floated on their backs, paddled along on their fronts, rode on the warm updraught from the High Street chimneys and got grubby in the smoke. A strand of old fog unravelling over the River Thames made them cough.

Owls blinked in astonishment. Nelson on top of his column raised his telescope to his one good eye. Statues of famous men pointed and jumped from foot to foot. (One on horseback even bolted.) Policemen on their beats heard squeals of laughter, but looked in vain for someone to arrest.

'Where is Nibs?' called Wendy.

'*Not coming!*' answered Fireflyer.

'Where is Slightly?' John wanted to know.

'*Not coming!*' cried Fireflyer, glowing with glee.

'*Oh, yes I am!*' And Slightly came porpoising through the air, his wavy hair a-glitter with fairy dust. He was wearing an evening shirt whose tails came down past his nine-year-old knees and whose sleeves flapped way beyond his fingers. In his hand he clutched a clarinet, like a dueller's sword. 'I went down to the foot of the bed, you see! Haven't done it for twenty years! Right down to the end and beyond! I remembered, you see! You can end up *anywhere* if you dare to go right down to the bottom! Which way now, Fireflyer?'

'*How should I know?*' snapped the fairy.

But everyone else answered for him: '*Second to the right and straight on till morning!*'

At set of moon, after they had gone, the rain came down in exclamation marks.

The further they flew, the more they forgot of being grown up and the better they remembered their days in Neverland. Sunshine! Leapfrog! Picnics! Into their heads tumbled daydreams and excitements. And all their feelings fizzed inside them, and all their muscles were twangy. They almost forgot to remember why they were making the journey.

'If the Redskins are on the warpath, I'm going too!'

'Do you think Tinker Bell will be pleased to see us?'

'*Oh, will she be there, then, this Tinker Bell?*'

'I can't wait to see Peter's face when I give him his presents!'

'I can't wait to see the mermaids!'

'I said, will Tinker Bell be there? Fairies die if you ignore them, you know?'

'I hope there are new villains to fight!'

'Do you think there will be *new* Lost Boys, as well?'

At the thought of that, there was a sudden silence. Of course it was altogether possible! Boys fall out of their prams all the time, and nursery maids are notoriously bad at noticing. In all likelihood Peter Pan had gathered a new band of followers around him since the days of Nibs, Curly, the Twins, Slightly, and Tootles.

'Will the underground den be big enough for us all to fit?' Curly wondered anxiously.

'Will the others even let us in?' whispered the Twins.

'They better had, or I'll beat down the door!'

'There might even be Lost Girls,' said Wendy, uneasily. 'Girls are so much sillier than they were when I was a baby.' She was not at all sure she wanted there to be Lost Girls; without the right upbringing, girls can be so very . . . *domestic.*

Fireflyer the fairy, scorching between them like a hot cinder, suggested gleefully, *'Maybe Peter Pan will cull you if there are too many! That's what Peters do, isn't it?'* and the younger boys turned pale with fright.

'There is always the Wendy House,' Wendy told them soothingly. 'If the den is too crowded, we shall live there.'

'Yes, and no one can stop us!' declared Tootles. 'We built that Wendy House our own selves, for Wendy! And you can't keep a Wendy out of her own Wendy House!'

A flock of clouds bleated its way across the High Way, causing a traffic jam. Fireflyer darted in among them, stinging and biting until the clouds broke into a trot. And as the flock scattered, there beneath lay . . .

NEVERLAND!

A circle without a perimeter, a square without corners, an island without bounds: Neverland. Imagination had pushed it up from the bottom of the sea and into the daylight. Now bad dreams had summoned them back to it: the place where children never grow up!

Little did they know (or care) that back in their various homes, on dressing tables and bathroom sills, their abandoned wristwatches stopped at that exact same moment. For when a child is in Neverland, time should stand still.

Their hearts rose into their mouths. There was nowhere like this! In all the round world there is nowhere like Neverland! And there it lay, spread out below them, totally and completely and utterly and absolutely . . .

changed.

Despite flying into the brightness of morning, Wendy, in her flimsy sundress, gave a shiver, for the sunlight was thinner and paler than she remembered. The shadows were longer – some rocky pinnacles and pine trees had three or four shadows all sprawling in different directions. Wendy knew they had been right to come: all was not well in Neverland.

As they flew over the Neverwood, an ocean of golden, orange, and scarlet trees tossed and rolled beneath them now, loosing, from time to time, a spray of crisp, autumn leaves. The Redskin totem poles leaned at crazy angles, felled by wind or war, and roped in creepers and ivy. Huge globes of mistletoe rolled about the treetops like Chinese lanterns. It was beautiful . . . but there was no birdsong.

The clearings, where once the League of Lost Boys had built camp fires or held councils of war, were gone: healed up and disappeared as surely as a hole in the sea. If there were wolves lurking, they could not be seen. If there were Redskins on the warpath, their warpaths were hidden from sight.

'How shall we ever find the den or the Wendy House?' said John, voicing everyone's fears. But they need not have worried, for the little house with its red walls and mossy green roof was the very next thing they saw. The smoke from its chimney coiled between them and they reefed themselves in by it, hand over hand.

Wendy's House stood balanced in the fork of a tree – a tree taller by the height of a church spire than any in the forest. On the wash-line that stretched between two branches, wispy clouds hung snagged, alongside a wind-ragged apron, a flag, and a single sock.

'That's my apron!' exclaimed Wendy.

The flying children rapped at the door; they rattled at the windows and clamoured round the chimney pot. But no one came to let them in. After a night's flying, they were starting to tire.

'He has shut us out!' cried Wendy. 'After all he said! Me, I've never closed my bedroom window, winter or summer! Not ever since Neverland!'

'Not even in a fog?' asked Curly.

Wendy was forced to admit it: 'Well, perhaps in a fog. You know how dangerous a London fog can be to the lungs.'

'Like breathing in bed fluff,' said Slightly. And they agreed that the owner of the house must have closed the windows because clouds were rather like a London fog.

'Fly down the chimney, Fireflyer, and slip the bolt,' said Tootles, and the fairy swooped into the chimney pot. They waited and waited, but when Tootles used one of her plaits to wipe a peep-hole in the dirt-caked windows, she could see that Fireflyer had got sidetracked and was swinging from a coat peg, eating the buttons off a jacket. 'Silly creature,' she said.

Wendy realized they must enter by a different route. 'You Lost Boys built the Wendy House,' she told them. 'You have a perfect right to take it apart again.' So, after knocking politely once more, they wrapped their fingers around the corner posts and wrenched off the end wall.

They were confronted by a boy, sword drawn, head tilted back and a ferocious scowl on his face. 'Have at you, Nightmares! You may breach my castle wall, but I shall fill up the gap with your dead bodies!' It was Peter Pan and it was not. His suit of skeleton leaves was gone, and in its place was a tunic of jay feathers and the blood-red leaves of autumn: Virginia creeper and maple.

'Now now, Peter,' said Wendy, stepping into the breach. 'Is that any way to greet your old friends?'

'*I have no friends who are old!*' cried the boy with the drawn sword. 'I am Boy and if things are big, I cut 'em down to size!'

Seeing that Peter did not recognize her, tears pricked behind Wendy's eyes, but she too tipped back her head. 'Don't be so silly,' she said briskly. 'You are Peter and I am Wendy, and we have come . . .' – she racked her brains trying to remember – 'in case you were in trouble.'

Peter looked at her, baffled. 'How "in trouble"? In a cooking pot with cannibals waiting to eat me, you mean?'

'Well, maybe not that exactly . . .'

'Fallen off a ship in shark-infested waters?'

'Possibly not, but . . .'

'Being carried through the sky by a giant mother eagle to her eyrie to feed her hungry chicks?' It was plain Peter rather liked the idea of being in trouble. It was equally plain that none of these things were happening to him. Wendy began to feel rather foolish, which was something she never enjoyed.

'Have you been saying your prayers?' she demanded (a question every bit as scary as a sword waved in your face).

'Well, I haven't been saying anyone else's!' retorted Peter.

Then, for the first time, he looked at them properly. His sword-tip wavered and a great smile lit up his face. 'Ah. You've come back, then, have you? I thought I was dreaming you. I have dreamt you a lot, lately.' He added accusingly, 'You were *much too big* . . . Why did you say you had come?'

'To do the Spring Cleaning, of course!' said Wendy, which was much simpler than explaining.

Carelessly Peter flung his sword into a corner. 'You can clean out the nightmares if you like,' he said.

Wendy was not exactly sure what Peter's nightmares looked like, so she swept down the black cobwebs from the corners of the ceiling. 'There! They are all gone now,' she said, and added breezily: 'We have been having nightmares, too. About Neverland. We thought something might be wrong.'

But either Peter did not know or he did not care about the dreams leaking out of Neverland: Neverland had dreams a-plenty to spare.

'Things outside look very . . . *different*,' said Wendy carefully.

But of course Peter loved Neverland in scarlet and gold just as much as in summer greens, so he saw nothing wrong in that. Wendy did not press him. Perhaps she had been mistaken, and nothing was wrong.

'Are you quite well, Chief?' said Tootles tenderly, feeling Peter's pulse and the temperature of his forehead. 'If you are not, we can play doctors and nurses!'

'I am dying!' exclaimed Peter, throwing an arm across his face.

Wendy gave a cry of distress: 'Oh, I *knew* it! I *knew* something was wrong! I do hope you are not!'

'I am dying of boredom!' groaned Peter. Then he changed his

mind and sprang to his feet. 'But now I have imagined you here, we can have the best adventures in the world!' And he uttered a triumphant crow that was thrilling and chilling and ear-splitting, all three:

'*Cock-a-doodle-doo!*'

Charlie's Birthday

From *Charlie and the Chocolate Factory*

Written by ROALD DAHL
Illustrated by QUENTIN BLAKE

The excerpt which follows comes from a wonderful book that lies very close to my heart – a dazzlingly entertaining morality tale that sets itself in a world where folk reap what they sow, and that, to the unreserved glee of us all, includes Charlie and his loving family.

In this particular chapter, 'Charlie's Birthday', we witness some of the key themes found throughout Roald Dahl's glorious body of work. There is the bond of a close-knit family unit and a solidarity that, despite the surrounding adversity, shines brightly through to warm the heart of everyone it touches. On top of that, there is of course the hope. The hope that the ticket will, at some point, turn up in Charlie's hands. And though we know from the start that it will, Roald Dahl still manages to have us on the edge of our seats throughout, every time we read it. For to good people does come what they deserve: great luck! – and we know Charlie and his family are nothing if not good, honest souls.

It is then the constant teasing with this sense of justice that thrills us so. There are few things sweeter than when Charlie's moment does finally arrive, but for now, you'll just have to wait a little longer and instead savour the delicious anticipation a birthday always brings of wonderful things waiting just around the corner!

Johnny Depp

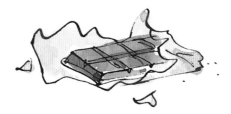

Charlie's Birthday

'Happy birthday!' cried the four old grandparents, as Charlie came into their room early the next morning.

Charlie smiled nervously and sat down on the edge of the bed. He was holding his present, his only present, very carefully in his two hands. WONKA'S WHIPPLE-SCRUMPTIOUS FUDGE-MALLOW DELIGHT, it said on the wrapper.

The four old people, two at either end of the bed, propped themselves up on their pillows and stared with anxious eyes at the bar of chocolate in Charlie's hands.

Mr and Mrs Bucket came in and stood at the foot of the bed, watching Charlie.

The room became silent. Everybody was waiting now for Charlie to start opening his present. Charlie looked down at the bar of chocolate. He ran his fingers slowly back and forth along the length of it, stroking it lovingly, and the shiny paper wrapper made little sharp crackly noises in the quiet room.

Then Mrs Bucket said gently, 'You mustn't be too disappointed, my darling, if you don't find what you're looking for underneath that wrapper. You really can't expect to be as lucky as all that.'

'She's quite right,' Mr Bucket said.

Charlie didn't say anything.

'After all,' Grandma Josephine said, 'in the whole wide world there are only three tickets left to be found.'

'The thing to remember,' Grandma Georgina said, 'is that whatever happens, you'll still have the bar of chocolate.'

'Wonka's Whipple-Scrumptious Fudgemallow Delight!' cried Grandpa George. 'It's the best of them all! You'll just *love* it!'

'Yes,' Charlie whispered. 'I know.'

'Just forget all about those Golden Tickets and enjoy the chocolate,' Grandpa Joe said. 'Why don't you do that?'

They all knew it was ridiculous to expect this one poor little bar of chocolate to have a magic ticket inside it, and they were trying as gently and as kindly as they could to prepare Charlie for the disappointment. But there was one other thing that the grown-ups also knew, and it was this: that however *small* the chance might be of striking lucky, *the chance was there.*

The chance *had* to be there.

This particular bar of chocolate had as much chance as any other of having a Golden Ticket.

And that was why all the grandparents and parents in the room were actually just as tense and excited as Charlie was, although they were pretending to be very calm.

'You'd better go ahead and open it up, or you'll be late for school,' Grandpa Joe said.

'You might as well get it over with,' Grandpa George said.

'Open it, my dear,' Grandma Georgina said. 'Please open it. You're making me jumpy.'

Very slowly, Charlie's fingers began to tear open one small corner of the wrapping paper.

The old people in the bed all leaned forward, craning their scraggy necks.

Then suddenly, as though he couldn't bear the suspense any longer, Charlie tore the wrapper right down the middle . . . and on to his lap, there fell . . . a light-brown creamy-coloured bar of chocolate.

There was no sign of a Golden Ticket anywhere.

'Well – that's *that!*' said Grandpa Joe brightly. 'It's just what we expected.'

Charlie looked up. Four kind old faces were watching him intently from the bed. He smiled at them, a small sad smile, and then he shrugged his shoulders and picked up the chocolate bar and held it out to his mother, and said, 'Here, Mother, have a bit. We'll share it. I want everybody to taste it.'

'Certainly not!' his mother said.

And the others all cried, 'No, no! We wouldn't dream of it! It's *all* yours!'

'*Please*,' begged Charlie, turning round and offering it to Grandpa Joe.

But neither he nor anyone else would take even a tiny bit.

'It's time to go to school, my darling,' Mrs Bucket said, putting an arm around Charlie's skinny shoulders. 'Come on, or you'll be late.'

The Government of Ted

Written by FRANK COTTRELL BOYCE
Illustrated by CHRIS RIDDELL

One of the most exciting things about birthdays is the way that as you get older you're allowed to do more things. You're twelve, so now you're allowed to go to a twelve-certificate film. You're eighteen, now you can vote. And in the end you're sixty-five, now you can finally get cheap train fares. Nowadays if you buy stuff on the Internet, they almost always ask you for your birth date for security reasons. And then you always get all kinds of free offers in with your birthday cards. I put these two things together and came up with a story about how one birthday you might be old enough to rule the world.

Frank Cottrell Boyce

The Government
of Ted

I love it when you wake up early on your birthday and you can lie there, imagining all the excellent new stuff that is coming your way. When I woke up on my twelfth birthday, my mum and dad were already moving about downstairs. I thought, That must be some monster surprise they're getting ready down there. It's only half past six. It had to be a quad bike at least. I stayed in bed as long as I could. I didn't want to spoil their big moment. In the end, I just couldn't wait. I ran downstairs and said, 'Hi, Mum, hi, Dad.'

Neither of them was tuning a quad bike. Or setting up a new PlayStation. Or wrapping up an iPhone. They were in fact asleep on the couch.

I said, 'Hi, Mum, hi, Dad,' again, a bit louder this time, and Mum lazily opened one eye and said, 'Oh. Ted. Hi. Turn the telly off, will you?'

Dad opened both eyes and said, 'Oh. Ted. I wanted to say something to you . . .'

'Was it happy birthday?'

'No. It'll come back to me.' And he went to sleep again.

I looked around the room for signs of extravagant spending. Nothing. I turned the telly off and that woke Dad again, who said, 'That's it. We've got a new prime minister. Goodnight.'

They'd stayed up all night to watch the election and completely forgotten my birthday. If I was the new Prime Minister I'd pass a law against this kind of behaviour right away.

I'd also pass a law against the increasing social problem of people who throw other people's bags off the back of the school bus. For instance Evil Owen. Evil Owen sat opposite me on the bus to school and laughed at my hair for three stops. 'Look at his hair,' he said. 'It's hilarious.'

I said, 'It's not hilarious. It's red.'

'Exactly. Red with a hint of hilarious.'

'Leave him alone,' said my friend, Benedict. 'It's his birthday.'

'Oh, is it?' said Owen. 'Then I must give you a surprise.' And in a single fluid movement, he grabbed my bag, opened the emergency window, and dropped the bag out of it.

I had to get off at the next stop, and walk half a mile back up the High Street to find it again. On my birthday. Honestly, if I was Prime Minister and stuff like that was going on in my country, I wouldn't sleep nights.

At birthday parties when I was growing up, my favourite thing was always Hula Hoops – not the actual hula hoops that you hula with; the crisps. I don't know what it is about them. I think it's because you can put one over the end of each finger and then pretend you're eating your fingers. Or something. Anyway, clearly I could no longer rely on Mum and Dad to come up with birthday Hula Hoops. So, on the way home that night, I stopped off at this new supermarket at the end of our road (it's called 'Neighbourhood') and I bought a massive party pack of Hula Hoops and some 'Happy Birthday' paper cups for myself. 'Somebody's birthday today?' asked the nice lady on the till. Obviously a descendant of Sherlock Holmes.

I said, 'Yes. Mine. I'm twelve.'

I was going to tell her about how my parents had practically slept through the whole day but she said, 'Twelve? Just the right age for our new loyalty card. There you go.' And she gave me a little purple plastic card. 'Every time you buy anything here, we'll put points on that card for you. And points mean prizes.'

I wasn't sure. I said, 'I'm not sure.'

'And as an introductory offer, and in view of the fact that it's your birthday, you can have this mammoth pack of Premier League collector's cards absolutely free. What football team do you support?' she said.

I explained that for reasons of family history I supported the historic but basically rubbish team of Stockport County. 'Oh,' she said. 'How character-building.'

When I got home, there was a big HAPPY BIRTHDAY poster stuck to the door and a table full of food, including a bowl of Hula Hoops big enough to swim in. Mum had made me a cake shaped like a bike. She'd made a boy out of marzipan to sit on top of it and given him red hair just like mine. Plus I got a real bike, a non-cake bike. With about a million gears. And my cousins came round and we had a massive on-bike water fight. So basically Mum and Dad had got their act together just in time and given me an outstanding birthday.

While we were clearing up, we watched the new Prime Minister give her first television interview. When she let slip that she supported Stockport County too, we thought it was surprising but not weird. Things didn't get unarguably weird for another week.

Next time I stopped off at Neighbourhood there was a different nice woman, standing by the fresh fruit and veg with a clipboard. 'Could you answer a few questions for our survey?' she said. She asked me my name and how I got to the store and whether I preferred soup in tins to soup in cartons, and then she said, 'And do you think it would be a good idea if all children were made to walk to school, just one day a week? It would cut carbon emissions, relieve congestion and raise fitness levels. What d'you think?'

I said, 'Sure. Some people in our school come quite a distance though. Maybe you could say everyone who lives within a mile of the school has to walk.'

'Great. I'll put that down.'

I noticed that party packs of Hula Hoops were on a two-for-one offer. But I'd moved on by then. I was just beginning my cheese-flavoured breadsticks phase.

That night, during the news, the new Prime Minister announced that she was introducing a scheme to make every child walk to school one day every week. The interviewer said, 'But what about those children who live miles away?'

She smiled and said, 'It only applies to children who live within a mile of the school.'

'Well,' said the interviewer, 'it sounds like a politician has finally had a good idea.'

'Thank you. I'm going to do it myself. On Fridays I shall be walking from Downing Street to Parliament. It should help me keep my weight down.'

The interviewer said something polite about the Prime Minister not being fat. And this is where it gets a bit weird. Because the Prime Minister said, 'Not yet maybe. But I've been really punishing the cheese-flavoured breadsticks recently.' And as she said this last bit, I swear she looked straight at me – from the telly – and winked. At me.

That Friday was the first ever compulsory walk to school. Evil Owen took my bag and threw it, but because we were no longer on a moving bus, it only went a few metres away. All I had to do was pick it up. Finally a government had passed a law that worked.

That was the day Mum asked me to pick up some carrots and potatoes on the way home from school. 'If you do it,' she said, 'you'll get extra points on your loyalty card.' Benedict came with me and I showed him the card. He said, 'That's a terrible photograph.' And that's when I thought, I don't remember them taking a photograph of me. And how come the card has my name printed on it? They didn't even ask me my name. Was that weird too?

Benedict said it wasn't. 'Supermarkets know everything about you,' he said. 'They probably know we're having this conversation. It's called market research.'

There was a massive queue at the checkout but the supervisor came up to me and whispered, 'Mustn't keep our loyal customers waiting. Till seven is opening.'

I slipped out of the queue and got to till seven just as the nice woman from the first night was sitting down at the machine. 'Hello,' she smiled. 'And how are things at Stockport County?'

'We need a defender who can distribute the ball as well as stopping it.'

'I see.'

And she checked out my vegetables and yawned. 'Don't you think it would be better if the weekends started on Fridays?'

I said, 'It would be better if they went on until Monday.'

'Oh. Maybe you're right. No Hula Hoops tonight then?'

'No. But I'll take a packet of Premier League collector's cards please.'

'Sold out, I'm afraid.'

That evening the Prime Minister appeared on TV to launch a new initiative. All public employees would get Mondays off. 'It will cut emissions and improve the work–life balance. We all know that work expands to fill the time you give it, so why not just give it less time?'

It was a massively popular move. 'You must be very happy, Prime Minister,' said the interviewer.

'I'd be happier,' she said – and she was definitely looking straight at me when she said it – 'if Stockport County had a defender who could distribute the ball instead of just blocking it.'

That was when I knew for certain. That was when the weirdness made sense. Clearly, the woman at the checkout was working for the Prime Minister. Clearly, the Prime Minister wanted my advice. Really she wanted me to run the country. I tried to explain this to Benedict.

'Why would the Prime Minister want you to run the country?' he said.

'Well, obviously I'm really clever. I came second in French, remember, and third in History. Why wouldn't she want me to help her run the country?'

'I think,' said Benedict, 'that you might be suffering from paranoid delusions brought on by excessive Hula Hoop consumption.'

'I'll show you,' I said.

We stopped off at Neighbourhood. They still didn't have any Premier League collector's cards. I went to the nice woman on the checkout and said, 'Still no Premier League collector's cards, I see. Someone should do something about that. It's distracting children from their studies. And putting them in danger. The fewer cards there are, the more valuable they are. Which means that bullies are more likely to beat you up to get your cards off you.'

'I'll see what I can do,' smiled the checkout lady.

Benedict came back to ours for tea. I put on *Newsround Extra*. There she was – my own little Prime Minister – and here is what she was saying:

'The Premier League collector's cards provide children with a valuable lesson in how the free market works. The rarer the card, the more it's worth. But things have reached crisis point and we are hearing stories of children being beaten up to get more valuable cards. I intend to restore order to our playgrounds by organizing the distribution of free Premier League cards to all our playgrounds in the next few days.'

Benedict looked at me. 'You,' he said, 'are the Leader.'

As we were queuing up for our free cards the next day, Benedict said, 'I just can't figure out why it would be you.'

I said, 'Think about it. They've been doing tests on us since we were little – Sats tests, cat tests, you name it. They know everything about us. Obviously they just put all the information together, stuck it in a computer, ran a test and I came out top.'

'I just can't see that,' said Benedict. 'I mean, you're not even top of our class, never mind Great Britain.'

'Not in exams, just top as in a top guy. Top person.'

'Clearly not,' said Benedict, 'or you would be making better use of this opportunity.'

'How do you mean?'

'Well, come on, you're in control of the whole country and all you've done is get us a few extra Premier League cards. You could really improve people's lives.'

Of course he was right. The Prime Minister had asked for my help. Why? Obviously because I'm a genius. Because I could save the world. But how? I lay awake all night thinking of schemes that might stop global warming, mass extinction, car crashes, poverty and the seemingly inevitable decline of Stockport County. On the way to school I saw litter in the streets, petrol fumes in the air, babies crying in pushchairs, and somehow they were all my fault.

Benedict said, 'I tell you what I found on YouTube – a film of a snake swallowing a whole antelope. Why don't they put stuff like that on the news instead of all about murders and wars? Why don't you pass a law about that?'

'Benedict,' I said, 'be quiet. And carry my bag, it's interfering with my concentration.'

'You've changed, Ted McKillop.'

'Of course I've changed. I'm trying to save the planet.'

During lunchtime I sent Benedict to queue for hot food for me while I tried to find a quiet moment in which to use my powerful brain. I couldn't help looking up from time to time at all the other kids laughing and shoving and eating. So carefree. Because they're not burdened with genius like I am.

Benedict brought me a pasta bake, an apple and some coffee. 'The apple is for energy and the coffee will stimulate your brain. The pasta is . . . well, it's horrible. You couldn't pass a law about school dinners, could you? Or – shall I tell you my idea? It's a way to end wars.'

'A way to end wars? Yeah. Definitely. Go on.'

'Well, what you could do – instead of sending planes to bomb ordinary people and innocent children – what about if each country used its top scientists to bring back a dinosaur?'

'Bring back a dinosaur?'

'From dinosaur DNA. Any dinosaur you like and then, instead of sending rockets and bombers, the countries just send their dinosaurs to fight each other. No one gets hurt. Except the dinosaurs. And instead of spending trillions of dollars, you make money because everyone would want to watch it. On subscription TV. I mean, say it was a Tyrannosaurus versus a Diplodocus, you'd want to watch that, wouldn't you? Who wouldn't?'

'Benedict,' I said, 'you don't understand.'

'I think the Diplodocus would probably win because of its tail. All it would need to do—'

'Sssh.' I was looking at the apple he'd brought me. It had a label on the side saying it was from South Africa. I suddenly thought about all the food that was flying around the world. Sometimes food from countries where people were starving was flown all the way to our country for rich people to eat. And if it was broccoli or something, people probably wouldn't even eat it. I could feel my idea coming. Something about leaving food where it was. You'd stop all the pollution from the planes. People in poor countries would have food. And there'd be less waste – broccoli, for instance – in this country. Genius. I was beginning to understand why the Prime Minister had picked me.

'What are you smiling at?' It was Evil Owen who said this. He was looking right at me.

I couldn't say, 'I may just have solved the problems of hunger and global warming in a single sentence,' could I? So I said, 'I'm not sure. I think the label must've fallen off.'

He growled, picked up my bag and lobbed it across the dining hall.

It hit Mr Mercer, our head of year, smack in the face. Mr Mercer gave me a detention. 'But, sir . . .' I wanted to explain that a) it wasn't me, and b) I was too busy saving the world to have detention. But he wouldn't listen.

'It's your bag,' he said. 'It hit me. You're in trouble.'

'But he threw it, not me.'

'Then you shouldn't let him throw it. Your bag is your responsibility.'

By the time I finally got out of school, there were massive queues in

Neighbourhood, but a nice voice came cooing over the tannoy saying, 'Would Ted McKillop please report to the information desk? That's Ted McKillop to the information desk please.'

When I got there, the nice woman from the till was waiting for me. 'Can't have you waiting at the till like an ordinary customer,' she smiled. 'How are you today?'

I said, 'I feel OK considering I'm a redhead. People with red hair are always getting into trouble. We're always blamed for stuff just because we're easier to spot. There should be a law saying if a redhead gets blamed for something, they probably didn't do it.'

I know I should have told her my brilliant idea for ending poverty and global warming in one go. But I was too upset about the undeserved detention.

My Prime Minister announced the Redheads Presumption of Innocence Act two days later. Any redhead who was arrested had to be set free again unless the police had actual photographs of them doing the crime. If a redhead went to court, he had two defence lawyers instead of the usual one. It was controversial. And not very practical. Criminals started dyeing their hair red so they'd have a better chance of getting away with it. People from Africa and China and the Caribbean – in fact, most people in the world – were annoyed because they hardly ever have red hair. There were Blond Riots in Manchester and Glasgow. Bald people went on strike in Wales.

I felt slightly responsible for all this. So I started avoiding Neighbourhood. Then a letter came in the post. *Congratulations!* it said. *Your loyalty card has been selected from millions of others. You have won a ride in our special Neighbourhood helicopter! It will collect you from your back garden any minute now!*

Any minute now? I looked out of the kitchen window. No sign of a helicopter. I carried on reading the letter. *Honestly*, it said. *Look out of the window again. It's just coming.*

And there was a helicopter, jerkily dropping down towards the garden, churning up grass clippings and compost. Dad came tearing downstairs. 'Who is that maniac!?' he yelled. 'Look what he's doing to my apple trees!' The apple trees were thrashing about like goths in a mosh pit. A ladder dropped down from the cockpit.

I said, 'Got to go, Dad. See you later.'

'You're not getting in there!' he yelled. 'What have I told you about taking lifts from strangers?'

But it wasn't a stranger. It was the nice lady from the checkout.

'Sorry about the helicopter,' she said. 'But the noise of the blades makes it impossible for anyone to bug our conversation. It is a secret conversation.'

'Right.'

'You know that we've been using you as a kind of unofficial adviser. You've been brilliant so far but now you've let us down.'

'I know. I'm sorry. I was upset. I can explain.'

She held up her hand. 'It's not your fault. It's ours. We never asked your permission. It was our idea. Not yours. Have you worked out why we chose you?'

'Because I'm a genius? I came second in French and third in History and—'

'We chose you because you were completely average. We looked at all the Sats scores, cat scores, school exams, shopping habits, TV habits – you are the most average boy in the whole country. We thought that anything you liked, most people would like too. Because you are like most people. There's nothing special about you. Or we thought there was nothing special about you. Then we found out about your hair. You see, on CCTV footage it looks like normal hair. But in fact, there's nothing normal about it. It's glorious. And a bit hilarious. It's definitely not average. I guess the lesson for us is that no one is average. Everyone is special. We'll try to remember that in future. In the meantime, please accept this helicopter ride as a kind of thank-you present . . .'

'Oh, thanks.'

'And as a reminder that if you ever mention this to anyone, you will be snatched by a squad of elite commandos in a helicopter like this one and smuggled out of the country to live out the rest of your days in a secret location with no TV and only goats for company.'

'Oh. Right. Well. I won't forget.'

'Good.'

*   *   *

So that was it. I went back to being Ted McKillop, most average boy in Britain. Everything was just the same except for the longer weekend and the Friday walk to school. People looked a bit happier. And that was down to me. Life went back to normal. The nearest thing to excitement after that was Benedict's birthday. He got a bike too and we had another massive combined bike joust and water fight. It was only later, when we were eating pizza, that I noticed the Neighbourhood loyalty card on his mantelpiece. I said, 'After this, do you fancy a quick go on the PlayStation?'

'No, I really want to watch the news tonight.'

'The news? On your birthday? Why?'

'I just do.'

So we watched the news. The lead story was 'Snake Swallows Antelope Whole'.

Mrs Flittersnoop's Birthday Present

From *Professor Branestawm's Great Revolution*

Written by NORMAN HUNTER
Illustrated by BRUCE INGMAN

I loved Professor Branestawm when I was a kid. He was a classic absent-minded inventor who came up with brilliantly mad inventions that always went wrong in some way. Sometimes he left out a vital part, but usually he failed to predict the awful consequences of his inventions, which would lead to chaos and destruction in the village of Great Pagwell (just next to Little Pagwell, Pagwell Gardens, Greater Pagwell, Lesser Pagwell, and so on).

The books were unusual in that they were comic stories, not about children or talking animals, but adults. The fact that they still make children laugh today tells you something about Norman Hunter's genius.

One of the reasons I was so drawn to the Professor was that, like me, he wore glasses. In fact he wore five pairs, ranged across the top of his bald head, one for reading, one for writing, one for out of doors, one for looking at you over the top of and one for looking for the others when they got lost.

He is often joined by his friend Colonel Dedshott of the Catapult Cavaliers, and rescued by his housekeeper, the long-suffering Mrs Flittersnoop, who rarely appreciates his inventions as they get in the way of the smooth running of the house (and also because they frequently attack her in some way).

In the following story it's Mrs Flittersnoop's birthday, but will the absent-minded Professor remember?

Charlie Higson

Mrs Flittersnoop's Birthday Present

Mrs Flittersnoop had a birthday coming on. And, goodness gracious, Professor Branestawm knew about it!

'Ah, Mrs Flittersnoop,' he said heartily, at breakfast. 'I believe next Tuesday is your birthday?'

Goodness knows how the Professor managed to remember that, as he certainly never remembered his own birthday, or how old he was, and very often he didn't remember where he lived. But Mrs Flittersnoop's sister Aggie had sent him a large secret letter reminding him of the date so that may have had something to do with it.

'I wonder,' went on the Professor, 'whether you would let me know what you would, er, like for a present.'

'Well, indeed, that's very kind of you, I'm sure, sir,' said Mrs Flittersnoop, thinking away like mad about what she would like to have that the Professor might possibly manage to buy without getting it too wrong.

'I think perhaps you might, ah, mark something you would like in this catalogue of Ginnibag and Knitwoddle's,' said the Professor.

That was an idea of sister Aggie's, too. The Professor handed over the Pagwell telephone directory in mistake for the catalogue.

'Thank you very much, sir,' said Mrs Flittersnoop, taking the telephone directory with the air of the Mayoress receiving an illuminated address. But she put it away and got out the catalogue instead, because she didn't really want the Great Pagwell Fire Station for a birthday present, or the second-hand bicycle shop in Lower Pagwell.

'Now, what shall I choose?' she murmured, when the breakfast was cleared away and the Professor was safely stowed in his inventory, happily clashing things about. 'I could do with a new hat,' she said to herself, turning the pages of the catalogue and watching the new hats flash by. Naturally no lady ever has enough new hats. But hats are a little on the tricky side. For one thing you can't be happy in a hat unless it's really you, and Mrs Flittersnoop didn't think Professor Branestawm would know at sight whether a hat was really her or not. And anyway, with another birthday coming on, she was reaching a slightly risky age where hats were concerned, having got past the time when she was afraid a hat was too old for her, which would have been awful, and was now rather worried in case a hat should be too young for her, which would be just as bad.

'Or again,' she said to herself, 'a pair of warm gloves would be nice, or perhaps some scent.' She giggled a bit at the thought of the Professor giving her an exotic flask of *Temptation of Eve* or *Venus Passion*.

Finally she settled for a nice new handbag, not too expensive, and big enough to take all the used bus tickets, out-of-date timetables, face tissues, packets of peppermints, nail scissors, nail files, lipstick, pencils, spare buttons, reels of cotton, safety pins, shopping lists, holiday snapshots, raffle tickets, and handbills of steamer trips which she might need to carry with her.

'That will be lovely!' she said to herself, and she made a nice thick cross against the handbag and put the catalogue on the Professor's desk.

'Ah, what's this?' mumbled the Professor, finding the catalogue. 'Ginnibag and Knitwoddle's catalogue! Dear me, did I order something from them and if so, what was it? Some new screwdrivers with self-ejecting ends? A set of heavy hammers? No, no, they don't sell things like that.' He turned over the pages and came on a page with something marked with a big cross.

'Ha!' he exclaimed, clapping his hand to his head and scattering his spectacles all over the carpet. 'Yes, yes, of course, fancy me forgetting! This is what Mrs Flittersnoop wants for her birthday. Let me see. Good gracious!'

No wonder the Professor was astonished. The mark was placed

against an elegant pipe rack, complete with a device for cleaning pipes, including a bowl scraper-out, a stem pusher-through and a tobacco shover-down.

'I really had no idea Mrs Flittersnoop smoked a pipe,' he said, 'but you never can tell these days.' And he went off to buy Mrs Flittersnoop a very special pipe rack that she certainly didn't want.

Well then, why had she marked it in the catalogue? Was she getting as absent-minded as the Professor? No, in fact she hadn't marked the pipe rack at all. She had made such a heavy inky cross against the handbag she wanted that the ink had gone right through the paper and marked itself against the pipe rack that was on the other side of the page. But how was the Professor to know that?

The Professor was looking at the pipe rack in his inventory, out of the way so that Mrs Flittersnoop shouldn't see it and spoil the surprise. 'Not that it could be much of a surprise,' he thought, 'as she already knows what I'm giving her.' Which just shows that things were not a bit as he thought, but then they hardly ever were with the Professor.

'I wonder what Mrs Flittersnoop can possibly want with this pipe rack?' he said to himself. He turned it over and round and round. He examined the pipe cleaning device. 'Perhaps she wants to use it for something else,' he thought. 'I know she uses an old coffee tin to put the milkman's money in and keeps an old knife with no handle to open tight lids. Yes, yes, that would be it. But I wonder what she is going to use this for?'

He started to think. And once Professor Branestawm started to think you never knew what it would lead to. In about ten minutes he had thought of fifteen different things he could use the pipe rack for and by tea time he had taken it to bits and invented it into several unlikely pieces of machinery.

Of course that put Mrs Flittersnoop's birthday clean out of his mind. And, when next Tuesday arrived there he was on Mrs Flittersnoop's birthday morning with no present to give her except a novelty pipe rack that was all in bits.

'Good morning, sir,' said Mrs Flittersnoop, putting a sausage in front of him.

'Ah, good morning, Mrs Flittersnoop,' said the Professor. Then he noticed a parcel beside his plate.

'Dear, dear, is it my birthday already?' he muttered.

He looked at the parcel and found a label on it that said, *To Mrs Flittersnoop, with birthday wishes from Professor Branestawm.*

Mrs Flittersnoop, who knew enough about the Professor to guess that he would never have managed to get her a present without getting himself in a muddle, had bought the handbag on his behalf. And she had gift-wrapped it for herself, too, so that all the Professor had to do was hand it graciously over with birthday remarks and plenty of smiles. And this he did without any trouble.

Oooh aah aah Oooh
When will I see you again

'Oh, thank you very much, I'm sure, sir,' she said. She unwrapped the parcel, folded the paper neatly, and said, 'A handbag! How lovely! Just what I wanted. It is most kind of you to remember my birthday, indeed, I'm sure, sir.'

And she helped him to another sausage.

Will There Be Cake?

Written by PHILIP ARDAGH
Illustrated by DAVID ROBERTS

There are plenty of adults who don't like to celebrate their birthdays or, at least, claim that they don't. I've never liked birthday *parties* – I don't think I've ever had one of my own – but I love birthdays themselves: the cards, the presents, the being special for a day. I was, therefore, quite surprised to find that I don't appear to have written more than a few fleeting lines about birthdays in my fiction . . . so I had to write this story specially.

All of it – apart from the made-up parts, of course – is absolutely true.

Philip Ardagh

Will There Be Cake?

'The Prince,' announced the duke, looking up from his breakfast newspaper, 'is going to be sixty.'

'Sixty what?' asked the duchess, who wasn't known for her razor-sharp intelligence but was remarkably good at throwing dinner parties. She was sipping very weak tea from a fine bone-china cup.

'Sixty years old,' said the duke. He looked back down at the article he'd been reading (next to an advertisement for carpet shampoo). 'It'll soon be his sixtieth birthday.'

'Will there be cake?' asked Pudge, their only son and heir. He was half hidden behind a plate piled high with everything from devilled kidneys to kippers.

Their six daughters remained silent.

'There's bound to be!' said the duke.

'Most definitely,' said the duchess. 'You can't be a prince

and not have a party on your birthday. And you can't have a birthday party without having cake.'

Pudge leaped to his feet, which was something he didn't do that often. His knees creaked as much in surprise as in protest. 'A thought has occurred to me, Papa!' he said.

'That's a first,' muttered Elvira, the eldest of the daughters. The remaining five girls giggled behind their thinly buttered slices of toast. They were sitting in a row down the opposite side of the breakfast table to their brother, in order of age (and, coincidentally, height).

As always, Pudge had a corner of the white linen tablecloth tucked into the collar of his sailor suit as a napkin, and as he jumped around with excitement – his knees now *groaning* – his plate began to slide precariously close to the edge of the table.

Gaunt, the footman, stood ready to pounce if the young marquis strayed too far. Hot food, plates, cups, toast-racks and pots of preserves often ended up on the floor. The family got through rather a lot of breakfast crockery this way, so the footman had to be ever vigilant. (The carpet in the breakfast room had been chosen for its thick pile and pattern of multi-coloured whorls, ideally suited for absorbing and incorporating everything from yoghurt stains to mustard smears.)

Breakfast in Wotton Hall was the one meal where family and guests served themselves. The food was left by an army of retreating servants in silver-domed serving dishes from which the duke and duchess and their seven delightful children made their own selection. (In Pudge's case this was less about choosing and more about 'having most of everything'.) Gaunt was simply there to clear up any breakages or administer first aid if and when required.

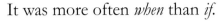

It was more often *when* than *if*.

Since childhood, the duchess had never been able to get the hang of using a fork. Firstly, she didn't know when to use it. For soup? A boiled egg? A cup of coffee? Opening a letter, perhaps? Secondly, she didn't know *how* to use it. Many was the occasion when Gaunt had found himself removing the tines – that's prongs to you or me – from her leg, or arm or eye. (That explained the eye-patch.)

'A thought?' said the duchess. 'You've had a thought, Pudge! Did you hear that, Hubert? Our boy has had a thought. How simply delightful!'

'Yes, Mama, if His Royal Highness is going to be sixty and have a sixtieth birthday cake, it'll need to be big enough to fit sixty candles . . .'

'Yes,' said his father, who wasn't the brightest star in the firmament but was remarkably good at throwing dwarfs and, later, Wellington boots (when dwarf-throwing was outlawed throughout the land).

'Which means that it's going to have to be a jolly BIG cake!'

'How right you are, m'boy! How right you are.'

Filly, the third-oldest (fourth-youngest) daughter, cleared her throat.

'Yes, Pansy?'

'I'm Filly, she's Pansy,' said Filly just as Pansy was saying, 'I'm Pansy, she's Filly.'

'What is it, Pansy – er – Filly?'

'I don't see why Pudge is getting all excited, Papa!' said Filly.

'Even if His Royal Highness does have a great big party with a great big cake, there's nothing to say we'll be invited.'

Their mother let out a strangled cry. Gaunt the footman stepped forward ready to pull the fork prongs – sorry, tines – from wherever it was she'd stuck them *now*. But this had been no cry of pain. This had been a cry of surely-not-how-could-that-be?!

'What ails you, dearest?' asked the duke. In a moment of lapsed concentration he was now buttering his ducal tie.

'Is it possible, Hubert? Might it really be so?'

'What, my darling?'

'Might the Prince hold a party and not . . . not' – she found it hard to say the words – 'not i-n-v-i-t-e u-s?'

'Anything is possible, my dear, but let me explain.' The duke pulled a well-thumbed copy of *Old Roxbee's Pocket Guide to Aristocracy* from an inside pocket of his marmalade-stained jacket (in a Prince of Wales check).

He flipped through the pages, reading a sentence here and there as he went. '*The very first duke was Edward, Duke of Cornwall, in 1337 . . . Duke Ellington wasn't really a duke . . .* Ah!' he said. 'Here we are. *Did Mary Ever Visit Brighton Beach?*'

'Mary who, dear?' asked the duchess. 'We know so many.' This wasn't strictly true because, although the duchess called all her housemaids Mary, this wasn't their actual name. Being called Mary, however, was in the terms and conditions of their employment. Mrs Harper, the housekeeper, who did all the hiring and firing of such maids, made a point of never actually employing a genuine twenty-four-carat Mary. She thought it would be unfair. In her book – a large dusty blue ledger – every maid should have to change her name without exception.

'I wasn't referring to a *real* Mary,' the duke explained (rather badly).

'You were wondering whether an *imaginary* Mary ever visited Brighton beach?' his wife asked. 'Whatever for?'

'It's a mnemonic, Mama,' explained Coriander. 'The first letter of each word refers to something else. In this instance to Duke, Marquis, Earl, Viscount, Baron and Baronet. It's the order of aristocracy—'

'With us dukes at the very top,' said her father, looking a little peeved that his second-eldest daughter should already know this. 'Which means that we are very likely to be near the top of any list of invitations to a royal sixtieth birthday party.'

'In one of his books, Philip Ardagh suggested *Dame Melba Eats Very Big Buns*,' said Elvira.

'Philip who?' asked the duke.

'An author,' said Elvira.

'Eating big buns might be bad for one's digestion and figure!' protested the duchess. 'And an author should know that the correct way of addressing her would have been Dame Nellie!' (She was, of course, referring to Dame Nellie Melba, after whom the pudding Peach Melba was named. Or was it the other way round? And wasn't there toast involved too, somewhere along the way?)

'*Do Mindless Eyes View Big Brother?*' suggested Pansy.

'Do eyes generally have minds, then?' asked a now totally confused duchess. 'And you're older than your brother, so what are you talking about?'

Intent on joining the fun, Filly piped up with: '*Don't Make Elvis Vocalize Boring Ballads!*' then whooped in a most unladylike fashion.

'What's got into you?' snapped the duke. 'The King is dead.' He had a sad faraway look in his eye.

'Dead?'

'He meant Elvis, Mama.'

'One of the cats?'

'A popular singer,' said the duke.

'I'm all shook up!' said Filly.

'I'm sorry to hear that,' said her mother.

'I've got it! I've got it!' said Pudge, with uncontained excitement. Then, to everyone's amazement, he shouted, '*Doughnuts Make Evil Vampires Barf Blood!*'

Pudge was amazed that he'd actually understood what a mnemonic was and then come up with one of his own.

So were his sisters. All six of them.

Utterly.

His father, the duke, was amazed that his only son and heir thought it acceptable behaviour to use the word 'barf' at the breakfast table, particularly in mixed company.

His mother, the duchess, was amazed to discover that undead creatures of the night ate doughnuts, even if it did make them sick. She'd always been under the impression – deliberately led to believe, in fact – that they fed solely off human blood. She was so distracted that she stabbed herself with the fork she'd been using to sweep the hair from her face. She screamed.

Pudge ran – yes, *ran* – to her, bringing the tablecloth with him. He collided with Gaunt (who'd been torn between saving the crockery and saving the duchess).

There was an almighty CRASH, and no more talk of the birthday party that morning. Or thereafter.

Ever.

A Letter from Tim Diamond

TIM DIAMOND INC.
23 THE CUTTING, CAMDEN TOWN, NW1

Dear Reader,

It's not every day I get invited to Buckingham Palace. In fact, if you want the truth, I've never been invited to Buckingham Palace. I went there once to watch the changing of the guard but I wasn't very impressed. The new guard looked exactly the same as the old one. And of course I've watched the Queen's Speech on TV at Christmas. I have to say she doesn't look too well these days with that green skin and those strange, flickering eyes. Or maybe I need a new TV.

It's never been the same since it was hit by a bullet during <u>Doctor Who</u>. I hadn't realized the gun was loaded. Anyway, since then it's only been able to get three channels and two of them are Scandinavian. Somehow it's not quite the same watching old episodes of <u>Doktor Hvem</u>. The daleks don't say 'exterminate'. They say 'tilintetgjøre'. And they look green and flickery too.

In a way, I'm a little surprised. You'd have thought something would have come my way by now – an OBE or even a knighthood for services to private detection. After all, I'm the man who found the Purple Peacock – the priceless Ming vase stolen from the British Museum. Admittedly, I sat on it – but the pieces are still on display and if the museum spent some of their grant on a tube of Araldite, everyone would be happy. I broke up a drug ring in Paris and a fake charity in London. And if it hadn't been for me, the Russian diplomat Kusenov would have been blown into so many pieces that he'd have made the Ming vase look good.

If none of this makes any sense to you, then either you're Scandinavian or you haven't read any of my books. My name is Tim Diamond. I used to be a policeman but I left the force after an incident in Hatton Gardens when two men asked me the way to the bank. How was I to know they were going to rob it? OK – maybe the stocking masks and the guns should have given me a clue, but this was Christmas and I thought they might be on their way to a party. At the time I was myself disguised as an elf.

After that I became a private detective, with offices in Camden Town and my own name on the door – although it was a while before I could afford the door. My first case was to find a dog that had gone missing on Hampstead Heath. For that, I got fifty pounds and fleas.

The owner was grateful and the dog bit me . . . although maybe it was the other way round. I can't remember now but since then I've made it a rule not to work with animals. You lose your hamster, go to the RSPCA. They're cheaper than me and they'll bring their own exercise wheel.

But once I'd got myself established, the cases begin to arrive thick and fast – and my first big client was certainly both. Not that 'big' is the right word for Johnny Naples. He was a South American gangster with a height problem. His problem was that he didn't have any. He can't have been more than four feet tall so that when he sat down, he disappeared. I'm glad he wasn't around for long because I couldn't talk to him eye-to-eye without getting a stiff neck. Naples had a fortune in diamonds hidden in a packet of Maltesers – not that it did him much good. I found him lying shot dead on a bed in a cheap hotel. I just hope they changed the sheets.

By now you get the general idea . . . There have been seven books written about me and if you haven't seen them, you've obviously been nowhere near your local Oxfam shop. They're written by a guy called Anthony Horowitz. He's a writer who's often been compared to J. K. Rowling. They say he's nowhere near as good. He's actually written quite a few bestsellers but those were quiet weeks in the publishing trade. And we're also talking Lithuania. Sell seventeen copies in Lithuania and they break open the champagne, although if you've ever tasted Lithuanian champagne, you'll wish they hadn't bothered.

Let's get to the point.

A couple of days ago, I got a knock on the door. It had been a bad week. Monday had been slapped around by Tuesday, and Wednesday might as well have stayed in bed. It was the sort of week that makes you glad there are only fifty-two of them in the year. By the time I got to Thursday, I was seriously thinking of cutting out Friday and going straight to the weekend. Outside, the rain was pattering down. It was pattering down inside too. It was definitely time I got someone to look at the roof.

I was sitting behind my desk. Or maybe I was in front of it. I'd just bought it from Ikea and you know how it is with this Swedish self-assembly stuff. The instructions might as well be in Greek. Even the angle-poise lamp seemed to be at the wrong angle. There was another knock, this time harder. Whoever it was didn't like to be kept waiting.

'Come in,' I called.

The door opened and a man walked in. Actually, he didn't walk. He marched. My first thought was that he had to be a soldier. He had square shoulders and a straight back, and looking at him, I wished he'd go straight back out again. Somehow, I knew he was trouble. His eyes were cold and unforgiving . . . a bit like his dress sense. He seemed to have left most of his hair outside, and as for what he'd brought in, he needn't have bothered. He took one look around the room and I could see him weighing it all up. Maybe he didn't like what he saw. I'd seen more pleasant smiles in the morgue.

'Are you Tim Diamond?' he demanded.

'Who wants to know?' I asked.

'Well, I do – obviously!' he snapped. 'I just asked you.' He sat down although he hadn't been invited. 'My name is Michael Morpurgo,' he said. 'And I need your help.'

'What sort of help do you have in mind, Mr Morburgo?' I said.

'Not Burgo. Purgo. The thing is, I'm putting together a book for the Prince of Wales.'

'You're writing a book for a pub?'

'Not a pub. For Prince Charles.' Two pinpricks of red appeared in his cheeks and I realized this was a man who got angry easily. I wished now I hadn't kept him waiting. I wished even more that I hadn't let him in. 'I'm talking about the heir to the throne,' he said.

'Why does he want you to write a book?'

'He doesn't know anything about it. It's a surprise for his sixtieth birthday.'

This was getting more unlikely by the minute. I'd met people who talked to the birds but that didn't mean the birds answered back. There are a lot of crazy people in North London and it looked like this might be one of them. What would he be suggesting next? A surprise party for the Pope?

'The thing is, I was wondering if you'd like to contribute . . .' he went on.

'You know the Prince of Wales?' I asked.

'Yes. But that's not the point. I'm doing this for charity—'

'Hold it right there, Mr Morcargo,' I cut in. 'The Prince doesn't need charity. He's got plenty of cash.'

'It's for the Prince's Foundation for Children and the Arts—'

'That's what you say. But the fact is, I've never heard of you—'

'You must have heard of me. I was the Children's Laureate for two years. And I wrote a book called <u>War Horse</u>. Didn't you see it at the National Theatre?'

'No. Did you leave it there?'

'They turned it into a play!' Those pinpricks had gone a little darker. 'Listen, Mr Diamond. I've come here to ask you to write something for the book. That's all. But if you're too busy or you can't be bothered . . .'

One of the drawers of my desk had slid out. I pushed it back in again. It slid out the other side. 'All right, Mr Embargo,' I said. 'This book of yours. What's in it?'

'It's going to be a collection of favourite writing by famous writers.'

'I mean . . . what's in it for you?'

'For me?' His voice wavered. He looked as if he was going to be sick. I wondered what he'd had for lunch because any minute now I was going to find out. 'There's nothing in it for me! There are no royalties involved.'

'I thought you said it was for Prince Charles.'

'All right.' He stood up with such force that the chair fell over. All the colour had left his face and there really hadn't been too much to begin with. 'All right,' he repeated. 'I knew it was going to be a waste of time coming here. You're even more stupid than I'd been led to believe and I can assure you, my book will be absolutely fine without you. I should never have asked in the first place.'

He strode out, slamming the door with full force behind him. One of the desk handles fell off. I was left on my own.

But not for long. About a minute later, the door opened and my kid brother, Nick, walked in. Maybe I should have mentioned him earlier. Nick is fourteen. He moved in with me after our parents emigrated to Australia and he somehow missed the flight. The strange thing is that they were somewhere over the English Channel before they even noticed the empty seat. And they were still laughing by the time they hit the coast of Spain. Since then, Nick has helped me with my cases. Not that I needed him, of course. But he often told me that I didn't have a clue. So then he'd help me find one.

He was just back from school. He goes to this really tough comprehensive just up the road. It's the sort of school where the teachers only leave the staff room in pairs and the uniform includes its own bullet-proof vest. He was looking excited.

'What was Michael Morpurgo doing here?' he asked.

'What?'

'I saw him leaving just now . . .'

I frowned. 'You know him?'

'Of course I know him. I've seen him on TV. He's a big-shot writer.' Nick threw down his school bag. 'Don't tell me he needs a private detective!'

Quickly, I explained what had happened. And when I described how Montego had left, Nick looked at me in horror.

'You're crazy, Tim,' he exclaimed. 'If he asked you to be in this book, you should have done it.'

'Why?'

Nick sighed. 'How about to help people less fortunate than yourself?' He thought for a moment. 'All right. There aren't any people less fortunate than yourself. But you could have done it for the publicity. This book will probably sell thousands of copies. And think of the contacts you'd make being in with all those famous writers . . .'

'Suppose I'm too busy?' I said.

'You're not busy, Tim. You haven't had any business for weeks. And in case you've forgotten, your last client is suing you.'

'I thought he was still in hospital.'

'When he gets out . . .' He looked sadly at my desk. And he was right. I didn't have any clients at the moment. The only thing in my in-tray was my out-tray, which I still hadn't managed to put together.

I didn't say anything right then. I waited until Nick had gone upstairs to do his homework and then I was straight onto the phone to the publishers. Maybe I'd been a bit hasty. This guy Michael Lumbago wasn't so crazy after all. How many words would they like? And in what order?

Because, you see, I was thinking. Lunch at Buckingham Palace. A sword gently touching my shoulders and a lady with green skin and flickering eyes muttering: 'Arise, Sir Tim.' Don't get me wrong. That isn't the reason why I've written this letter. I'm a great supporter of the Prince's Foundation for Children and the Arts.

But you never know . . .

Best wishes,

Tim Diamond

My Party

Written by KIT WRIGHT
Illustrated by POSY SIMMONDS

This is the first poem I wrote to feature a disreputable boy called Dave Dirt, in a collection called *Rabbiting On*. He has appeared in several later books of mine for children and seems loath to go away. He is capable of a certain devious ingenuity, but is more likely, as here, to be plain gross. As the Anti-guest, Dave can be relied upon to bring something to the party! I've been doing the piece in primary schools and elsewhere for thirty years and find the kids like joining in the chorus, especially its last line, bellowing and finally whispering, '*And my dear old friend, Dave Dirt.*' It makes for a slightly unruly occasion . . . like a party, I hope!

Kit Wright

My Party

My parents said I could have a party
And that's just what I did.

Dad said, 'Who had you thought of inviting?'
I told him. He said, 'Well, you'd better start writing,'
And that's just what I did

To:
Phyllis Willis, Horace Morris,
Nancy, Clancy, Bert and Gert Sturt,
Dick and Mick and Nick Crick,
Ron, Don, John,
Dolly, Molly, Polly –
Neil Peel –
And my dear old friend, Dave Dirt.

I wrote, 'Come along, I'm having a party,'
And that's just what they did.

They all arrived with huge appetites
As Dad and I were fixing the lights.
I said, 'Help yourself to the drinks and bites!'
And that's just what they did,
All of them:

Phyllis Willis, Horace Morris,
Nancy, Clancy, Bert and Gert Sturt,
Dick and Mick and Nick Crick,
Ron, Don, John,
Dolly, Molly, Polly –
Neil Peel –
And my dear old friend, Dave Dirt.

Now, I had a good time and as far as I could tell,
The party seemed to go pretty well –
Yes, that's just what it did.

Then Dad said, 'Come on, just for fun,
Let's have a *turn* from everyone!'
And a turn's just what they did,

All of them:

Phyllis Willis, Horace Morris,
Nancy, Clancy, Bert and Gert Sturt,
Dick and Mick and Nick Crick,
Ron, Don, John,
Dolly, Molly, Polly –
Neil Peel –
And my dear old friend, Dave Dirt.

AND THIS IS WHAT THEY DID:

Phyllis and Clancy
And Horace and Nancy
Did a song and dance number
That was really fancy –

Dolly, Molly, Polly,
Ron, Don and John
Performed a play
That went on and on and on –

Gert and Bert Sturt,
Sister and brother,
Did an imitation of
Each other.
(Gert Sturt put on Bert Sturt's shirt
And Bert Sturt put on Gert Sturt's skirt.)

Neil Peel
All on his own
Danced an eightsome reel.

Dick and Mick
And Nicholas Crick
Did a most *ingenious*
Conjuring trick

And my dear old friend, Dave Dirt,
Was terribly sick
All over the flowers.
We cleaned it up.
It took *hours*.

But as Dad said, giving a party's not easy.
You really
Have to
Stick at it.
I agree. And if Dave gives a party
I'm certainly
Going to be
Sick at it.

The Royal Sulphur

From *The Firework-Maker's Daughter*

Written by Philip Pullman
Illustrated by Ian Beck

If you write a story called *The Firework-Maker's Daughter*, you really have to end with a firework display. But everything in a story has to help the story work, or it gets in the way; and this isn't just any old firework display, it's one on which the very life of the heroine's father depends. Lila is a girl who has defied tradition by travelling to the grotto of the Fire-fiend himself in order to bring back some of the Royal Sulphur which, she's learned, is the one ingredient every true Firework-Maker needs. And she is determined to be a Firework-Maker, come what may.

But in the course of the story, her father Lalchand has set free the Royal Elephant, Hamlet, and the King has decreed that he will only spare Lalchand's life if he and Lila win the great firework contest that is about to take place. The other Firework-Makers – Signor Scorcini from Italy, Dr Puffenflasch from Germany, and Colonel Sam Sparkington from America – put on their displays, which are greeted with enormous applause; and finally it's Lila and Lalchand's turn.

And – it's giving the ending away, but this is a fairy tale, after all, and our heroes have to live happily ever after – when it's all over, there is a celebration. When things that have nearly gone terribly wrong all come out right in the end, what else can we do but celebrate?

Philip Pullman

The Royal
Sulphur

Lila and Lalchand looked at each other. There was nothing to say. But then they hugged each other very tightly, and ran to their places, and as soon as the audience was settled again, they began their display.

The first thing that happened was that little lotus flowers made of white fire suddenly popped open on the water, with no hint of where the fire had come from. The audience fell silent, and when the flowers began to float across the dark lake like little paper boats, they were completely hushed.

Then a beautiful green light began to glow beneath the water, and rose slowly upwards to become a fountain of green fire. But it didn't look like fire – it looked like water, and it splashed and danced like a bubbling spring.

And while the fountain played over the lake, something quite different was happening under the trees. A carpet of living moss seemed to have spread itself across the grass, a million million little points of light all so close together that they looked as soft as velvet. A sort of 'Aaah' sound came from the audience.

Then came the most difficult part. Lila had designed a sequence of fireworks based on what she had seen in the Grotto of the Fire-fiend, but it all depended on the delayed-action fuses working as they should – and of course they hadn't had time to test them properly. If some of the fireworks went off a second too early or a second too late, the whole show would make no sense.

But there was no time to worry about that now. Quickly and expertly she and Lalchand touched fire to the end of the master fuses, and held their breath.

First came a series of slow dull explosions like the beat of a muffled drum. Everything was dark. Then a red light shivered downwards, leaving a trail of red sparks hanging in the air, like a crack opening in the night. The solemn drumbeats got louder and louder, and everyone sat very still, holding their breath, because of the irresistible feeling that *something* was going to happen.

Then it did. Out of the red crack in the night a great cascade of brilliant red, orange, and yellow lava seemed to pour down and spread out like the carpet of fire in the Grotto. Lila couldn't resist glancing

up very swiftly at Dr Puffenflasch, Signor Scorcini, and Colonel Sparkington, and saw them all watching wide-eyed like little children.

When the lava carpet had flowed down almost to the edge of the lake, the speed of the drumbeat got faster, and sharp bangs and cracks beat the air between them. And suddenly, dancing as he had in the Grotto, Razvani himself seemed to be there, whirling and stamping and laughing for joy in the play of the eternal fire.

Both Lila and Lalchand forgot everything else, and seized each other's hands and danced as well. Never had they produced such a display! No matter what happened, it was worth it, everything was worth it, for a moment of joy like this! They laughed and danced for happiness.

But their fire was not Razvani's, of course, and it couldn't last for ever. The great red firework-demon burnt himself out, and the last of the red lava poured slowly into the lake, and then the little white lotus-boats, now scattered over the water like the stars in the sky, flared up and burnt more brightly than ever for a moment before all going out at once.

Then there was silence. It was a silence that got longer and longer until Lila could hardly bear it, and she gripped Lalchand's hand so tightly it nearly cracked.

And when she thought it was all over, Lalchand was doomed, everything was ruined, there came a mighty yell from Colonel Sparkington.

'*Yeee-haa!*' he cried, waving his hat. And—

'*Bravissimo!*' shouted Signor Scorcini, clapping his hands above his head. And—

'*Hoch! Hoch! Hoch!*' roared Dr Puffenflasch, seizing the cymbals from his *Bombardenorgelmitsparkenpumpe* in order to clap more loudly.

The audience, not to be out-applauded by the visiting Firework-Makers, joined in with such a roar and a stamping and a clapping and a thumping of one another on the back and a whistling and a shouting that four hundred and thirty-eight doves roosting in a tree ten miles away woke up and said, 'Did you hear that?'

Of course the court official timing the applause had to give up. It was obvious to everyone who had won, and Lalchand and Lila went up to the Royal platform where the King was waiting to present the prize.

'I keep my word,' the King said quietly. 'Lalchand, you are free. Take this prize, the pair of you, and enjoy the Festival!'

Hardly knowing what was happening, Lila and Lalchand wandered back to the darkness of the firing area under the trees. And he might have been going to say something, and she might have spoken too, but suddenly the air was filled with the sound of a mighty trumpet.

'It's Hamlet!' said Lila. 'Look! He's excited about something!'

A moment later they saw what the elephant had seen, and Lila clapped her hands for joy. A little figure came strolling on to the grass in front of the Royal platform and bowed elegantly to the King. It was Chulak.

'Your Majesty!' he said, and everyone stopped to hear what he was going to say. 'In honour of your great wisdom and generosity to all your subjects, and in celebration of your many glorious years on the throne and in the hope of many even more glorious ones ahead, and as a tribute to the splendour of your courage and your dignity, and in recognition . . .'

'He's on the verge of being cheeky,' Lalchand said, as Chulak went on. 'I can see the King tapping his foot. That's a bad sign.'

'. . . So, Your Majesty,' Chulak finished, 'I have the honour to present to you a group of the finest musicians ever heard, who will sing a selection of vocal gems, for your delight. Your Majesty, my lords, ladies and gentlemen – Rambashi's Melody Boys!'

'I don't believe it!' said Lila.

But she had to, because there were Rambashi's ex-pirates in person, wearing smart scarlet jackets and tartan sarongs. Rambashi himself, beaming all over his broad face, gave a deep bow and prepared to conduct them – but before he could begin, there was an interruption.

One of the dancing-girls who had accompanied the Royal procession from the Palace suddenly squealed and cried, 'Chang!'

And one of the Melody Boys held out his arms and cried, 'Lotus Blossom!'

'What did he say?' said Lalchand. 'Locust Bottom?'

The young couple ran to each other with their arms outstretched, but stopped, embarrassed, as they realized that everyone was watching.

'Well, go on,' said the King. 'You might as well.'

So they kissed shyly, and everyone cheered.

'And now I'd like an explanation, please,' said the King.

'I was a carpenter, Your Majesty,' said Chang, 'and I thought I ought to seek my fortune before I asked Lotus Blossom to marry me. So I went off and sought it, and that's what I'm doing here, Your Majesty.'

'Well, you'd better start singing then,' said the King.

So Chang ran back to the Melody Boys, and Rambashi counted them in, and they began to sing a close-harmony song called *Down by the Old Irrawaddy*.

'They're very good, aren't they?' said Lalchand.

'I'm amazed!' said Lila. 'After all the trouble they've had finding the right thing to do! Who would have thought it?'

The song came to an end and the King led the applause. While Rambashi was announcing the next one, Lila went to talk to Chulak, and found him stroking Hamlet's trunk. The Elephant looked happy, but of course he couldn't say so with everyone around.

'Have you heard?' said Chulak. 'Hamlet's going to get married! Oh, well done, by the way. We heard the racket they made when you won. I always knew you would. And I've got my job back!'

Hamlet cuffed him gently around the head.

'So Frangipani said yes?' said Lila. 'Congratulations, Hamlet! I'm so pleased. What made her change her mind?'

'Me!' said Chulak. 'I went and told her about his gallant deeds up on Mount Merapi, and she was conquered. Actually she said she'd loved him all the time, but she hadn't liked to say so. Old Uncle Rambashi's doing well, isn't he?'

The audience was clapping and cheering as Rambashi announced the next song. When the Melody Boys were singing and swaying to *Save the Last Mango for Me*, Lila wandered back to Lalchand, who was deep in talk with the three other Firework-Makers. They all stood up politely and asked her to join them.

'I was just congratulating yer pa on that mighty fine display,' said Colonel Sparkington. 'And half the credit goes to you, Miss. That trick with the little bitty boats that all went out at once – that's a lulu. How d'you work that stunt?'

So Lila told them about the delayed action fuses, because there are no secrets among true artists. And Dr Puffenflasch told them the art of pink fire, and Signor Scorcini told them how he made the octopus's legs wave, and they all talked for hours and liked one another enormously.

And very late, when they were extremely tired and when even Rambashi's Melody Boys had run out of songs to sing, Lila and Lalchand found themselves alone in the great garden, on the grass under the warm stars; and Lalchand cleared his throat and looked embarrassed.

'Lila, my dear,' he said, 'I've an apology to make.'

'Whatever for?'

'Well, you see, I should have trusted you. I brought you up as a Firework-Maker's daughter; I should have expected you to want to be a Firework-Maker yourself. After all, you have the Three Gifts.'

'Oh yes! The Three Gifts! Razvani asked if I had them, and I didn't know – but then he said I must have brought them after all. And what with rushing back to the city and preparing the display, and worrying about whether we'd manage to save your life, I forgot all about them. And I still don't know what they are.'

'Well, my dear, did you see the ghosts?' said Lalchand.

'Yes, I did. They didn't bring the Gifts, and they failed . . . But what *are* the Three Gifts?'

'They are what all Firework-Makers must have. They are all equally important, and two of them are no good without the third. The first one is talent, and you have that, my dear. The second has many names: courage, determination, will-power . . . It's what made you carry on climbing the mountain when everything seemed hopeless.'

Lila was silent for a moment, and then she said, 'What is the third?'

'It's simply luck,' he said. 'It's what gave you good friends like Chulak and Hamlet, and brought them to you in time. Those are the Three Gifts, and you took them and offered them to Razvani as a Firework-Maker should. And he gave you the Royal Sulphur in exchange.'

'But he didn't!'

'Yes, he did.'

'He said it was illusion!'

'In the eyes of Razvani, no doubt it is. But human beings call it wisdom. You can only gain that by suffering and risk — by taking the journey to Mount Merapi. It's what the journey is for. Each of our friends the other Firework-Makers has made his own journey in a similar way, and so has Rambashi. So you see, you didn't come home empty-handed, Lila. You did bring back the Royal Sulphur.'

Lila thought of Hamlet and Frangipani, now happily engaged. She thought of Chulak, restored to his job, and Chang and Lotus Blossom, restored to each other. She thought of Rambashi and the Melody Boys, happily snoring in the Hotel Intercontinental, dreaming of the triumphant show-business career that lay ahead of them. She thought of the other Firework-Makers and how they'd welcomed her as one of them.

And then she realized what she had learned. She suddenly saw that Dr Puffenflasch loved his pink fire, and Signor Scorcini loved his octopus, and Colonel Sparkington loved his funny moon-people. To make good fireworks you had to love them, every little sparkler or Crackle-Dragon. That was it! You had to put love into your fireworks as well as all the skill you had.

(And Dr Puffenflasch's pink fire really was very pretty. If they combined some of it with a little glimmer-juice, and some of that doubling-back powder they'd never found a use for, they might be able to—)

She laughed, and turned to Lalchand.

'*Now* I see!' she said.

And so it was that Lila became a Firework-Maker.

August

From *Ballet Shoes*

Written by NOEL STREATFEILD
Illustrated by ALEXIS DEACON

You don't have to like ballet to read this, honest! It's about an eccentric one-legged fossil-hunting professor, Gum, who, in the course of his travels, brings home three babies, dumps them on his niece, Sylvia, and for most of the book is never seen again. The babies, Pauline, Petrova and Posy, are given the surname Fossil (so that one set of nametapes, P. Fossil, will do for all!) and live a quite happy but dull life in their huge house in the Cromwell Road in London with Sylvia and Nana. And then the money Gum has left them runs out.

Sylvia takes drastic action – she fills the house with boarders, and the girls are enrolled at a theatrical academy. The fun of the story is in their struggles as they are plunged into this alien world of auditions, tap shoes and curtseys. Pauline can act but can't afford a dress to audition in, Posy can dance brilliantly but can't stop taking the mickey while she's doing it, and Petrova, who everyone thinks should dance because she's Russian, hates the whole thing and just wants to mend cars.

It was one of my favourite books as a child – in fact my copy still has chocolate cake crumbs amongst the pages: it's full of great detail about life in the theatre, but it's also about making things happen for yourself, and in this extract Pauline, Petrova and Posy are making their annual vow – to get their names in the history books and make some money!

Victoria Wood

August

On Petrova's birthday Mr Simpson took a holiday from the garage, and invited everybody in the house to a picnic. The doctors were still away, and so was Theo, and Clara was having her holiday; but the children, Sylvia, Nana, and Cook, were delighted to accept. His car was not big enough to take them all, so he borrowed a second one from the garage, and they drove to a wood outside Westerham in Kent. Mrs Simpson had bought all the lunch, so that Cook had a real holiday too. It was a terrific meal from Fortnum and Mason's, and after they had eaten, they all felt too fat to do anything for a bit. They lay on the pine needles, and looked at the sun coming through the trees, and felt absolutely contented. Even Sylvia forgot to worry, it was so hot, and the pine needles smelt so good. Presently Posy got up and took off her frock and sandals, and gave a dance for each of them; she danced Cook making a cake, and Sylvia teaching lessons, and Nana ironing, and Mr Simpson mending a car, and Mrs Simpson going to church, and Pauline as a leading lady, and Petrova

watching an aeroplane while she got dressed. She made them all laugh till the tears ran down their cheeks and they begged her to stop because laughing made them hot. Cook said she had not enjoyed anything so much since she saw Charlie in 'The Gold Rush', and Nana that it was a pity she was bent on being a dancer, as she could keep them all if she went on 'the halls'; but Mr Simpson, though he could not stop laughing, said she was a cruel little devil, and far too observant for her years.

After Posy's dances, Pauline signalled to her, and to Petrova, to come behind a tree out of earshot of the grown-ups, because they had not done their vowing, and it was Petrova's birthday.

'I've an idea,' she said. 'Do you think that we could add to our vows? Something to vow and try and earn money to help Garnie?'

After arguing a bit, they decided it would not do any harm, so Pauline raised her right arm, and said in a suitably churchy voice:

'We three Fossils vow to try and put our name into history books, because it's our very own, and nobody can say it's because of our Grandfathers, and we vow to try and earn money for Garnie until Gum comes home, Amen.'

Petrova and Posy both made faces at her, but they raised their right arms and said 'We vow'. Then Petrova burst out:

'Why did you say Amen? If you say it, we've got to too, like in church, and then it spoils the "We vow".'

'I don't know why I said it.' Pauline looked puzzled. 'It sort of came. We do need money so much, it seemed like a prayer almost.'

Posy turned a pirouette.

'If it's a prayer, we ought to be kneeling down.'

Pauline felt a bit embarrassed.

'I'm sorry; I won't say it next time.'

'You can. We don't mind, do we, Posy?' Petrova ran off. 'Come on, let's play hide-and-seek until tea.'

Tea was a gorgeous affair, with a birthday cake with twelve candles. Petrova was very pleased, as she had not had any proper presents, because neither Pauline nor Posy had any money, and Nana none to spare, and Sylvia had sold all her jewellery, and though she gave her a book, it was only one of her own, and an old book does not make a very good birthday present.

Nothing had come by the post either, which was disappointing, as both the doctors and Theo usually gave them birthday presents. So a pink-and-white birthday cake with her name on it, and candles, was a great comfort. Mrs Simpson told her to cut it, and showed her a mark which was where she was to make the cut. When the slice came out something was shining in it, and there was a golden half-sovereign. None of the children had ever seen a gold ten shillings before, and they thought it the best present any of them had ever had, though, as Pauline said, it would be a dreadful thing spending it; but Mr Simpson said, if she took it to a bank, she would get more than ten shillings for it, so it was worth the sacrifice of parting with it. At the end of tea, Cook handed Petrova her birthday present, which was a box of crackers; they were the really good kind with daylight fireworks in them as well as a cap, and pulling them and lighting the fireworks made a wonderful end to the picnic. The last firework was a little ball which, when a match was put to it, unwound until it was a large twisted snake. It looked so handsome that they made it a stand of two bricks, and put it on the top as a monument to mark where they had spent Petrova's birthday.

When they got home there were two letters for Petrova and one for Sylvia. In Petrova's were ten shillings from the two doctors and five shillings from Theo, and in Sylvia's was a letter from Miss Jay. A management were putting on 'A Midsummer Night's Dream' in September, and Pauline was to go and see them about the part of Pease-blossom, and Petrova was to be seen for the ballet of fairies.

In bed that night, Pauline said:

'Do you think adding the bit about making money to our vow had anything to do with the letter Garnie got?'

'I don't see how it could have,' Petrova pointed out. 'It came by the afternoon post, and was written before we vowed.'

Posy sat up and hugged her knees.

'It might have all the same; you never can tell what's magic.'

A Place on the Piano

Written by EVA IBBOTSON
Illustrated by DAVID GENTLEMAN

I was born in Vienna many years ago and when I was a small girl
Hitler began rounding up all the people he didn't care for – Jews
and gypsies and democrats – and sending them to camps where
most of them died.

My own family and close friends all escaped and made happy
new lives in Britain, but I had a small cousin called Marianne, aged
seven, who vanished with her family and was never heard of again.

She must, I suppose, have perished along with millions of
others, but it seemed so terrible that I, who was the same age,
should find safety and happiness in my new country and that
she should disappear into darkness; and so I have never quite
stopped wondering about her. Sometimes I've imagined that
somehow, somewhere, she was still alive. And because I'm a writer
I have thought of many ways in which her story could after all
have turned out to have a different ending.

'A Place on the Piano' is one such story – the events I have described did happen – mothers did save their babies by throwing them out of trains . . . and perhaps, who knows, my little cousin Marianne was one such child, and lived.

And if that happened what a rebirth that would be!

Eva Ibbotson

A Place on
the Piano

I always thought the war would end suddenly but it didn't – it sort of dribbled away. Six months after I stood with the other boys in my class outside Buckingham Palace – yelling for the king and queen because we'd defeated Hitler – the barrage balloons still floated like great silver grandfathers over the roofs of London. The park railings were still missing, St Paul's Cathedral stood in a sea of rubble, and there was nothing to be bought in the shops.

My teacher had explained it to me. 'Wars are expensive, Michael,' he said. 'They have to be paid for.'

Rationing got tighter – you still had to have coupons for clothes and fuel. Worst of all was the food. You could hardly see the meat ration with the naked eye, and some very weird things were issued by the government for us to eat. Tinned snoek, for example. Snoek is a South African fish and when Cook opened the tin, it turned out to be a bluish animal with terrifying spikes, swimming in a sea of gelatinous goo – and the smell was unspeakable.

'This time they've gone too far,' she said, and she tried to give it to the cat, who sneered and turned away.

I knew quite a lot about rationing because I was a sort of kitchen boy. Not that I worked in the kitchen exactly; I'd just won a scholarship to the grammar school, but I lived below stairs in the basement of a large house belonging to a family called Glossop, where my mother was the housekeeper. We'd lived there, in London, all through the war.

I remember the snoek particularly because we were just wondering what to do with it when the bell went and my mother was called upstairs.

When she came back she looked really happy and excited. 'Little Marianne Gerstenberger has been found. She's alive!'

It was incredible news. Marianne had been thrown out of a cattle train when she was a baby. It was her own mother who had done it. She'd been rounded up with some other Jews and she was on her way to a concentration camp when she found a weak place in one of the boards behind the latrine. She got the others to help her work on it to make a small hole. And then she bundled up the baby, and when the train stopped for a moment she managed to push her out onto the track.

We'd heard a lot about bravery during the last six years of war: soldiers in Burma stumbling on, dying of thirst; parachutists at Arnhem; and of course the Spitfire pilots who had saved us in the Blitz. But the story of Marianne caught us all.

'To do that,' said my mother; 'to push your own baby out onto the track because you knew you were going to your death . . .'

At first my mother had tried not to speak of what had happened when Hitler went mad and tried to exterminate the Jews. But my school was the kind where they told you things, and I'd seen the newsreels. I'd seen the bodies piled up when the Allies opened up the camps, and the skeletons which were supposed to be people. Marianne's parents had both perished, but now, as the news came through from the Red Cross in Switzerland, it seemed that the baby had survived. She had been found by a peasant family who had taken her in and was living in East Germany, close to the border with Poland.

'They're going to fetch her,' said my mother. 'They're going to take her in.' And there were tears in her eyes.

'They' were her employers – the Glossops – who lived in the house above us and who she served. The Glossops were not Jewish, but Marianne's mother had been married to the son of their Jewish business partners in Berlin. Glossop and Gerstenberger had been a well-known firm of exporters.

'They're going to adopt her,' my mother went on. She didn't often speak warmly about the Glossops, but I could hear the admiration in her voice.

'She'll live like a little princess,' said Cook. 'Imagine, after being brought up with peasants.'

Everyone agreed with this: the kids in my school, the people in the shops, the tradesmen who came to deliver goods to the basement. Because the Glossops weren't just well off, they were properly rich.

Their house was the largest in the square, double-fronted – and furnished as though the war had never been. To go up the service stairs and through the green baize door into the house was like stepping into a different world.

Mrs Glossop and her mother-in-law had spent the war in a hotel in the Lake District to get away from the bombs; and her daughter, Daphne, who was ten years old, had been away at boarding school, but the house stayed open because Mr Glossop used it when he was in town on business, which meant that the servants had to keep it ready for him whenever he wanted.

So my mother and I went upstairs most days to check the blackout curtains and make sure the shutters were closed and none of the windowpanes had cracked in the raids – and I knew the house as well as I knew the dark rooms in the basement where we lived, along with the cook and old Tom, the chauffeur-handyman.

I knew the dining room with its heavy button-backed chairs and the carved sideboard where they kept the napkin rings and the cruets which Tom polished every week. I knew the drawing room with its thick Turkish carpet and massive sofas – and I knew old Mrs Glossop's boudoir on the first floor with the gilt mirrors and claw-footed tables – and the piano.

I knew the piano very well. I remember once when I was upstairs helping my mother, I heard a V1 rocket cut out above me, which meant I had about half a minute before it came down and exploded – and without thinking I dived under the piano.

It was an enormous piano – a Steinway Concert Grand – but I'd never heard anybody play it. It was a piano for keeping relations on.

On the dark red chenille cover which protected it were rows of Glossops in silver frames: old Glossops and young ones, Glossops on their horses and Glossops in their university gowns. There were Glossop children in their school uniforms or holding cricket bats, and there were Glossop women in their presentation dresses ready to go to court. There was even a Glossop who had been knighted, and as I lay there, waiting for the rocket to fall, I wasn't in the least bit scared – I didn't feel anyone would dare to destroy a whole army of Glossops, and I was right. It came down three streets away.

And now Marianne Gerstenberger, who was just seven years old, would have her own place on the piano, and be a Glossop too.

* * *

The preparations for Marianne began straight away, and we all threw ourselves into the work. It may sound silly, but I think it was then that we realized that the war was well and truly over, and that good things were happening in the world.

'We'll put her in the room next to Daphne's,' said Mrs Glossop – and she gave my mother a list of all the things that needed to be done. New curtains of pale blue satin to be sewn, and the bed canopied with the same material. A white fur rug on the floor, the walls re-papered with a design of forget-me-nots and rosebuds, and a new dressing table to be lined with a matching pattern. Furniture was difficult to get – you had to have coupons for almost everything – but when you own three department stores the rules don't really apply. The Glossops had always had everything they wanted, and that included food. Parcels from America had come all through the war and they were coming still.

'She can have my dolls – I don't play with them any more,' said Daphne, but Mrs Glossop ordered a whole batch of new dolls and fluffy toys and games from the store.

'Of course she'll be a little savage,' said old Mrs Glossop. 'We must be patient with her.'

She sent my mother out to get one of the napkin rings engraved with Marianne's name and I imagined the little girl sitting in the big solemn dining room with all the Glossop ancestors looking down from the wall, carefully rolling up her damask napkin after every meal.

Actually, I knew exactly the sort of life Marianne was going to lead, because of Daphne.

Daphne didn't speak to me much; she was not the sort of girl who spoke to servants. A year earlier I'd pulled off an Alsatian who was holding her at bay as she played in the gardens of the square, and got quite badly bitten, and while my hands were bandaged she was positively friendly, but it didn't last.

Mostly Daphne was away at boarding school, but when she was at home she led a very busy life. On Saturday morning she put on her jodhpurs and Tom drove her to the park where she went riding – trotting down the sanded paths and greeting other children on well-groomed ponies. On Monday afternoon, she carried her dancing shoes in a velvet bag to Miss Bigelow's Academy and learned ballet, and on Thursdays she did elocution with a lady called Madame Farnari.

Marianne would do all this – but not for long, because as soon as she had her eighth birthday she would be taken to a school outfitter to buy a brown velour hat and a brown gymslip and a hockey stick and go off with Daphne to St Hilda's, where the school motto was 'Play straight and play the game'.

'When you think what that school costs, and the kind of children who go there – all those honourables and what have you – it'll be a wonderful thing for the little thing,' said old Tom, the chauffeur. 'Mind you, she'll have a lot to learn.'

As it turned out, we had several months to get ready for Marianne, because even the Glossops didn't find it easy to get the passports and permits and papers that were needed to bring Marianne to Britain. Things were made more difficult because the village where Marianne now lived was in the part of Germany that was occupied by the

Russians and they were very strict about who could come into their zone and who could not.

But at last a permit came through, allowing two people to travel to Orthausen and pick up the little girl. The permit was for a particular week in July and now my mother was sent for again. What's more, she was asked to sit down, which was unusual.

'It's so awkward, such a nuisance,' said Mrs Glossop to my mother. 'But the permit covers the day of the royal garden party and I've been asked to attend. I simply couldn't miss that – and two days later it's Daphne's prize-giving at St Hilda's and of course I must go down for that.'

My mother waited, wondering why she had been summoned.

'My husband would go and fetch the little girl, but he has the annual meeting of the cricket club and then a very important Rotary dinner in Aberdeen at which he's been asked to speak.' She bent forward and fixed my mother with a stern eye. 'So I want you to fetch Marianne. It's so convenient because you speak German.'

This was true. My mother had been studying modern languages at university when my father had married and deserted her, all in three months.

But my mother said she couldn't leave me. This was nonsense, of course, but she said it very firmly. I think she felt that the Glossops should go themselves to fetch their new daughter – or perhaps she was nervous. Since my father betrayed her, she had looked for a quiet life – a life where the two of us would be safe.

'Well, the permit is for two people. I don't see why Michael shouldn't go with you; we don't have to say that he's only twelve years old.'

So it was my mother and I who went to fetch Marianne Gerstenberger, but before we left we were given some very important instructions.

'Marianne has a birthmark on her arm,' said Mrs Glossop. 'Her mother wrote to us about it when she was born. It's on her right arm and it runs from her shoulder to her elbow – and you must make absolutely sure that she does have that mark and in the right place. It's one thing to adopt the daughter of one's husband's partner and another to take in any stray that wants a comfortable home.' And she told us that though Marianne's name had been pinned to her blanket, it was possible that in those frightful times the baby's things had been stolen and given to some other child.

'We will make sure,' promised my mother – and two weeks later we set off.

It was quite a journey. Ordinary people hadn't been allowed to travel all through the war and of course I was excited, crossing the Channel, getting a train to go through the Netherlands and Germany.

Or rather, five trains. Most of the rolling stock had been destroyed in Allied bombing raids. We stopped and started and were pushed out onto the platform and back in again. There was no food to be had on the train, or water, and I couldn't help wondering if it was because she knew how uncomfortable the journey was going to be that Mrs Glossop had decided to send my mother instead. We went through towns that were nothing but heaps of rubble and countryside with burned and empty fields. It was odd to think that it was we who had caused all this destruction. I'd thought of bombing as something that the Germans did.

We spent the night in a cold and gloomy little hotel on the Belgian border, and the next day we travelled east through Germany.

I asked my mother if this was the route that Marianne's mother would have travelled on her last journey but she didn't know.

We were going through farmland now: fields and copses and little villages. The houses looked poor and small but there were a few animals: cows and sheep. The peasants were struggling to get back to a normal life.

We had to change twice more onto branch lines, travelling on trains so old that we didn't think they would manage to pull their loads. Then in the late afternoon we reached Orthausen.

The village that Marianne lived in was not directly on the railway. The woman who found her must have carried her bundle a long way to her house. My mother and I now walked that road, trudging along

the white dust village street with our bags and turning off along a track which ran beside a stream.

Then, late in the afternoon, we crossed a small bridge and came to a wooden house standing by itself in a clearing.

Marianne was sitting on the steps of the porch. She was holding a tortoiseshell kitten on her lap and talking to it – not fussing over it, just telling it to behave. She spoke in German, but I knew exactly what she was saying.

She had thick, fawn, curly hair and brown eyes and she wore a dirndl, and over it a knitted jersey which covered her arms. When she saw us she put down the kitten and then she reached for the bag my mother carried and led us into the house.

The woman who had found Marianne on the railway track was called

Mrs Wasilewski. She was very pale with a screwed-down bun of fair hair and a tight mouth. To me she looked like a death's head, so white and forbidding, and I was glad that we were going to take Marianne away from such a cold, stern woman. But Marianne went up to her trustingly and said, here were the visitors from England, and I realized that she did not yet know why we had come.

Mrs Wasilewski offered us some ersatz coffee and slices of dark bread spread with dripping. Her husband was away, working in a sawmill in the north of the country for the summer, to earn some extra money. When we had eaten, Marianne turned to me and took me by the hand, and said, '*Komm*,' and I got up and followed her.

When somebody takes you by the hand and says, '*Komm*,' it is not difficult to guess what they are saying, but it still seems odd to me that from the first moment I understood Marianne so completely, and that she understood me.

The Wasilewskis had a smallholding, but the Germans had commandeered the horse at the beginning of the war and the Russians had taken the cow at the end of it. All the same, the animals that were left seemed to satisfy Marianne. She introduced me to the two goats – a white one, called Bella, and a bad-tempered brown one, called Sidonia, after a disagreeable lady who scowled at everybody in the church. She showed me the five hens and told me their names and the rabbits and the new piglet, honking in the straw.

Actually, it was more than showing . . . she sort of presented them to me, giving me the animals to hold as if hanging onto a squawking chicken or a lop-eared rabbit must make me the happiest person in the world.

It was far too late to try and make our way back that night – no one knew how the trains would run. Mrs Wasilewski – still unsmiling and gaunt – led us to a loft with two goosedown duvets on a slatted wooden board and we went to bed.

I was sure we'd leave the next morning, but we didn't. My mother helped Mrs Wasilewski with the housework and once again Marianne put out her hand and said, '*Komm*,' and once again I came.

She led me to a part of the stream where the water ran clear over a bed of pebbles. Both of us took off our shoes, but she kept on her jersey, and we walked along the river bed, dredging up bright and glittering stones.

'*Nicht Gold*,' she said, holding out a yellow-veined stone and shaking her head, but she was smiling. She didn't want gold, I could see that. She wanted brightness.

The stream was full of sticklebacks and newts and tiny frogs; all the creatures too small to have been stolen or pillaged in war.

After a while a boy and a girl appeared – a brother and sister – and Marianne introduced me, carefully pronouncing my name in the English way I'd taught her.

We came to a bridge where the current ran quite fast and we each chose a stick and raced it from one side to the other. I hadn't done that since I was at infant school, but you can't go wrong with Pooh sticks, and I found myself wondering if they played it at St Hilda's.

Mrs Wasilewski, still grim and silent, gave us lunch – pieces of salt bacon with beetroot and cabbage from her garden – and afterwards Marianne took me out and showed me the rows of vegetables, and picked a pea pod from the vine and opened it, dropping the shelled peas into my palm.

All that day Marianne stretched out her hand and said, '*Komm.*' She showed me a hedgehog asleep in the potting shed and a place where raspberries grew wild, and I made her a whistle out of a hazel twig. I'd brought my Swiss Army knife, and the whistle was a good one. They don't always work but this one did.

Even the next day my mother said nothing about leaving. We slept on the floor; the work she was helping with was far harder than any that she did in England and Mrs Wasilewski still went round like a zombie, but my mother didn't seem in any hurry to return.

That day Marianne showed me her special tree. It was an ancient oak standing on its own on a small hill and it was the kind of tree that is a whole world in itself. There were hollows in the trunk where squirrels had stored their nuts; beetles sheltered under the bark and a woodpecker tapped in the branches.

Marianne had not *built* a tree-house because the tree *was* her house.

She explained this as we climbed up – and that it was in this house that she kept her treasures. They lived in a tin with a picture of cough lozenges on the lid, and she showed them to me, one by one. There was a tortoiseshell hair slide, a little bent; a bracelet made out of glass beads; a propelling pencil – and her most important possession: a small bear, carved roughly out of wood, which Mr Wasilewski had made on her last birthday. Then she took the whistle I had made for her out of her pocket and laid it carefully in the tin beside the other things, and closed the lid.

But the best thing about the tree was the view. Because it stood on a knoll you could see the surrounding countryside for miles. Marianne pointed to a small farm and told me that the man who had lived there had been killed on the Eastern Front. He'd been a German, of course – maybe a Nazi – but Marianne's face grew sad as she told me about him, which was strange because her mother's people had been so horribly persecuted by men like him.

If she was the child we thought she was . . .

But in the opposite direction was a low, red-roofed house and she told me that the man who owned it had a litter of sheepdog puppies and he was going to let her have one. There was enough food now to keep a dog, she said joyfully; it was no longer forbidden.

I didn't say anything. She would never be able to bring a dog into England; the quarantine regulations were far too strict, and the Glossops said it wasn't fair to keep animals in town. Even the cat we kept in the basement knew better than to make her way upstairs.

Then on the morning of the third day my mother called me into the kitchen. Mrs Wasilewski was there, more silent and morose than ever. There was a bundle on the table: the blanket Marianne had been wrapped in, I guessed, when she was found on the track, and a few baby clothes. Mrs Wasilewski called Marianne to her side and she came. For the first time, she looked puzzled and anxious.

'Wait,' said my mother. 'We must make sure we have the right child.' And very gently she said, 'Will you take your jersey off, Marianne, and your blouse?'

Marianne looked at Mrs Wasilewski, who nodded. Then she took off her jersey and undid the drawstring of her blouse.

Now she stood before us with both arms bare. From her shoulder to her elbow, her right arm was covered in a dark brown birthmark.

It was exactly what the Glossops had described to us. Without a doubt, the child who stood before us was the child who had been thrown from the train.

My mother and I looked at each other. Mrs Wasilewski stood like a ramrod, her mouth tight shut. Marianne, still puzzled, reached for her blouse and began to put it on.

The room was very still. Then my mother cleared her throat and looked at me again. She looked at me hard.

'What a pity,' she said clearly to Mrs Wasilewski. 'I'm so sorry. I'm afraid this is the wrong child. We can't take her back with us – her birthmark is on the wrong arm.' And then, softly: 'She will have to stay with you.'

The silence was broken suddenly by a gasp – followed by a kind of juddering sound. Then Mrs Wasilewski went mad. Her head dropped forward onto the table and she began to cry – but you can't call it crying. She erupted in tears, she became completely drenched in them, her hair came down and fell in damp strands across the table. I have never in all my life heard anybody cry like that.

When she lifted her head again she was a totally different woman; she was rosy, she laughed, she hugged my mother and me. And I understood what my mother had understood at once — that this woman who had made Marianne's world with such loving care had been almost destroyed at the thought of losing her.

In the train my mother said, 'I think we'll just say there was no birthmark. We don't want any further fuss about left or right.'

'Yes.' The train chugged on through what had once been enemy territory and was now just the great plain of central Europe. 'I'm going back,' I said. 'Later.' And then: 'Not much later.'

'Yes, I know,' said my mother. 'And I'm going on.'

(And she did too. She gave up her job with the Glossops and went back to finish her degree. We lived in two small rooms and were very happy.)

When we got back we were called up to the boudoir so that the old lady too could hear our story.

'Oh, well,' said Mrs Glossop, when we'd finished. 'It's a pity, when we had so much to offer a child. But it doesn't sound as though she would have fitted in.'

And my mother looked at the piano, with its two dozen important Glossops in silver frames, and said no, she wouldn't have fitted in. She wouldn't have fitted in at all.

The Gardens of Treachery

From *The Eye of the Horse*

Written by JAMILA GAVIN
Illustrated by ANNA BHUSHAN

Why do I think it appropriate? Because Gandhi was assassinated in the January of 1948 when I was a child, aged six, in London, having been brought there by my mother to escape the horrors of Partition. We were still there when Prince Charles was born the following November, and my mother took us down to wait among the crowds outside Buckingham Palace for the announcement. A few months later, we returned to India, but I wrote a song/poem for him, which I sent to Princess Elizabeth, and was really proud to receive a reply (albeit from her lady-in-waiting).

> Bonnie Charles my darling
> England's little princeling

What do you see on your ride?
Policemen and soldiers
Horse men and sailors,
Down by the old Thames' side.

So not only is the year of great importance to me – but it was
a significant year, with India having been the first country to leave
the Empire in 1947, now embroiled in such bitter division. Prince
Charles's birth must have seemed like a good omen for the future.

Jamila Gavin

The Gardens of Treachery

Marvinder had been dreaming about a horse. Sitting astride a white horse, she had been galloping . . . galloping . . . along twisting mountain trails; jumping gulleys and ditches and bubbling streams; ducking her head beneath the low branches of pine and spruce; then breaking out onto an open plain, where a silver horizon ran unimpeded from end to end; where the wind caught the horse's tail and made it fan out behind it like a silver cataract; and her heart beat with the drumming of its hooves, as they sped along so fast, that any minute now, she felt they would leap up into the skies and gallop among the stars.

But the sounds which awoke her were slow and heavy. Marvinder heard the early morning clip-clop of the milkman's cart coming down to Whitworth Road, and the faint tinkle of bottles as he unloaded the quota destined for No. 30.

She eased herself silently out of bed and sped, barefoot, down the freezing lino-covered stairs, to the front door. She opened it in time to see the milkman climbing the front steps with cheery face beaming out at her from beneath his peaked cap.

'Hello, my little early bird,' he whispered, as with practised silence he set down the various groups of milk bottles in their proper places. 'Looking for worms?'

She grinned back, remembered how it was he who taught her the saying, 'It's the early bird that catches the worm.'

Then, suddenly, his face became grave, and he bent forward confidentially. 'There was news on the wireless this morning that'll interest you,' he murmured.

'Oh?' Marvinder was puzzled.

'Mahatma Gandhi.' The milkman said the name with reverence. 'He's been shot.'

It was Friday, 30th January 1948.

So, Marvinder in England heard the news before the clerk in India. The clerk didn't hear till almost evening. He had been accounting all day, sitting in front of large dusty ledger books, with his specs balanced on his nose, pencil in hand, roaming up and down columns of figures, calculating, adding and subtracting and dividing, his brain revolving and clicking like the beads on an abacus.

'What do you want?' he demanded of the gangly youth who lingered somewhat insolently in the doorway.

The clerk knew he was something of a laughing-stock with his colleagues, who liked to tease him for being such a faithful disciple of the Mahatma – especially as he came to work wearing a coarse khadi dhoti, instead of refined white cotton trousers and shirts or even western-style suits. What's more, he had insisted on removing the top of his desk from its frame, placing it on the floor and working

cross-legged. 'We Indians should do things the Indian way, not ape the Britishers,' he had declared with an air of moral superiority. However, it irked him no end, to think that he was being smirked at behind his back, by the cocky young messengers who hung about the office.

'You haven't heard the news, then?' asked the youth with mock concern.

'What news?' The clerk frowned. He straightened his back from his cross-legged position, and adjusted his spectacles which had slipped down his nose. As he did so, he was aware of the sound of women wailing in the background and agitated voices, rising and falling in repeating sequences of distress. Anxiously, he gathered up his dhoti and got to his feet.

'It's your beloved leader; the Father of the People . . . Bapu . . .' The youth drawled out the words slowly and sarcastically, relishing the puzzled anxiety he could see beginning to furrow the clerk's face.

'Gandhiji? Gandhiji?'

'He's been shot!'

'Is he dead?'

'Oh yes.' The youth tittered, then fled.

Slipping . . . slipping . . . the ground was slipping away from beneath his feet. The clerk clutched his heart and then his head. The whole world became dark and began to spin around him as if out of control . . . it was a past betrayed . . . a future lost . . . what would happen . . . what would become of them? All that slaughter . . . destruction . . . and a terrible sickness of the soul . . . who could heal the wounds? Who could save them now? What revenge would God take for the death of a saint? Slipping . . .

slipping . . . there was nothing solid for his feet to stand on.

The clerk crumpled to the ground, his arms clutched around his head as if waiting to be sucked away into oblivion.

In his distraught mind, he wandered through beautiful gardens of ornamental lakes and perfumed fountains; down shaded avenues of cypresses; into fruit groves and walled gardens, where flowering bushes were bursting with colour and profusion. They were gardens of order and peace created out of a jungle of danger and chaos. Yet a voice whispered in his brain. Beware! Beware the beast that lurks; the enemy disguised as a friend; the serpent coiled among the boughs of the tree in the garden of Eden, waiting for Eve; beware the Judas seeking out Jesus in the Garden of Gethsemane to embrace him with the kiss of betrayal; Ravana, king of the demons disguised as a holy man; the devil who has gained access into the inner sanctuary.

But it was too late for warnings. In a garden in Delhi, an assassin lurked among the shrubberies of Birla House. A man, pretending to be a disciple, waited for Gandhi.

The Mahatma was still frail and impossibly thin after his long fast. Flanked by his faithful women followers, on whose shoulders he rested a hand for support, he walked trustingly to a prayer meeting. The assassin stepped forward. So close. As close as friends. He faced him, looked him in the eye, then shot him three times.

'Hiya Ram, Ram, Ram!' were the last words on the Mahatma's dying breath.

'The light has gone out of our world,' wept the Prime Minister.

My Father Is a Polar Bear

From *From Hereabout Hill*

Written by MICHAEL MORPURGO
Illustrated by MICHAEL FOREMAN

I remember friends at school thinking it was rather strange that I called my parents Jack and Kippe, whilst they talked of Daddy and Mummy, or Dad and Mum, or Father and Mother. I didn't mind. I quite liked being odd. I took a particular pride in the oddity of my mother's name. But it took some while for me to discover why it was so frowned upon in our family to call Kippe 'Mummy', or Jack 'Daddy'. Later I found out it was part of a cunning plan to disguise an unspoken family secret.

In the 1940s and 50s a divorce in the family was a cause for deep shame. My father and mother divorced just after the end of World War II, and my father went off to live in Canada to start a new life. My mother remarried. So my brother and I now had a stepfather, and very soon a half-brother and a half-sister. Our stepfather gave us his surname. So now, to the outside world, we were all one happy family, the Morpurgo family. All four of us children called our 'parents' Jack and Kippe, thus avoiding any embarrassing questions.

The divorce was never spoken of. Our birth father was simply airbrushed out of the picture. Not only was our father not spoken of, but my brother and I did not even see him, not once, until we were in our twenties, and back home for Christmas.

It was Christmas Eve. They were showing *Great Expectations* on the BBC. We didn't know it but we were in for the surprise of our lives . . .

Michael Morpurgo

My Father
Is a Polar Bear

Tracking down a polar bear shouldn't be that difficult. You just
follow the paw prints. My father is a polar bear. Now if you had
a father who was a polar bear, you'd be curious, wouldn't you? You'd
go looking for him. That's what I did, I went looking for him, and I'm
telling you he wasn't at all easy to find.

In a way I was lucky, because I always had two fathers. I had a father who *was* there – I called him Douglas – and one who wasn't there, the one I'd never even met – the polar bear one. Yet in a way he was there. All the time I was growing up he was there inside my head. But he wasn't only in my head, he was at the bottom of our Start-Rite shoe box, our secret treasure box, with the rubber bands round it, which I kept hidden at the bottom of the cupboard in our bedroom. So how, you might ask, does a polar bear fit into a shoebox? I'll tell you.

My big brother Terry first showed me the magazine under the bedclothes, by torchlight, in 1948 when I was five years old. The magazine was called *Theatre World*. I couldn't read it at the time, but he could. (He was two years older than me, and already mad about acting and the theatre and all that – he still is.) He had saved up all his pocket money to buy it. I thought he was crazy. 'A shilling! You can get about a hundred lemon sherbets for that down at the shop,' I told him.

Terry just ignored me and turned to page twenty-seven. He read it out: '"*The Snow Queen*, a dramat— something or other – of Hans Christian Andersen's famous story, by the Young Vic Company."' And there was a large black and white photograph right across the page – a photograph of two fierce-looking polar bears baring their teeth and about to eat two children, a boy and a girl, who looked very frightened.

'Look at the polar bears,' said Terry. 'You see that one on the left, the fatter one? That's our dad, our real dad. It says his name and everything – Peter Van Diemen. But you're not to tell. Not Douglas, not even Mum, promise?'

'My dad's a polar bear?' I said. I was a little confused.

'Promise you won't tell,' he went on, 'or I'll give you a Chinese burn.'

Of course I wasn't going to tell, Chinese burn or no Chinese burn. I was hardly going to go to school the next day and tell everyone that I had a polar bear for a father, was I? And I certainly couldn't tell my mother, because I knew she never liked it if I ever asked about my real father. She always insisted that Douglas was the only father I had. I knew he wasn't, not really. So did she, so did Terry, so did Douglas. But for some reason that was always a complete mystery to me, everyone in the house pretended that he was.

Some background might be useful here. I was born, I later found out, when my father was a soldier in Baghdad during the Second World War. (You didn't know there were polar bears in Baghdad, did you?) Sometime after that my mother met and fell in love with a dashing young officer in the Royal Marines called Douglas Macleish. All this time, evacuated to the Lake District away from the bombs, blissfully unaware of the war and Douglas, I was learning to walk and talk and do my business in the right place at the right time. So my father came home from the war to discover that his place in my mother's heart had been taken. He did all he could to win her back. He took her away on a week's cycling holiday in Suffolk to see if he could rekindle the light of their love. But it was hopeless. By the end of the week they had come to an amicable arrangement. My father would simply disappear, because he didn't want to 'get in the way'. They would get divorced quickly and quietly, so that Terry and I could be brought up as a new family with Douglas as our father. Douglas would adopt us and give us Macleish as our surname.

All my father insisted upon was that Terry and I should keep Van Diemen as our middle name. That's what happened. They divorced. My father disappeared, and at the age of three I became Andrew Van Diemen Macleish. It was a mouthful then and it's a mouthful now.

So Terry and I had no actual memories of our father whatsoever. I do have some vague recollections of standing on a railway bridge somewhere near Earls Court in London, where we lived, with Douglas's sister – Aunty Betty, as I came to know her – telling us that we had a brand new father who'd be looking after us from now on. I was really not that concerned, not at the time. I was much more interested in the train that was chuffing along under the bridge, wreathing us in a fog of smoke.

My first father, my real father, my missing father, became a taboo person, a big hush-hush taboo person that no one ever mentioned, except for Terry and me. For us he soon became a sort of secret phantom father. We used to whisper about him under the blankets at night. Terry would sometimes go snooping in my mother's desk and he'd find things out about him. 'He's an actor,' Terry told me one night. 'Our dad's an actor, just like Mum is, just like I'm going to be.'

It was only a couple of weeks later that he brought the theatre magazine home. After that we'd take it out again and look at our polar bear father. It took some time, I remember, before the truth of it dawned on me – I don't think Terry can have explained it very well. If he had, I'd have understood it much sooner – I'm sure I would. The truth, of course – as I think you might have guessed by now – was that my father was both an actor *and* a polar bear at one and the same time. Douglas went out to work a lot and when he was home he was a bit silent, so we didn't really get to know him. But we did get to know Aunty Betty. Aunty Betty simply adored us, and she loved giving us treats. She wanted to take us on a special birthday treat, she said – it was her birthday, not ours. Would we like to go to the zoo? Would we like to go to the pantomime? There was *Dick Whittington* or *Puss in Boots*. We could choose whatever we liked.

Quick as a flash, Terry said, '*The Snow Queen*. We want to go to *The Snow Queen*.'

So there we were a few days later, Christmas Eve 1948, sitting in the stalls at a matinée performance of *The Snow Queen* at the Young Vic theatre, waiting, waiting for the moment when the polar bears come on. We didn't have to wait for long. Terry nudged me and pointed, but I knew already which polar bear my father had to be. He was the best one, the snarliest one, the growliest one, the scariest one. Whenever he came on he really looked as if he was going to eat someone, anyone. He looked mean and hungry and savage, just the way a polar bear should look.

I have no idea whatsoever what happened in *The Snow Queen*. I just could not take my eyes off my polar bear father's curling claws, his slavering tongue, his killer eyes. My father was without doubt the finest polar bear actor the world had ever seen. When the great red curtains closed at the end and opened again for the actors to take their bows, I clapped so hard that my hands hurt. Three more curtain calls and the curtains stayed closed. The safety curtain came down and my father was cut off from me, gone, gone for ever. I'd never see him again.

Terry had other ideas. Everyone was getting up, but Terry stayed sitting. He was staring at the safety curtain as if in some kind of trance. 'I want to meet the polar bears,' he said quietly.

Aunty Betty laughed. 'They're not bears, dear, they're actors, just actors, people acting. And you can't meet them, it's not allowed.'

'I want to meet the polar bears,' Terry repeated.

So did I, of course, so I joined in. 'Please, Aunty Betty,' I pleaded. 'Please.'

'Don't be silly. You two, you do get some silly notions sometimes. Have a choc ice instead. Get your coats on now.'

So we each got a choc ice. But that wasn't the end of it.

We were in the foyer caught in the crush of the crowd when Aunty Betty suddenly noticed that Terry was missing. She went loopy. Aunty Betty always wore a fox stole, heads still attached, round her shoulders. Those poor old foxes looked every bit as pop-eyed and frantic as she did, as she plunged through the crowd, dragging me along behind her and calling for Terry.

Gradually the theatre emptied. Still no Terry. There was quite a to-do, I can tell you. Policemen were called in off the street. All the programme sellers joined in the search, everyone did. Of course, I'd worked it out. I knew exactly where Terry had gone, and what he was up to. By now Aunty Betty was sitting down in the foyer and sobbing her heart out. Then, cool as a cucumber, Terry appeared from nowhere, just wandered into the foyer. Aunty Betty crushed him to her, in a great hug. Then she went loopy all over again, telling him what a naughty, naughty boy he was, going off like that. 'Where were you? Where have you been?' she cried.

'Yes, young man,' said one of the policemen. 'That's something we'd all like to know as well.'

I remember to this day exactly what Terry said, the very words: 'Jimmy riddle. I just went for a jimmy riddle.' For a moment he even had me believing him. What an actor! Brilliant.

We were on the bus home, right at the front on the top deck where you can guide the bus round corners all by yourself – all you have to do is steer hard on the white bar in front of you. Aunty Betty was sitting a couple of rows behind us. Terry made quite sure she wasn't looking. Then, very surreptitiously, he took something out from under his coat and showed me. The programme. Signed right across it were these words, which Terry read out to me:

'To Terry and Andrew,
With love from your polar bear father, Peter. Keep happy.'

Night after night I asked Terry about him, and night after night under the blankets he'd tell me the story again, about how he'd gone into the dressing room and found our father sitting there in his polar bear costume with his head off (if you know what I mean), all hot and sweaty. Terry said he had a very round, very smiley face, and that he laughed just like a bear would laugh, a sort of deep bellow of a laugh – when he'd got over the surprise that is. Terry described him as looking like a 'giant pixie in a bearskin'.

For ever afterwards I always held it against Terry that he never took me with him that day down to the dressing room to meet my polar bear father. I was so envious. Terry had a memory of him now, a real memory. And I didn't. All I had were a few words and a signature on a theatre programme from someone I'd never even met, someone

who to me was part polar bear, part actor, part pixie – not at all easy to picture in my head as I grew up.

Picture another Christmas Eve fourteen years later. Upstairs, still at the bottom of my cupboard, my polar bear father in the magazine in the Start-Rite shoebox; and with him all our accumulated childhood treasures: the signed programme, a battered champion conker (a sixty-fiver!), six silver ball bearings, four greenish silver threepenny bits (Christmas pudding treasure trove), a Red Devil throat pastille tin with three of my milk teeth cushioned in yellow cotton wool, and my collection of twenty-seven cowrie shells gleaned over many summers from the beach on Samson in the Scilly Isles.

Downstairs, the whole family were gathered in the sitting room: my mother, Douglas, Terry and my two sisters (half-sisters really, but of course no one ever called them that), Aunty Betty, now married, with twin daughters, my cousins, who were truly awful – I promise you. We were decorating the tree, or rather the twins were fighting over every single dingly-dangly glitter ball, every strand of tinsel. I was trying to fix up the Christmas tree lights which, of course, wouldn't work – again – whilst Aunty Betty was doing her best to avert a war by bribing the dreadful cousins away from the tree with a Mars bar each. It took a while, but in the end she got both of them up onto her lap, and soon they were stuffing themselves contentedly with Mars bars. Blessed peace.

This was the very first Christmas we had had the television. Given half a chance we'd have had it on all the time. But, wisely enough I suppose, Douglas had rationed us to just one programme a day over Christmas. He didn't want the Christmas celebrations interfered with by 'that thing in the corner', as he called it. By common consent, we had chosen the Christmas Eve film on the BBC at five o'clock.

Five o'clock was a very long time coming that day, and when at last Douglas got up and turned on the television, it seemed to take for ever to warm up. Then, there it was on the screen: *Great Expectations* by Charles Dickens. The half-mended lights were at once discarded, the decorating abandoned, as we all settled down to watch in rapt anticipation. Maybe you know the moment: Young Pip is making his way through the graveyard at dusk, mist swirling around him, an owl screeching, gravestones rearing out of the gloom, branches like ghoulish fingers whipping at him as he passes, reaching out to snatch him. He moves through the graveyard timorously, tentatively, like a frightened fawn. Every snap of a twig, every barking fox, every *aarking* heron, sends shivers into our very souls.

Suddenly, a face! A hideous face, a monstrous face, looms up from behind a gravestone. Magwitch, the escaped convict, ancient, craggy and crooked. A wild man with wild eyes, blazing eyes, the eyes of a wolf.

The cousins screamed in unison, long and loud, which broke the tension for all of us and made us laugh. All except my mother.

'Oh my God,' she breathed, grasping my arm. 'That's your father! It is. It's him. It's Peter.'

All the years of pretence, the whole long conspiracy of silence, were undone in that one moment. The drama on the television paled into sudden insignificance. The hush in the room was palpable.

Douglas coughed. 'I think I'll fetch some more logs,' he said.

And my two half-sisters went out with him, in solidarity I think. So did Aunt Betty and the twins; and that left my mother, Terry and me alone together.

I could not take my eyes off the screen. After a while I said to Terry, 'He doesn't look much like a pixie to me.'

'Doesn't look much like a polar bear either,' Terry replied. At Magwitch's every appearance I tried to see through his make-up (I just hoped it *was* make-up!) to discover how my father really looked. It was impossible. My polar bear father, my pixie father, had become my convict father.

Until the credits came up at the end my mother never said a word. Then all she said was, 'Well, the potatoes won't peel themselves, and

I've got the Brussels sprouts to do as well.' Christmas was a very subdued affair that year, I can tell you.

They say you can't put a genie back in the bottle. Not true. No one in the family ever spoke of the incident afterwards – except Terry and me, of course. Everyone behaved as if it had never happened. Enough was enough. Terry and I decided it was time to broach the whole forbidden subject with our mother, in private. We waited until the furore of Christmas was over, and caught her alone in the kitchen one evening. We asked her point-blank to tell us about him, our 'first' father, our 'missing' father.

'I don't want to talk about him,' she said. She wouldn't even look at us. 'All I know is that he lives somewhere in Canada now. It was another life. I was another person then. It's not important.' We tried to press her, but that was all she would tell us.

Soon after this I became very busy with my own life, and for some years I thought very little about my convict father, my polar bear father. By the time I was thirty I was married with two sons, and was a teacher trying to become a writer, something I had never dreamt I could be.

Terry had become an actor, something he had always been quite sure he would be. He rang me very late one night in a high state of excitement. 'You'll never guess,' he said. 'He's here! Peter! Our dad. He's here, in England. He's playing in *Henry IV*, *Part II* in Chichester. I've just read a rave review. He's Falstaff. Why don't we go down there and give him the surprise of his life?'

So we did. The next weekend we went down to Chichester together. I took my family with me. I wanted them to be there for this. He was a wonderful Falstaff, big and boomy, rumbustious and raunchy, yet full of pathos. My two boys (ten and eight) kept whispering at me every time he came on. 'Is that him? Is that him?' Afterwards we went round to see him in his dressing room. Terry said I should go in first, and on my own. 'I had my turn a long time ago, if you remember,' he said. 'Best if he sees just one of us to start with, I reckon.'

My heart was in my mouth. I had to take a very deep breath before I knocked on that door. 'Enter.' He sounded still jovial, still Falstaffian. I went in.

He was sitting at his dressing table in his vest and braces, boots and britches, and humming to himself as he rubbed off his make-up. We looked at each other in the mirror. He stopped humming, and swivelled round to face me. For some moments I just stood there looking at him. Then I said, 'Were you a polar bear once, a long time ago in London?'

'Yes.'

'And were you once the convict in *Great Expectations* on the television?'

'Yes.'

'Then I think I'm your son,' I told him.

There was a lot of hugging in his dressing room that night, not enough to make up for all those missing years, maybe. But it was a start.

My mother's dead now, bless her heart, but I still have two fathers. I get on well enough with Douglas; I always have done in a detached sort of way. He's done his best by me, I know that; but in all the years I've known him he's never once mentioned my other father. It doesn't matter now. It's history best left crusted over, I think.

We see my polar bear father – I still think of him as that – every year or so, whenever he's over from Canada. He's well past eighty now, still acting for six months of every year – a real trouper. My children and my grandchildren always call him Grandpa Bear because of his great bushy beard (the same one he grew for Falstaff!), and because they all know the story of their grandfather, I suppose.

Recently I wrote a story about a polar bear. I can't imagine why. He's upstairs now reading it to my smallest granddaughter. I can hear him a-snarling and a-growling just as proper polar bears do. Takes him back, I should think. Takes me back, that's for sure.

The Pride of Perks

From *The Railway Children*

Written by E. NESBIT
Illustrated by CHARLOTTE VOAKE

I first read *The Railway Children* when I was about twelve, and I found myself identifying with the children wholeheartedly. Edith Nesbit's understanding of being a child comes directly from her memories of childhood; she does not reinvent childhood from an adult perspective. However, she puts her children into an adult world full of injustices where, without the prejudices learned in later life, they are able to confront difficulties and overcome them.

In *The Railway Children*, she draws on fond memories from her teens when the family lived in Kent, near the railway line. Father, who mysteriously disappears at the beginning of the story, returns to the family in a magically written scene (its tone is almost mystical). The children are reassured by Mother in the first chapter that 'It'll all come right in the end.' Edith's need to believe in happy endings and perfect families, with Mother and Father both there, gives her stories immense poignancy.

Celebrations of 'birthdays and great occasions such as the christening of the new kittens or the refurnishing of the dolls house' are of great importance to Mother and, one feels, to Edith herself. The story of the Railway Children begins shortly after Peter's birthday – one of his presents is a most beautiful toy steam engine. When it blows up, this seems to be the first sign of their perfect life falling apart. Father is taken away. The children have to 'play at being poor' and move to the country. However, their lack of money does not stop Mother wanting to make Roberta's birthday a very special occasion, with a surprise party and the present of a brooch 'which she thought she would never own'. (I have fond memories of playing Roberta and filming this scene. Lionel Jefferies, the director, wanted to create a dreamlike sequence in which the character floated through the room. I sat on a camera stool attached to the dolly, a camera on wheels, and moved with the camera in front of the lens.)

It is in a conversation with Perks about the brooch that the three children discover the date of his birthday, which of course they are determined to celebrate. In this funny and touching chapter, 'The Pride of Perks', Nesbit is able to point up the peculiarities of the Edwardian class system, about which the children are painfully unaware.

Jenny Agutter

The Pride of Perks

It was breakfast-time. Mother's face was very bright as she poured the milk and ladled out the porridge.

'I've sold another story, Chickies,' she said; 'the one about the King of the Mussels, so there'll be buns for tea. You can go and get them as soon as they're baked. About eleven, isn't it?'

Peter, Phyllis, and Bobbie exchanged glances with each other, six glances in all. Then Bobbie said:

'Mother would you mind if we didn't have the buns for tea tonight, but on the fifteenth? That's next Thursday.'

'I don't mind when you have them, dear,' said Mother, 'but why?'

'Because it's Perks's birthday,' said Bobbie; 'he's thirty-two, and he says he doesn't keep his birthday any more, because he's got other things to keep – not rabbits or secrets – but the kids and the missus.'

'You mean his wife and children,' said Mother.

'Yes,' said Phyllis; 'it's the same thing, isn't it?'

'And we thought we'd make a nice birthday for him. He's been so awfully jolly decent to us, you know, Mother,' said Peter, 'and we agreed that next bun-day we'd ask you if we could.'

'But supposing there hadn't been a bun-day before the fifteenth?' said Mother.

'Oh, then, we meant to ask you to let us anti – antipate it, and go without when the bun-day came.'

'Anticipate,' said Mother. 'I see. Certainly. It would be nice to put his name on the buns with pink sugar, wouldn't it?'

'Perks,' said Peter, 'it's not a pretty name.'

'His other name's Albert,' said Phyllis; 'I asked him once.'

'We might put A.P.,' said Mother; 'I'll show you how when the time comes.'

This was all very well as far as it went. But even fourteen halfpenny buns with A.P. on them in pink sugar do not of themselves make a very grand celebration.

'There are always flowers, of course,' said Bobbie, later, when a really earnest council was being held on the subject in the hay-loft where the broken chaff-cutting machine was, and the row of holes to drop hay through in to the hay-racks over the mangers of the stables below.

'He's got lots of flowers of his own,' said Peter.

'But it's always nice to have them given you,' said Bobbie, 'however many you've got of your own. We can use flowers for trimmings to the birthday. But there must be something to trim besides buns.'

'Let's all be quiet and think,' said Phyllis; 'no one's to speak until it's thought of something.'

So they were all quiet and so very still that a brown rat thought that there was no one in the loft and came out very boldly. When Bobbie sneezed, the rat was quite shocked and hurried away, for he saw that a hay-loft where such things could happen was no place for a respectable middle-aged rat that liked a quiet life.

'Hooray!' cried Peter, suddenly, 'I've got it.' He jumped up and kicked at the loose hay.

'What?' said the others, eagerly.

'Why, Perks is so nice to everybody. There must be lots of people in the village who'd like to help to make him a birthday. Let's go round and ask everybody.'

'Mother said we weren't to ask people for things,' said Bobbie doubtfully.

'For ourselves, she meant, silly, not for other people. I'll ask the old gentleman too. You see if I don't,' said Peter.

'Let's ask Mother first,' said Bobbie.

'Oh, what's the use of bothering Mother about every little thing?' said Peter, 'especially when she's busy. Come on. Let's go down to the village now and begin.'

So they went. The old lady at the Post-office said she didn't see why Perks should have a birthday any more than anyone else.

'No,' said Bobbie. 'I should like everyone to have one. Only we know when his is.'

'Mine's tomorrow,' said the old lady, 'and much notice anyone will take of it. Go along with you.'

So they went.

And some people were kind, and some were crusty. And some would give and some would not. It is rather difficult work asking for things, even for other people, as you have no doubt found if you have ever tried it.

When the children got home and counted up what had been given and what had been promised, they felt that for the first day it was not so bad. Peter wrote down the lists of the things in the little pocket-book where he kept the numbers of his engines. These were the lists:

Given.

A tobacco pipe from the sweet shop.

Half a pound of tea from the grocer's.

A woollen scarf slightly faded from the draper's, which was the
    other side of the grocer's.

A stuffed squirrel from the Doctor.

Promised.

A piece of meat from the butcher.

Six fresh eggs from the woman who lived in the old turnpike
    cottage.

A piece of honeycomb and six bootlaces from the cobbler, and an
    iron shovel from the blacksmith's.

Very early next morning Bobbie got up and woke Phyllis. This had been agreed on between them. They had not told Peter because they thought he would think it silly. But they told him afterwards, when it had turned out all right.

They cut a big bunch of roses, and put it in a basket with the needle-book that Phyllis had made for Bobbie on her birthday, and a very pretty blue necktie of Phyllis's. Then they wrote on a paper: 'For Mrs Ransome, with our best love, because it is her birthday,' and they put the paper in the basket, and 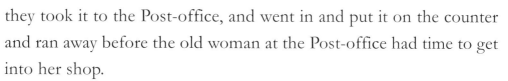 they took it to the Post-office, and went in and put it on the counter and ran away before the old woman at the Post-office had time to get into her shop.

When they got home Peter had grown confidential over helping Mother to get the breakfast and had told her their plans.

'There's no harm in it,' said Mother, 'but it depends *how* you do it. I only hope he won't be offended and think it's *charity*. Poor people are very proud, you know.'

'It isn't because he's poor,' said Phyllis; 'it's because we're fond of him.'

'I'll find some things that Phyllis has outgrown,' said Mother, 'if you're quite sure you can give them to him without his being offended. I should like to do some little thing for him because he's been so kind to you. I can't do much because we're poor ourselves. What are you writing, Bobbie?'

'Nothing particular,' said Bobbie, who had suddenly begun to scribble. 'I'm sure he'd like the things, Mother.'

The morning of the fifteenth was spent very happily in getting the buns and watching Mother make A.P. on them with pink sugar. You know how it's done, of course? You beat up whites of eggs and mix powdered sugar with them, and put in a few drops of cochineal. And then you make a cone of clean white paper with a little hole at the pointed end, and put the pink egg-sugar in at the big end. It runs slowly out at the pointed end, and you write the letters with it just as though it were a great fat pen full of pink sugar-ink.

The buns looked beautiful with A.P. on every one, and, when they were put in a cool oven to set the sugar, the children went up to the village to collect the honey and the shovel and the other promised things.

The old lady at the Post-office was standing on her doorstep. The children said 'Good morning,' politely, as they passed.

'Here, stop a bit,' she said.

So they stopped.

'Those roses,' said she.

'Did you like them?' said Phyllis; 'they were as fresh as fresh. *I* made the needle-book, but it was Bobbie's present.' She skipped joyously as she spoke.

'Here's your basket,' said the Post-office woman. She went in and brought out the basket. It was full of fat, red gooseberries.

'I dare say Perks's children would like them,' said she.

'You *are* an old dear,' said Phyllis, throwing her arms around the old lady's fat waist. 'Perks *will* be pleased.'

'He won't be half so pleased as I was with your needle-book and the tie and the pretty flowers and all,' said the old lady, patting Phyllis's shoulder. 'You're good little souls, that you are. Look here. I've got a

pram round the back in the wood-lodge. It was got for my Emmie's first, that didn't live but six months, and she never had but that one. I'd like Mrs Perks to have it. It 'ud be a help to her with that great boy of hers. Will you take it along?'

'*Oh!*' said all the children together.

When Mrs Ransome had got out the perambulator and taken off the careful papers that covered it, and dusted it all over, she said:

'Well, there it is. I don't know but what I'd have given it to her before if I'd thought of it. Only I didn't quite know if she'd accept it from me. You tell her it was my Emmie's little one's pram—'

'Oh, *isn't* it nice to think there is going to be a real live baby in it again!'

'Yes,' said Mrs Ransome, sighing and then laughing; 'here, I'll give you some peppermint cushions for the little ones, and then you must run along before I give you the roof off my head and the clothes off my back.'

All the things that had been collected for Perks were packed into the perambulator, and at half past three Peter and Bobbie and Phyllis wheeled it down to the little yellow house where the Perkses lived.

The house was very tidy. On the window ledge was a jug of wild flowers, big daisies, and red sorrel, and feathery, flowery grasses.

There was a sound of splashing from the wash-house, and a partly washed boy put his head round the door.

'Mother's a-changing of herself,' he said.

'Down in a minute,' a voice sounded down the narrow, freshly scrubbed stairs.

The children waited. Next moment the stairs creaked and Mrs Perks came down, buttoning her bodice. Her hair was brushed very smooth and tight, and her face shone with soap and water.

'I'm a bit late changing, Miss,' she said to Bobbie, 'owing to me having had a extry clean-up today, along o' Perks happening to name its being his birthday. I don't know what put it into his head to think of such a thing. We keeps the children's birthdays, of course; but him and me – we're too old for such like, as a general rule.'

'We knew it was his birthday,' said Peter, 'and we've got some presents for him outside in the perambulator.'

As the presents were being unpacked, Mrs Perks gasped. When they were all unpacked, she surprised and horrified the children by sitting suddenly down on a wooden chair and bursting into tears.

'Oh, don't!' said everybody; 'oh, please don't!' And Peter added, perhaps a little impatiently: 'What on earth is the matter? You don't mean to say you don't like it?'

Mrs Perks only sobbed. The Perks children, now as shiny-faced as anyone could wish, stood at the wash-house door, and scowled at the intruders. There was a silence, an awkward silence.

'*Don't* you like it?' said Peter, again, while his sisters patted Mrs Perks on the back.

She stopped crying as suddenly as she had begun.

'There, there, don't you mind me. *I'm* all right!' she said. 'Like it? Why, it's a birthday such as Perks never 'ad, not even when 'e was a boy and stayed with his uncle, who was a corn-chandler on his own account. He failed afterwards. Like it? Oh—' and then she went on and said all sorts of things that I won't write down, because I am sure that Peter and Bobbie and Phyllis would not like me to. Their ears got hotter and hotter, and their faces redder and redder, at the kind things Mrs Perks said. They felt they had done nothing to deserve all this praise.

At last Peter said: 'Look here, we're glad you're pleased. But if you go on saying things like that, we must go home. And we did want to stay and see if Mr Perks is pleased, too. But we can't stand this.'

'I won't say another single word,' said Mrs Perks, with a beaming face, 'but that needn't stop me thinking, need it? For if ever—'

'Can we have a plate for the buns?' Bobbie asked abruptly. And then Mrs Perks hastily laid the table for tea, and the buns and the honey and the gooseberries were displayed on plates, and the roses were put in two glass jam jars, and the tea-table looked, as Mrs Perks said, 'fit for a Prince'.

'To think!' she said, 'me getting the place tidy early, and the little 'uns getting the wild flowers and all – when never did I think there'd be anything more for him except the ounce of his pet particular that I got o' Saturday and been saving up for 'im ever since. Bless us! 'e *is* early!'

Perks had indeed unlatched the latch of the little front gate.

'Oh,' whispered Bobbie, 'let's hide in the back kitchen, and *you* tell him about it. But give him the tobacco first, because you got it for him. And when you've told him, we'll all come in and shout, "Many happy returns!"'

It was a very nice plan, but it did not quite come off. To begin with, there was only just time for Peter and Bobbie and Phyllis to rush into the wash-house, pushing the young and open-mouthed Perks children in front of them. There was not time to shut the door, so that, without at all meaning it, they had to listen to what went on in the kitchen. The wash-house was a tight fit for the Perks children and the Three Chimneys children, as well as all the wash-house's proper furniture, including the mangle and the copper.

'Hullo, old woman!' they heard Mr Perks's voice say; 'here's a pretty set-out!'

'It's your birthday tea, Bert,' said Mrs Perks, 'and here's a ounce of your extry particular. I got it o' Saturday along o' your happening to remember it was your birthday today.'

'Good old girl!' said Mr Perks, and there was a sound of a kiss.

'But what's that pram doing here? And what's all these bundles? And where did you get the sweetstuff, and—'

The children did not hear what Mrs Perks replied, because just then Bobbie gave a start, put her hand in her pocket, and all her body grew stiff with horror.

'Oh!' she whispered to the others, 'whatever shall we do? I forgot to put the labels on any of the things! He won't know what's from who. He'll think it's all *us*, and that we're trying to be grand or charitable or something horrid.'

'Hush!' said Peter.

And then they heard the voice of Mr Perks, loud and rather angry.

'I don't care,' he said; 'I won't stand it, and so I tell you straight.'

'But,' said Mrs Perks, 'it's them children you make such a fuss about – the children from the Three Chimneys.'

'I don't care,' said Perks, firmly, 'not if it was a angel from Heaven. We've got on all right all these years and no favours asked. I'm not going to begin these sort of charity goings-on at my time of life, so don't you think it, Nell.'

'Oh, hush!' said poor Mrs Perks; 'Bert, shut your silly tongue, for goodness' sake. The all three of 'em's in the wash-house a-listening to every word you speaks.'

'Then I'll give them something to listen to,' said the angry Perks; 'I've spoke my mind to them afore now, and I'll do it again,' he added, and he took two strides to the wash-house door, and flung it wide open – as wide, that is, as it would go, with the tightly packed children behind it.

'Come out,' said Perks, 'come out and tell me what you mean by it. 'Ave I ever complained to you of being short as you comes this charity lay over me?'

'*Oh!*' said Phyllis, 'I thought you'd be so pleased; I'll never try to be kind to anyone else as long as I live. No, I won't, not never.'

She burst into tears.

'We didn't mean any harm,' said Peter.

'It ain't what you means so much as what you does,' said Perks.

'Oh, *don't!*' cried Bobbie, trying hard to be braver than Phyllis, and to find more words than Peter had done for explaining it. 'We thought you'd love it. We always have things on our birthdays.'

'Oh, yes,' said Perks, 'your own relations; that's different.'

'Oh, no,' Bobbie answered. '*Not* our own relations. All the servants always gave us things at home, and us to them when it was their birthdays. And when it was mine, and Mother gave me the brooch like a buttercup, Mrs Viney gave me two lovely glass pots, and nobody thought she was coming the charity lay over us.'

'If it had been glass pots here,' said Perks, 'I wouldn't ha' said so much. It's there being all this heap and heaps of things I can't stand. No – nor won't neither.'

'But they're not all from us —' said Peter, 'only we forgot to put the labels on. They're from all sorts of people in the village.'

'Who put 'em up to it, I'd like to know?' asked Perks.

'Why, we did,' said Phyllis.

Perks sat down heavily in the elbow-chair and looked at them with what Bobbie afterwards described as withering glances of gloomy despair.

'So you've been round telling the neighbours we can't make both ends meet? Well, now you've disgraced us as deep as you can in the neighbourhood, you can just take the whole bag of tricks back where it came from. Very much obliged, I'm sure. I don't doubt but what you meant it kind, but I'd rather not be acquainted with you any longer if it's all the same to you.' He deliberately turned the chair round so that his back was turned to the children. The legs of the chair grated on the brick floor, and that was the only sound that broke the silence.

Then suddenly Bobbie spoke.

'Look here,' she said, 'this is most awful.'

'That's what I says,' said Perks, not turning round.

'Look here,' said Bobbie, desperately, 'we'll go if you like — and you needn't be friends with us any more if you don't want, but—'

'*We* shall always be friends with *you*, however nasty you are to us,' sniffed Phyllis, wildly.

'Be quiet,' said Peter, in a fierce aside.

'But before we go,' Bobbie went on desperately, 'do let us show you the labels we wrote to put on the things.'

'I don't want to see no labels,' said Perks, 'except proper luggage ones in my own walk of life. Do you think I've kept respectable and outer debt on what I gets, and her having to take in washing, to be give away for a laughing-stock to all the neighbours?'

'Laughing?' said Peter; 'you don't know.'

'You're a very hasty gentleman,' whined Phyllis; 'you know you were wrong once before, about us not telling you the secrets about the Russian. Do let Bobbie tell you about the labels!'

'Well. Go ahead!' said Perks, grudgingly.

'Well, then,' said Bobbie, fumbling miserably, yet not without hope, in her tightly-stuffed pocket, 'we wrote down all the things everybody said when they gave us the things, with the people's names, because Mother said we ought to be careful – because – but I wrote down what she said – and you'll see.'

But Bobbie could not read the labels just at once. She had to swallow once or twice before she could begin.

Mrs Perks had been crying steadily ever since her husband had opened the wash-house door. Now she caught her breath, choked, and said:

'Don't you upset yourself, Missy. *I* know you meant it kind if he doesn't.'

'May I read the labels?' said Bobbie, crying on to the slips as she tried to sort them. 'Mother's first. It says:

'"Little Clothes for Mrs Perks's children." Mother said, "I'll find some of Phyllis's things that she's grown out of if you're quite sure Mr Perks wouldn't be offended and think it's meant for charity. I'd like to do some little thing for him, because he's so kind to you. I can't do much because we're poor ourselves."'

Bobbie paused.

'That's all right,' said Perks, 'your Ma's a born lady. We'll keep the little frocks, and what-not, Nell.'

'Then there's the perambulator and the gooseberries, and the sweets,' said Bobbie, 'they're from Mrs Ransome. She said: "I dare say Mr Perks's children would like the sweets. And the perambulator was got for my Emmie's first – it didn't live but six months, and she's never had but that one. I'd like Mrs Perks to have it. It would be a help with her fine boy. I'd have given it before if I'd been sure she'd accept of it from me." She told me to tell you,' Bobbie added, 'that it was her Emmie's little one's pram.'

'I can't send the pram back, Bert,' said Mrs Perks, firmly, 'and I won't. So don't you ask me—'

'I'm not a-asking anything,' said Perks, gruffly.

'Then the shovel,' said Bobbie. 'Mr James made it for you himself. And he said – where is it? Oh, yes, here! He said, "You tell Mr Perks it's a pleasure to make a little trifle for a man as is so much respected," and then he said he wished he could shoe your children and his own children, like they do the horses, because, well, he knew what shoe leather was.'

'James is a good enough chap,' said Perks.

'Then the honey,' said Bobbie, in haste, 'and the bootlaces. *He* said he respected a man that paid his way – and the butcher said the same. And the old turnpike woman said many was the time you'd lent her a hand with her garden when you were a lad – and things like that came home to roost – I don't know what she meant. And everybody who gave anything said they liked you, and it was a very good idea of ours; and nobody said anything about charity or anything horrid like that.

And the old gentleman gave Peter a gold pound for you, and said you were a man who knew your work. And I thought you'd *love* to know how fond people are of you, and I never was so unhappy in my life. Good-bye. I hope you'll forgive us some day—'

She could say no more, and she turned to go.

'Stop,' said Perks, still with his back to them; 'I take back every word I've said contrary to what you'd wish. Nell, set on the kettle.'

'We'll take the things away if you're unhappy about them,' said Peter; 'but I think everybody'll be most awfully disappointed as well as us.'

'I'm not unhappy about them,' said Perks; 'I don't know,' he added, suddenly wheeling the chair round and showing a very odd-looking screwed-up face, 'I don't know as ever I was better pleased. Not so much with the presents – though they're an A1 collection – but the kind respect of our neighbours. That's worth having, eh, Nell?'

'I think it's all worth having,' said Mrs Perks, 'and you've made a most ridiculous fuss about nothing, Bert, if you ask me.'

'No, I ain't,' said Perks, firmly; 'if a man didn't respect hisself, no one wouldn't do it for him.'

'But everyone respects you,' said Bobbie; 'they all said so.'

'I knew you'd like it when you really understood,' said Phyllis, brightly.

'Humph! You'll stay to tea?' said Mr Perks.

Later on Peter proposed Mr Perks's health. And Mr Perks proposed a toast, also honoured in tea, and the toast was, 'May the garland of friendship be ever green,' which was much more poetical than anyone had expected from him.

* * *

'Jolly good little kids, those,' said Mr Perks to his wife as they went to bed.

'Oh, they're all right, bless their heart,' said his wife; 'it's you that's the aggravatingest old thing that ever was. I was ashamed of you – I tell you—'

'You didn't need to be, old gal. I climbed down handsome soon as I understood it wasn't charity. But charity's what I never did abide, and won't neither.'

All sorts of people were made happy by that birthday party. Mr Perks and Mrs Perks and the little Perkses by all the nice things and by the kind thoughts of their neighbours; the Three Chimneys children by the success, undoubted though unexpectedly delayed, of their plan; and Mrs Ransome every time she saw the fat Perks baby in the perambulator. Mrs Perks made quite a round of visits to thank people for their kind birthday presents, and after each visit felt that she had a better friend than she had thought.

'Yes,' said Perks reflectively, 'it's not so much what you does as what you means; that's what I say. Now if it had been charity.'

'Oh, drat charity,' said Mrs Perks; 'nobody won't offer you charity, Bert, however much you was to want it, I lay. That was just friendliness, that was.'

When the clergyman called on Mrs Perks, she told him all about it. 'It *was* friendliness, wasn't it, Sir?' said she.

'I think,' said the clergyman, 'it was what is sometimes called loving-kindness.'

So you see it was all right in the end. But if one does that sort of thing, one has to be careful to do it in the right way. For, as Mr Perks said, when he had time to think it over, it's not so much what you do, as what you mean.

Fishing

From *In the Blood*

Written by ANDREW MOTION
Illustrated by PATRICK BENSON

The following is an extract from my memoir *In the Blood* – an account of my childhood, written from a child's point of view. In this passage I'm about eight years old, watching my mother catch a salmon in the River Feshie in Scotland. Usually, when my family took fishing holidays in that part of the world, it was a competitively male business (in spite or because of the fact that the women generally caught more fish than the men) – so there was a slightly seditious pleasure in watching her succeed. Why might the extract belong in a birthday book? Because we never paid much attention to birthdays when I was growing up, and looked to moments such as the one described here for the kind of thrill that other children got from cakes and presents. Though having said that, the fish was a kind of present: a present from the world.

Andrew Motion

Fishing

We went on the second day, simple as that, and took Beauty with us. 'She'll be very good,' mum told the ghillie, when he handed her a rod by the outhouse where Kit had seen the deer with no head. 'Can I have one too?' I asked, scanning the floor for bloodstains, then staring at the ghillie's caterpillar eyebrows. 'You, sonny?' he said. 'You're a bit wee for the salmon, but you can have a swing with your mother's rod if she'll let you.' I'd have been disappointed, if his voice hadn't been like hypnosis. Mackay at school had a Scottish accent, but it was nothing compared to this. This was like listening to a completely different language, which I understood even though I couldn't speak it. I told him I'd already been fishing in Ireland. 'Oh, you have, have you?' he murmured. 'Catch anything?' 'Yes,' said mum before I had time to answer. 'Some brownies.' That was two lies in one, and I looked at the ground again, hoping Kit wouldn't say anything. He didn't. He just whistled and put his hands in his pockets. 'Very nice too,' said the ghillie. Then he fiddled a pair of half-moon glasses from his top pocket, and perched them on his nose. They looked as out of place as a moustache on the Mona Lisa, but he needed them to check the fly was tied on properly. Then we were off.

The rod was too long and too heavy, so I soon gave up. When mum took over, she wasn't much good either. Her line kept collapsing in spaghetti-tangles, and every time this happened she gave a shriek, which the ghillie said didn't matter because salmon couldn't hear as well as trout. After five minutes she got into a rhythm – which was fine, except it meant she started to look alone, like dad had done in Ireland. I took the hint, and went to sit under the pine trees with Kit and Beauty, out of the way. The silver light bouncing off the river, and the way she had to stretch to get the line back properly: it all made me think she was about to hurt herself.

'Sorry, darlings,' she said in a half-shout because she couldn't turn round. 'I'm hopeless.' 'No,' said the ghillie softly, as if he was a darling too. 'You're doing fine.' He leaned forward to jiggle the line where it came off the reel, making the fly move a fraction in the water. At exactly that moment, his hands were magic as well as his voice. Just

by making the tiny tweak, he'd got the fly into a salmon's mouth. He must have, because suddenly the line was going wild. First in slow motion, while Kit and I scrambled to our feet, and then in speeded-up time, ripping off the reel as though it wanted to stretch all the way to Fort William. Everything else was going crazy too. The rod bucked in mum's hands, and the ghillie wrapped his arms round her, like dad when he'd been teaching me. Then he squatted down like a games coach at school, telling her to keep the rod hoisted and her line tight. To let the fish run, and eventually to start reeling in – because look, here was the net, and we were going to catch this fellow, it was a good one, a big one, and we'd show the men when they got back, oh yes we would.

My heart had bounced between my teeth and swelled up, so I could hardly breathe. Kit was goggle-eyed beside me, his mouth sagging. 'Come on, mum,' we said, which was also like games at school. 'Come on, mum.' She liked that. She kept giving her gurgling laugh, leaning backwards sometimes and gasping 'Blimey' or 'He weighs a ton.' Her face was red, redder than I'd ever seen it, with cloudy blotches on her cheeks. She wasn't exaggerating. It really was a heavy fish. And only five or six yards out, now. A bar in the water, like silver. Beauty saw it at the same time and growled. 'She's going to jump in,' I thought. 'She's going to ruin everything.' So I leaped forward just as she dipped into her collie-crouch and flung my arms round her neck, pinning her down. 'Good job, Master Andrew,' said the ghillie, which made me feel like Gordon Banks, and he went back to mum. 'Keep him coming,' he told her. 'Keep him coming.' He was almost whispering, and dipped his net into the water without making a ripple. I tried to bury my face in the hair on Beauty's neck, where the bull terrier had bitten her, but she wriggled her head round and licked my face. There was biscuit-smell on her breath. When I turned back to mum again, I'd missed the crucial moment. The ghillie was already springing to his feet, holding the net in mid-air with both hands and showing the whole world what mum had done. 'Well done, madam,' he said, with a funny crack in his voice.

'Thank you, thank you,' mum said in a rush, the rod straight in her hand again, and the line blowing across her face so she had to brush it away. She gave such a huge smile I could see all her teeth, even the one with the lead filling. It made me feel the heat inside her, and her blood tearing round. Then the ghillie laid his net on the bank, fiddled the fly from the salmon's mouth, whisked the priest out of his bag, clonked the fish on the head, and lifted it by the tail so we could see it completely. 'A fresh one,' he said. 'A fresh one and a fine one.' I thought archaeologists must feel like this, when they pulled treasure up from the earth. The salmon was like a buried warrior, suddenly yanked into the light. We gazed in silence at the dented silver on his head and jaw. Then Beauty sneezed, and mum said she'd have to sit down. I stayed looking while the ghillie laid the fish on the grass. I told myself I'd never forget, then went over to mum under the pine trees and hugged her so hard she told me to be careful, she felt creaky after all that hard work.

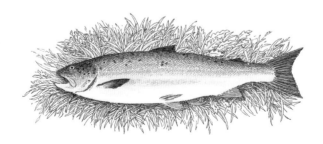

Early Morning

Written by MAURA DOOLEY
Illustrated by HANNAH FIRMIN

There are nights when you can't sleep for excitement and there are mornings when you are bright awake before anyone else in the house, the street, the town. These are special times, like those before birthdays or Christmas or holidays, when we burn with the thought of what's to come but have to wait for the hands of the clock to move slowly, oh so slowly round, or the person in charge to say, *Yes, OK, let's get started.*

I wrote this poem at one of those times. I had crept out of bed and into the garden before anyone else had stirred. Frost was thick on the grass, dawn was breaking and the garden seemed just to be waking up. I had never seen the garden like that before. No one was there and I felt a kind of wild thrill. I felt the day belonged only to me.

Maura Dooley

Early Morning

The garden
rising
from its bed
of frost
is green
as a raw glass
swilled
with faint colour,
crude sparkle.
I run my eyes
around its rim
and hear it ring.

Midwinter's Eve

From *The Dark Is Rising*

Written by SUSAN COOPER
Illustrated by QUENTIN BLAKE

The birthday that Will Stanton is facing, in the first chapter of *The Dark Is Rising*, will change his life completely. He thinks he is an ordinary English boy, the youngest of a large but ordinary family. He hasn't the remotest idea that on his eleventh birthday he will come into his powers as an Old One, one of the immortals destined to save the human race from being consumed by evil. He has no idea that he will be revealed on that day as the Seeker, who must find the Six Signs of the Light in order to help vanquish the powers of the Dark. He doesn't know – but the great lords of the Light and the Dark do, and they're waiting for him. So is a strange, sinister creature known as The Walker.

Certain birthdays are given an extra significance by the culture into which you are born. If Will were your average English child, traditionally he would grow up, and get 'the key of the door' – or at least a bubbly party – when he turned twenty-one. If he were a Jewish boy, his growing up would be marked by a bar mitzvah when he turned thirteen. But Will is neither average nor Jewish nor even human: he's magic. Through all the centuries of human consciousness, some numbers have always been thought magical. Generally they're prime numbers: three, five, seven.

And eleven.

Happy birthday, Will Stanton . . .

Susan Cooper

Midwinter's Eve

'Too many!' James shouted, and slammed the door behind him. 'What?' said Will.

'Too many kids in this family, that's what. Just too *many*.' James stood fuming on the landing like a small angry locomotive, then stumped across to the window-seat and stared out at the garden. Will put aside his book and pulled up his legs to make room. 'I could hear all the yelling,' he said, chin on knees.

'Wasn't anything,' James said. 'Just stupid Barbara again. Bossing. Pick up this, don't touch that. And Mary joining in, twitter twitter twitter. You'd think this house was big enough, but there's always *people*.'

They both looked out of the window. The snow lay thin and apologetic over the world. That wide grey sweep was the lawn, with the straggling trees of the orchard still dark beyond; the white squares were the roofs of the garage, the old barn, the rabbit hutches, the chicken coops. Further back there were only the flat fields of Dawsons' Farm, dimly white-striped. All the broad sky was grey, full of more snow that refused to fall. There was no colour anywhere.

'Four days to Christmas,' Will said. 'I wish it would snow properly.'

'And your birthday tomorrow.'

'Mmm.' He had been going to say that too, but it would have been too much like a reminder. And the gift he most wished for on his birthday was something nobody could give him: it was snow, beautiful, deep, blanketing snow, and it never came. At least this year there was the grey sprinkle, better than nothing.

He said, remembering a duty: 'I haven't fed the rabbits yet. Want to come?'

Booted and muffled, they clumped out through the sprawling kitchen. A full symphony orchestra was swelling out of the radio; their eldest sister Gwen was slicing onions and singing; their mother was bent broad-beamed and red-faced over an oven. 'Rabbits!' she shouted, when she caught sight of them. 'And some more hay from the farm!'

'We're going!' Will shouted back. The radio let out a sudden hideous crackle of static as he passed the table. He jumped. Mrs Stanton shrieked, 'Turn that thing DOWN.'

Outdoors, it was suddenly very quiet. Will dipped out a pail of pellets from the bin in the farm-smelling barn, which was not really a barn at all, but a long, low building with a tiled roof, once a stable. They tramped through the thin snow to the row of heavy wooden hutches, leaving dark foot-marks on the hard frozen ground.

Opening doors to fill the feed-boxes, Will paused, frowning. Normally the rabbits would be huddled sleepily in corners, only the greedy ones coming twitch-nosed forward to eat. Today they seemed restless and uneasy, rustling to and fro, banging against their wooden walls; one or two even leapt back in alarm when he opened their doors. He came to his favourite rabbit, named Chelsea, and reached in as usual to rub him affectionately behind the ears, but the animal scuffled back away from him and cringed into a corner, the pink-rimmed eyes staring up blank and terrified.

'Hey!' Will said, disturbed. 'Hey James, look at that. What's the matter with him? And all of them?'

'They seem all right to me.'

'Well, they don't to me. They're all jumpy. Even Chelsea. Hey, come on, boy—' But it was no good.

'Funny,' James said with mild interest, watching. 'I dare say your hands smell wrong. You must have touched something they don't like. Same as dogs and aniseed, but the other way round.'

'I haven't touched anything. Matter of fact, I'd just washed my hands when I saw you.'

'There you are then,' James said promptly. 'That's the trouble. They've never smelt you clean before. Probably all die of shock.'

'Ha very ha.' Will attacked him, and they scuffled together, grinning, while the empty pail toppled rattling on the hard ground. But when he glanced back as they left, the animals were still moving distractedly, not eating yet, staring after him with those strange frightened wide eyes.

'There might be a fox about again, I suppose,' James said. 'Remind me to tell Mum.' No fox could get at the rabbits, in their sturdy row, but the chickens were more vulnerable; a family of foxes had broken into one of the henhouses the previous winter and carried off six nicely-fattened birds just before marketing-time. Mrs Stanton, who relied on the chicken-money each year to help pay for eleven Christmas presents, had been so furious she had kept watch afterwards in the cold barn two nights running, but the villains had not come back.

Tugging the handcart, a home-made contraption with a bar joining its shafts, he and James made their way down the curve of the overgrown drive and out along the road to Dawsons' Farm. Quickly past the churchyard, its great dark yew trees leaning out over the crumbling wall; more slowly by Rooks' Wood, on the corner of Church Lane. The tall spinney of horse-chestnut trees, raucous with the calling of the rooks and rubbish-roofed with the clutter of their sprawling nests, was one of their familiar places.

'Hark at the rooks! Something's disturbed them.' The harsh irregular chorus was deafening, and when Will looked up at the treetops he saw the sky dark with wheeling birds. They flapped and drifted to and fro; there were no flurries of sudden movement, only this clamorous interweaving throng of rooks.

'An owl?'

'They're not chasing anything. Come on, Will, it'll be getting dark soon.'

'That's why it's so odd for the rooks to be in a fuss. They all ought to be roosting by now.' Will turned his head reluctantly down again, but then jumped and clutched his brother's arm, his eye caught by a movement in the darkening lane that led away from the road where they stood. Church Lane: it ran between Rooks' Wood and the churchyard to the tiny local church, and then on to the River Thames.

'Hey!'

'What's up?'

'There's someone over there. Or there was. Looking at us.'

James sighed. 'So what? Just someone out for a walk.'

'No, he wasn't.' Will screwed up his eyes nervously, peering down the little side road. 'It was a weird-looking man all hunched over, and when he saw me looking he ran off behind a tree. *Scuttled*, like a beetle.'

James heaved at the handcart and set off up the road, making Will run to keep up. 'It's just a tramp, then. I dunno, everyone seems to be going batty today – Barb and the rabbits and the rooks and now you, all yak-twitchetty-yakking. Come on, let's get that hay. I want my tea.'

The handcart bumped through the frozen ruts into Dawsons' yard, the great earthen square enclosed by buildings on three sides, and they smelt the familiar farm-smell. The cowshed must have been mucked out that day; Old George, the toothless cattleman, was piling dung across the yard. He raised a hand to them. Nothing missed Old George; he could see a hawk drop from a mile away. Mr Dawson came out of a barn.

'Ah,' he said. 'Hay for Stantons' Farm?' It was his joke with their mother, because of the rabbits and the hens.

James said, 'Yes, please.'

'It's coming,' Mr Dawson said. Old George had disappeared into the barn. 'Keeping well, then? Tell your mum I'll have ten birds off her tomorrow. And four rabbits. Don't look like that, young Will. If it's not their happy Christmas, it's one for the folks as'll have them.'

He glanced up at the sky, and Will thought a strange look came over his lined brown face. Up against the lowering grey clouds, two black rooks were flapping slowly over the farm in a wide circle.

'The rooks are making an awful din today,' James said. 'Will saw a tramp up by the wood.'

Mr Dawson looked at Will sharply. 'What was he like?'

'Just a little old man. He dodged away.'

'So the Walker is abroad,' the farmer said softly to himself. 'Ah. He would be.'

'Nasty weather for walking,' James said cheerfully. He nodded at the northern sky over the farmhouse roof; the clouds there seemed to be growing darker, massing in ominous grey mounds with a yellowish tinge. The wind was rising too; it stirred their hair, and they could hear a distant rustling from the tops of the trees.

'More snow coming,' said Mr Dawson.

'It's a horrible day,' said Will suddenly, surprised by his own violence; after all, he had wanted snow. But somehow uneasiness was growing in him. 'It's – creepy, somehow.'

'It will be a bad night,' said Mr Dawson.

'There's Old George with the hay,' said James. 'Come on, Will.'

'You go,' the farmer said. 'I want Will to pick up something for your mother from the house.' But he did not move, as James pushed the handcart off towards the barn; he stood with his hands thrust deep into the pockets of his old tweed jacket, looking at the darkening sky.

'The Walker is abroad,' he said again. 'And this night will be bad, and tomorrow will be beyond imagining.' He looked at Will, and Will looked back in growing alarm into the weathered face, the bright dark eyes creased narrow by decades of peering into sun and rain and wind. He had never noticed before how dark Farmer Dawson's eyes were: strange, in their blue-eyed county.

'You have a birthday coming,' the farmer said.

'Mmm,' said Will.

'I have something for you.' He glanced briefly round the yard, and withdrew one hand from his pocket; in it, Will saw what looked like a kind of ornament, made of black metal, a flat circle quartered by two crossed lines. He took it, fingering it curiously. It was about the size of his palm, and quite heavy; roughly forged out of iron, he guessed, though with no sharp points or edges. The iron was cold to his hand.

'What is it?' he said.

'For the moment,' Mr Dawson said, 'just call it something to keep. To keep with you always, all the time. Put it in your pocket, now. And later on, loop your belt through it and wear it like an extra buckle.'

Will slipped the iron circle into his pocket. 'Thank you very much,' he said, rather shakily. Mr Dawson, usually a comforting man, was not improving the day at all.

The farmer looked at him in the same intent, unnerving way, until Will felt the hair rise on the back of his neck; then he gave a twisted half-smile, with no amusement in it but a kind of anxiety. 'Keep it safe, Will. And the less you happen to talk about it, the better. You will need it after the snow comes.' He became brisk. 'Come on, now, Mrs Dawson has a jar of her mincemeat for your mother.'

They moved off towards the farmhouse.

* * *

With the big pot of mincemeat wedged between two bales of hay, Will and James pushed the handcart out of the yard. The farmer stood in his doorway behind them; Will could feel his eyes, watching. He glanced up uneasily at the looming, growing clouds, and half-unwillingly slipped a hand into his pocket to finger the strange iron circle. '*After the snow comes.*' The sky looked as if it were about to fall on them. He thought: *what's happening?*

One of the farm dogs came bounding up, tail waving; then it stopped abruptly a few yards away, looking at them.

'Hey, Racer!' Will called.

The dog's tail went down, and it snarled, showing its teeth.

'James!' said Will.

'He won't hurt you. What's the matter?'

They went on, and turned into the road.

'It's not that. Something's wrong, that's all. Something's awful. Racer, Chelsea – the animals are all scared of me.' He was beginning to be really frightened now.

The noise from the rookery was louder, even though the daylight was beginning to die. They could see the dark birds thronging over the treetops, more agitated than before, flapping and turning to and fro. And Will had been right; there was a stranger in the lane, standing beside the churchyard.

He was a shambling, tattered figure, more like a bundle of old clothes than a man, and at the sight of him the boys slowed their pace and drew instinctively closer to the cart and to one another. He turned his shaggy head to look at them.

Then suddenly, in a dreadful blur of unreality, a hoarse, shrieking flurry was rushing dark down out of the sky, and two huge rooks swooped at the man. He staggered back, shouting, his hands thrust up to protect his face, and the birds flapped their great wings in a black vicious whirl and were gone, swooping up past the boys and into the sky.

Will and James stood frozen, staring, pressed against the bales of hay.

The stranger cowered back against the gate.

'Kaaaaaak . . . kaaaaak . . .' came the head-splitting racket from the frenzied flock over the wood, and then three more whirling black shapes were swooping after the first two, diving wildly at the man and then away. This time he screamed in terror and stumbled out into the road, his arms still wrapped in defence round his head, his face down; and he ran. The boys heard the frightened gasps for breath as he dashed headlong past them, and up the road past the gates of Dawsons' Farm and on towards the village. They saw bushy, greasy grey hair below a dirty old cap; a torn brown overcoat tied with string, and some other garment flapping beneath it; old boots, one with a loose sole that made him kick his leg oddly sideways, half-hopping, as he ran. But they did not see his face.

The high whirling above their heads was dwindling into loops of slow flight, and the rooks began to settle one by one into the trees. They were still talking loudly to one another in a long cawing jumble, but the madness and the violence were not in it now. Dazed, moving his head for the first time, Will felt his cheek brush against something, and putting his hand to his shoulder, he found a long black feather there. He pushed it into his jacket pocket, moving slowly, like someone half-awake.

Together they pushed the loaded cart down the road to the house, and the cawing behind them died to an ominous murmur, like the swollen Thames in spring.

James said at last, 'Rooks don't do that sort of thing. They don't attack people. And they don't come down low when there's not much space. They just don't.'

'No,' Will said. He was still moving in a detached half-dream, not fully aware of anything except a curious vague groping in his mind. In the midst of all the din and the flurry, he had suddenly had a strange feeling stronger than any he had ever known: he had been aware that someone was trying to tell him something, something that had missed him because he could not understand the words. Not words exactly; it had been like a kind of silent shout. But he had not been able to pick up the message, because he had not known how.

'Like not having the radio on the right station,' he said aloud.

'What?' said James, but he wasn't really listening. 'What a thing,' he said. 'I s'pose the tramp must have been trying to catch a rook. And they got wild. He'll be snooping around after the hens and the rabbits, I bet you. Funny he didn't have a gun. Better tell Mum to leave the dogs in the barn tonight.' He chattered amiably on as they reached home and unloaded the hay. Gradually Will realized in amazement that all the shock of the wild, savage attack was running out of James's mind like water, and that in a matter of minutes even the very fact of its happening had gone.

Something had neatly wiped the whole incident from James's memory; something that did not want it reported. Something that knew this would stop Will from reporting it too.

'Here, take Mum's mincemeat,' James said. 'Let's go in before we freeze. The wind's really getting up – good job we hurried back.'

'Yes,' said Will. He felt cold, but it was not from the rising wind. His fingers closed round the iron circle in his pocket and held it tightly. This time, the iron felt warm.

The grey world had slipped into the dark by the time they went back to the kitchen. Outside the window, their father's battered little van stood in a yellow cave of light. The kitchen was even noisier and hotter than before. Gwen was setting the table, patiently steering her way round a trio of bent figures where Mr Stanton was peering at some small, nameless piece of machinery with the twins, Robin and Paul; and with Mary's plump form now guarding it, the radio was blasting out pop music at enormous volume. As Will approached, it erupted again into a high-pitched screech, so that everyone broke off with grimaces and howls.

'Turn that thing OFF!' Mrs Stanton yelled desperately from the sink. But though Mary, pouting, shut off the crackle and the buried music, the noise level changed very little. Somehow it never did when more than half the family was at home. Voices and laughter filled the long stone-floored kitchen as they sat round the scrubbed wooden table; the two Welsh collies, Raq and Ci, lay dozing at the far end of the room beside the fire. Will kept away from them; he could not have borne it if their own dogs had snarled at him. He sat quietly at tea and kept his plate and his mouth full of sausage to avoid having to talk. Not that anyone was likely to miss your talk in the cheerful babble of the Stanton family, especially when you were its youngest member.

Waving at him from the end of the table, his mother called, 'What shall we have for tea tomorrow, Will?'

He said indistinctly, 'Liver and bacon, please.'

James gave a loud groan.

'Shut up,' said Barbara, superior and sixteen. 'It's his birthday, he can choose.'

'But *liver*,' said James.

'Serves you right,' Robin said. 'On your last birthday, if I remember right, we all had to eat that revolting cauliflower cheese.'

'I made it,' said Gwen, 'and it wasn't revolting.'

'No offence,' said Robin mildly. 'I just can't bear cauliflower. Anyway you take my point.'

'I do. I don't know whether James does.'

Robin, large and deep-voiced, was the more muscular of the twins and not to be trifled with. James said hastily, 'Okay, okay.'

'Double-ones tomorrow, Will,' said Mr Stanton from the head of the table. 'We should have some special kind of ceremony. A tribal rite.' He smiled at his youngest son, his round, rather chubby face crinkling in affection.

Mary sniffed. 'On my eleventh birthday, I was beaten and sent to bed.'

'Good heavens,' said her mother, 'fancy you remembering that. And what a way to describe it. In point of fact you got one hard wallop on the bottom, and well-deserved, too, as far as I can recollect.'

'It was my birthday,' Mary said, tossing her pony-tail. 'And I've never forgotten.'

'Give yourself time,' Robin said cheerfully. 'Three years isn't much.'

'And you were a very young eleven,' Mrs Stanton said, chewing reflectively.

'Huh!' said Mary. 'And I suppose Will isn't?'

For a moment everyone looked at Will. He blinked in alarm at the ring of contemplating faces, and scowled down into his plate so that nothing of him was visible except a thick slanting curtain of brown hair. It was most disturbing to be looked at by so many people all at once, or at any rate by more people than one could look at in return. He felt almost as if he were being attacked. And he was suddenly convinced that it could in some way be dangerous to have so many people thinking about him, all at the same time. As if someone unfriendly might *hear* . . .

'Will,' Gwen said at length, 'is rather an old eleven.'

'Ageless, almost,' Robin said. They both sounded solemn and detached, as if they were discussing some far-off stranger.

'Let up, now,' said Paul unexpectedly. He was the quiet twin, and the family genius, perhaps a real one: he played the flute and thought about little else. 'Anyone coming to tea tomorrow, Will?'

'No. Angus Macdonald's gone to Scotland for Christmas, and Mike's staying with his grannie in Southall. I don't mind.'

There was a sudden commotion at the back door, and a blast of cold air; much stamping, and noises of loud shivering. Max stuck his head into the room from the passage; his long hair was wet and white-starred. 'Sorry I'm late, Mum, had to walk from the Common. Wow, you should see it out there – like a blizzard.' He looked at the blank row of faces, and grinned. 'Don't you know it's snowing?'

Forgetting everything for a moment, Will gave a joyful yell and scrambled with James for the door. 'Real snow? Heavy?'

'I'll say,' said Max, scattering drops of water over them as he unwound his scarf. He was the eldest brother, not counting Stephen, who had been in the Navy for years and seldom came home. 'Here.' He opened the door a crack, and the wind whistled through again; outside, Will saw a glittering white fog of fat snowflakes – no trees or bushes visible, nothing but the whirling snow. A chorus of protest came from the kitchen: 'SHUT THAT DOOR!'

'There's your ceremony, Will,' said his father. 'Right on time.'

* * *

Much later, when he went to bed, Will opened the bedroom curtain and pressed his nose against the cold windowpane, and he saw the snow tumbling down even thicker than before. Two or three inches already lay on the sill, and he could almost watch the level rising as the wind drove more against the house. He could hear the wind, too, whining round the roof close above him, and in all the chimneys. Will slept in a slant-roofed attic at the top of the house; he had moved into it only a few months before, when Stephen, whose room it had always been, had gone back to his ship after a leave. Until then Will had always shared a room with James — everyone in the family shared with someone else. 'But my attic ought to be lived in,' his eldest brother had said, knowing how Will loved it.

The snow flurried against the window, with a sound like fingers brushing the pane. Again Will heard the wind moaning in the roof, louder than before; it was rising into a real storm. He thought of the tramp, and wondered where he had taken shelter. '*The Walker is abroad . . . this night will be bad . . .*' He picked up his jacket and took the strange iron ornament from it, running his fingers round the circle, up and down the inner cross that quartered it. The surface of the iron was irregular, but though it showed no sign of having been polished it was completely smooth — smooth in a way that reminded him of a certain place in the rough stone floor of the kitchen, where all the roughness had been worn away by generations of feet turning to come round the corner from the door. It was an odd kind of iron: deep, absolute black, with no shine to it but no spot anywhere of discoloration or rust. And once more now it was cold to the touch; so cold this time that Will was startled to find it numbing his fingertips. Hastily he put it down. Then he pulled his belt out of his trousers, slung untidily as usual over the back of a chair, took the circle, and threaded it through like an extra buckle, as Mr Dawson had told him. The wind sang in the window-frame. Will put the belt back in his trousers and dropped them on the chair.

It was then, without warning, that the fear came.

The first wave caught him as he was crossing the room to his bed. It halted him stock-still in the middle of the room, the howl of the wind outside filling his ears. The snow lashed against the window. Will was suddenly deadly cold, yet tingling all over. He was so frightened that he could not move a finger. In a flash of memory he saw again the lowering sky over the spinney, dark with rooks, the big black birds wheeling and circling overhead. Then that was gone, and he saw only the tramp's terrified face and heard his scream as he ran. For a moment, then, there was only a dreadful darkness in his mind, a sense of looking into a great black pit. Then the high howl of the wind died, and he was released.

He stood shaking, looking wildly round the room. Nothing was wrong. Everything was just as usual. The trouble, he told himself, came from thinking. It would be all right if only he could stop thinking and go to sleep. He pulled off his dressing-gown, climbed into bed, and lay there looking up at the skylight in the slanting roof. It was covered grey with snow.

He switched off the small bedside lamp, and the night swallowed the room. There was no hint of light even when his eyes had grown accustomed to the dark. Time to sleep. Go on, go to sleep. But although he turned on his side, pulled the blankets up to his chin, and lay there relaxed, contemplating the cheerful fact that it would be his birthday when he woke up, nothing happened. It was no good. Something was wrong.

Will tossed uneasily. He had never known a feeling like this before. It was growing worse every minute. As if some huge weight were pushing at his mind, threatening, trying to take him over, turn him into something he didn't want to be. That's it, he thought: make me into someone else. But that's stupid. Who'd want to? And make me into what? Something creaked outside the half-open door, and he jumped. Then it creaked again, and he knew what it was: a certain floorboard that often talked to itself at night, with a sound so familiar that usually he never noticed it at all. In spite of himself, he still lay listening. A different kind of creak came from further away, in the other attic, and he twitched again, jerking so that the blanket rubbed against his chin. You're just jumpy, he said to himself; you're remembering this afternoon, but really there isn't much to remember. He tried to think of the tramp as someone unremarkable, just an ordinary man with a dirty overcoat and worn-out boots; but instead all he could see once more was the vicious diving of the rooks. '*The Walker is abroad . . .*' Another strange crackling noise came, this time above his head in the ceiling, and the wind whined suddenly loud, and Will sat bolt upright in bed and reached in panic for the lamp.

The room was at once a cosy cave of yellow light, and he lay back in shame, feeling stupid. Frightened of the dark, he thought: how awful. Just like a baby. Stephen would never have been frightened of the dark, up here. Look, there's the bookcase and the table, the two chairs and the window seat; look, there are the six little square-riggers of the mobile hanging from the ceiling, and their shadows sailing over there on the wall. Everything's ordinary. Go to sleep.

He switched off the light again, and instantly everything was even worse than before. The fear jumped at him for the third time like a great animal that had been waiting to spring. Will lay terrified, shaking, feeling himself shake, and yet unable to move. He felt he must be going mad. Outside, the wind moaned, paused, rose into a sudden howl, and there was a noise, a muffled scraping thump, against the skylight in the ceiling of his room. And then in a dreadful furious moment, horror seized him like a nightmare made real; there came a wrenching crash, with the howling of the wind suddenly much louder and closer, and a great blast of cold; and the Feeling came hurtling against him with such force of dread that it flung him cowering away.

Will shrieked. He only knew it afterwards; he was far too deep in fear to hear the sound of his own voice. For an appalling pitch-black moment he lay scarcely conscious, lost somewhere out of the world, out in black space. And then there were quick footsteps up the stairs outside his door, and a voice calling in concern, and blessed light warming the room and bringing him back into life again.

It was Paul's voice. 'Will? What is it? Are you all right?'

Slowly Will opened his eyes. He found that he was clenched into the shape of a ball, with his knees drawn up tight against his chin. He saw Paul standing over him, blinking anxiously behind his dark-rimmed spectacles. He nodded, without finding his voice. Then Paul turned his head, and Will followed his looking and saw that the skylight in the roof was hanging open, still swaying with the force of its fall; there was a black square of empty night in the roof, and through it the wind was bringing in a bitter midwinter cold. On the carpet below the skylight lay a heap of snow.

Paul peered at the edge of the skylight frame. 'Catch is broken – I suppose the snow was too heavy for it. Must have been pretty old anyway, the metal's all rusted. I'll get some wire and fix it up till tomorrow. Did it wake you? Lord, what a horrible shock. If I woke up like that, you'd find me somewhere under the bed.'

Will looked at him in speechless gratitude, and managed a watery smile. Every word in Paul's soothing, deep voice brought him closer back to reality. He sat up in bed and pulled back the covers.

'Dad must have some wire with that junk in the other attic,' Paul said. 'But let's get this snow out before it melts. Look, there's more coming in. I bet there aren't many houses where you can watch the snow coming down on the carpet.'

He was right: snowflakes were whirling in through the black space in the ceiling, scattering everywhere. Together they gathered what they could into a misshapen snowball on an old magazine, and Will scuttled downstairs to drop it in the bath. Paul wired the skylight back to its catch.

'There now,' he said briskly, and though he did not look at Will, for an instant they understood one another very well. 'Tell you what, Will, it's freezing up here – why don't you go down to our room and sleep in my bed? And I'll wake you when I come up later – or I might even sleep up here if you can survive Robin's snoring. All right?'

'All right,' Will said huskily. 'Thanks.'

He picked up his discarded clothes – with the belt and its new ornament – and bundled them under his arm, then paused at the door as they went out, and looked back. There was nothing to see, now, except a dark damp patch on the carpet where the heap of snow had been. But he felt colder than the cold air had made him, and the sick, empty feeling of fear still lay in his chest. If there had been nothing wrong beyond being frightened of the dark, he would not for the world have gone down to take refuge in Paul's room. But as things were, he knew he could not stay alone in the room where he belonged. For when they were clearing up that heap of fallen snow, he had seen something that Paul had not. It was impossible, in a howling snow-storm, for anything living to have made that soft unmistakable thud against the glass that he had heard just before the skylight fell. But buried in the heap of snow, he had found the fresh black wing-feather of a rook.

He heard the farmer's voice again: *This night will be bad. And tomorrow will be beyond imagining.*

The Grail Feast

From *Corbenic*

Written by CATHERINE FISHER
Illustrated by PETER BAILEY

I was very pleased to be asked to contribute a piece of writing to this celebration. I chose this excerpt from *Corbenic* because it describes the feast of a king, but this is a banquet with its own significance. I've always been interested in the legend of the Holy Grail, its grandeur and mystery.

Here, a young man, Cal, benighted at a dark building known only as Corbenic, witnesses and denies the procession that passes before him. He can't fit its strangeness into his own drab life. Such things are not possible, he thinks.

And yet the Grail legend insists on the power of the spiritual to burst into the everyday and change it for ever.

Catherine Fisher

The Grail Feast

It was a banquet. A feast. The courses were more elaborate than anything Cal had ever dreamed of, and they kept coming. Fish first, curls and delicately sauced bite-sized pieces of it, and though he disliked fish Cal was amazed at the variety of tastes. Tureens of hot, spicy meats were placed in front of him, and tiny exotic vegetables, and dips and dressings he didn't even know the names of. Between courses there were intricate little nothings of melt-in-the-mouth cheese and seafood and savoury pastries, and a rich pâté dressed with peacock feathers, which he hoped wasn't peacock but might have been. Steamy puddings followed, creamy with honey, and cool confections of chocolate and coffee, and mounds of tangy citrus fruits too small to be oranges. Under his fingers the bread rolls broke open, white and soft, the piled cherries shining in the massed candlelight.

Cal ate everything. He was ravenous, and though he tried to be cool about such abundance the flavours were so amazing that he attacked everything steadily, until his belt felt tight and he was hot and slightly woozy with the pale white wine Bron poured for him.

The dark man spoke little, and ate less. He pushed the small portions round his plate, listening restlessly to the musicians in the gallery somewhere above playing dreamy melodies of flute and harp. Behind him his giant servant stood, arms folded, attentive. Once when Bron coughed and reached for water the big man had it there instantly, his cheery face clouded. Bron sipped it, and sat back. 'Thank you, Leo,' he murmured. He looked pale with fever.

Cal put his spoon down in the empty syllabub dish and Bron almost smiled. 'You enjoyed it.'

'It was fantastic!' He picked up the heavy crystal glass, turning it so the rainbow facets glinted. 'All of it. If you knew what sort of place I live in . . .' He stopped abruptly. Never talk about home. Never. It was one of his rules.

Carefully, as if some moment had come, Bron laid his own fork down and looked out at the crowded tables. 'We all have our hidden pain, Cal. We've all been wounded.'

'Not me,' he said recklessly. 'I've walked away.'

'You're lucky.' Bron gave him a strange glance. 'I could have said that once but not now. I can never walk anywhere again.' His face was drawn, his skin clammy. In that brilliant room the dark clothes he wore seemed out of place, even though they were rich velvets and glinted here and there with discreet emeralds. He leaned forward for a moment and held the table's edge with an indrawn breath that was unmistakably pain. The osprey screeched, pecking at its harness. Cal looked round hasti , but the big man had gone. 'Are you all right? Can I get someone?'

'I am as well as I can be.' Bron tried to pour water but the jug shook in his long frail fingers, so Cal took it and poured. The man sipped, his eyes, a deep green to match the jewels on his coat, closed and hidden. Then he rubbed his forehead with one palm, pushing up his dark hair. 'Cal, listen to me. I wasn't born like this. Do you know how it is to have a wound that will not heal, a torment of pain? To want to die and not be able to? I think you might know something of that, or you would not be here.'

'Not me,' Cal interrupted quickly. He felt embarrassed. He hated illness in any form and the wine was making him feel bold and harsh; he looked away and said, 'Can't the doctors do anything?'

Bron stopped. He seemed tense. He said, in a quieter voice, 'There may be one cure.'

'Then go for it. You've got money. Go private. Money can get you anything.'

'Can it?' The King's green eyes were watching him. 'You believe that?'

'I'd like the chance to find out. Yes, I do. Why not?'

Bron frowned wryly. 'Maybe I thought that once.' He held out a coiled piece of fish; the osprey snatched it greedily. 'I cannot walk, Cal, or ride or hunt, and because of that I amuse myself by fishing. Leo carries me down to the boat, and we row out onto the lake, under the moon. How cool it is there, and the waves lap so calmly. And we fish. All the silver, teeming life of the lake comes into our nets, big and small, good and evil. Many we throw back. Some we bring here, to the Castle. And Leo jokes that one night we might catch a real treasure, a great fish with a ring in its belly as in the old stories.' He glanced at Cal, sidelong. 'Maybe tonight we did.'

Cal drank. The wine was blurring his eyesight; he felt dizzy and awkward. He wasn't sure what all this was getting at. Maybe now he'd eaten he could make some excuse and get to bed.

'Where were you going,' Bron asked quietly, 'on the train?'

'To live with my uncle.'

'For good?'

'Too right.'

'Your mother will miss you.'

'She'll get by.'

'And your father?'

It was against his rules to answer but something made him say, 'My father walked out when I was two.' He shrugged, watching the candles, how they put themselves out, one by one. 'I don't know why I'm telling you this anyway. She doesn't care. Not really. She drinks. Says she hears voices. Now she can get on without me.'

'And will she?'

'I'm past caring.' Grimly, Cal filled his glass and drank again. It was the music that was doing it. The music had turned into a fog; it was winding down from the gallery and was snuffing all the candles out with deft grey fingers. Even the great fire that had roared in the hearth behind them was sinking, clouding over. The clatter of knives and forks, the chatter of the guests was fading under the weight of it, an obscurity in the room, a gathering mist. Someone was turning down the world's volume.

Cal tugged at his collar. 'It's hot in here.'

Bron's fingers were white on the wine glass. 'Cal, I need you to help. You must . . .' He stopped abruptly, then turned and said with sudden desperation, 'This agony runs through all my realm. The kingdom is laid waste. You can heal it. If you went back . . .'

'Back?' In front of Cal three candles winked out; he stared at them in bewilderment. 'Back where?'

'Home.'

He stared at the man in amazement, his narrow, oddly familiar face. Then he stood up. 'No chance!'

Bron swivelled his wheeled chair with his bony hands. He seemed consumed with a secret torment. 'Please. The Grail is coming. Only see it. Look at it. Do what you can to help us.'

And the music stopped. It stopped instantly, like a CD switched off in mid-note. The room was black. All the people had gone. Cal swallowed; for a second he knew he was somewhere lost, a palace nowhere in the world, deep in darkness, and then the doors opened, and a boy came in. He was one of the tall, fair-haired ones from the door, and he carried what looked to be a long rod, upright in both  hands. He walked across the room quickly, without looking at Cal, and Cal stared, stunned at what the wine had done to his eyes. Because this was no rod, but a spear. *And the spear was bleeding.* Slowly, horribly, a great globule of blood welled from its tip; it ran down, trickling stickily over the boy's fingers, down the rough shaft, dripping in dark splashes on the wooden floor.

Cal felt sick. 'This is crazy,' he whispered.

Behind the boy came two more, each carrying a branched golden candlestick, and the candles that burned in them seemed to have such light that it made Cal bring

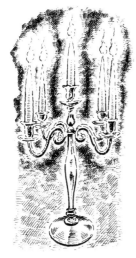

his hands together and clench them on the table. Beside him, he sensed Bron's rigid pain.

The doorway was empty. But something else was coming. Something so inexplicable, so terrible that it made the very air shiver, a sudden breath of icy purity, so that Cal stepped right back without knowing it, shocked into fear. Sweat chilled on his spine, the very darkness in the doorway seeming to crackle and swell as if the room breathed in, all the curtains flapping, the casements gusting open with terrifying cracks. He caught the edge of the table.

She had times like these. She'd see things, she'd scream, clutch her ears. How many times had he phoned the hospital, got a taxi, got her to Casualty. As if her head was bursting with visions, she'd say. Visions and angels. As if they were all in there with her.

A girl came in. She was taller than the boys, and her hair was fair and her dress green. She carried a cup. She carried it carefully, as if it was precious, and he could see how ancient it was, how dented and scarred, and that it was gold, and there were jewels in its rim. For a moment he could see, but it shone, it shone so fiercely it almost burned and quivered in her hands, and he wondered how she could bear it, how he could bear to see it. Because it burned him too, in his eyes until he closed them and then like a heat and glow against his body, and yet none of it was real, none of it existed, he had to remember that.

Bron's fingers were tight on his arm.

There was another room. There had been no door before, but there was now, and the boys with the spear and the candlesticks walked in there, and the girl did too, and as she passed she raised her face from the glory of the Grail and gave Cal one look, quick and rapt. And he was seared with the sudden joy of it, the nameless, unbelievable joy, but the door swung shut and the light was gone and the music was back. As if it had never stopped.

Knives and forks clattered. Glasses tinkled. All the candles glimmered. Cal rubbed his hand weakly down his face. He felt shaky, his whole body was wet with sweat. He collapsed into the chair.

'Cal?'

He turned. Bron was watching him, eyes bright, and behind him the red-bearded man waited, and the osprey stared, hawk-sharp.

'Did you see?'

'See?'

'You must ask me about it, Cal.' Bron's grip was so tight it hurt. 'You must ask me. That's all you need to do. Ask me about what you saw.'

Cal shook him off, shivering. 'Leave me alone. I've got to get out.'

'But you saw! You must have seen.'

Dully, Cal licked his lips, obstinate. He wasn't drunk. He wouldn't be like her. Never. He'd sworn long ago he'd never be like her. *'I didn't see a thing,'* he whispered.

My Birthday

From At the Crossing-Places

Written by KEVIN CROSSLEY-HOLLAND
Illustrated by CHRIS WORMELL

In the year 1200 most people in England were illiterate and few were absolutely sure of the exact date of their birthdays. Arthur de Caldicot's friend, the field-girl Gatty, can only say that her birthday was 'just after the harvest'.

But some people did know they were born on particular saint's days in a particular year of a king's reign. So, Arthur's birthday is on Saint David's Day (1 March) in the thirty-third year of the reign of Henry II.

No one is quite sure how children's birthdays were celebrated in medieval England. But I thought that a supper at which Lord Stephen honours Arthur by exchanging roles with him would show how much trust he is placing in his squire. This matters a great deal to Arthur because it's not long since he discovered the bitter truth about his own parentage. He feels between worlds and rather lost.

The two of them are about to leave the Welsh Marches to join the Fourth Crusade, and Gubert's wobbling birthday jelly, the centrepiece of Arthur's fourteenth-birthday supper, is not only exotic but a taste of the unknown ahead of them.

Kevin Crossley-Holland

My Birthday

Tomorrow, Ash Wednesday, is my birthday.

'The first day of Lent,' said Lord Stephen. 'Very disappointing, Arthur. But we can't change the Church calendar. Ash Wednesday follows Shrove Tuesday, and Shrove Tuesday follows Collop Monday, and they always have done. However! What we're going to do is recognise your birthday eve.'

Shrove Tuesday is a holiday, the first since I came to Holt, and this afternoon many of the people living on the manor gathered in the South Yard.

First Anian and Catrin tied little spurs to two cocks, but I don't really like watching them stab each other's eyes and rip each other to pieces. After that, I wrestled with Anian and threw him although he's two years older than I am. But then Sayer, the kennelman, threw me, and so did Simon – he's stronger than he looks. All the same, I know I'm stronger than I was last year.

'Arthur!' Rowena called out. 'Izzie wants to wrestle with you.'

Everyone laughed, and Izzie blushed.

'I won't,' I said. 'You're both stupid.'

'What about Rahere?' Alan said in a sneering voice. 'You'd like to wrestle with Arthur, wouldn't you?'

'Certainly not!' said Rahere huffily. 'Jesters don't wrestle. And wrestlers don't jest!'

When we met in the hall for supper, Lord Stephen bowed to me. 'Will you sit down, sir?' he said.

Lord Stephen showed me to my place and brought me a little basin of water. He kissed the towel draped over his right forearm, and I washed and dried my hands. Then Lord Stephen served me, and not until I'd eaten the first mouthful of my egg-and-butter pancake was anyone else allowed to start.

After we'd finished our pancakes, and boiled chicken stuffed with garlic and apricots – the last meat and butter we'll eat until after Easter – Lord Stephen rang his little handbell, and Gubert carried in a wobbling, striped jelly. It had fourteen layers, and each one was a different colour.

'Gubert!' exclaimed Lord Stephen, and he smiled and opened his hands.

'Ah!' sighed Rahere. 'The very sight of it . . . turns my insides to jelly.'

'Strained saffron, my lady,' said Gubert.

'Which?' asked Lady Judith.

'The bottom stripe. Then parsley-juice green, and pink rose petals . . . that violet-blue, that's sunflower. Egg-white . . .' Gubert explained each stripe until he'd reached the top layer.

'Poppy,' guessed Rowena.

'I know,' said Izzie. 'Plum-skin.'

'Or blood,' said Lord Stephen.

'Sandalwood red,' said Gubert proudly.

'Imported from Venice,' Lady Judith announced. 'My merchant buys sandalwood and pepper and caraway from Venice.'

'Let Arthur sniff!' Lord Stephen said.

I leaned over the jelly, and the sweet confusion of scents and spices swirled inside my head.

'Arthur's smelly!' Rahere said quite fondly.

'You'll bring home lots of spices from the Holy Land, I hope,' Lady Judith said. 'They cost so much here, when you can get them at all. I've heard the Saracens even serve their meats with sauces of different colours.'

After this, everyone shook hands with me, and wished me a happy birthday.

'Happy as a clam,' Rahere said, and he opened and snapped his mouth several times. 'Well! As happy as you can be with ash on your forehead.'

Then Lord Stephen and Lady Judith stood up. They bid us all a peaceful night and left the hall. Gubert and Anian and Catrin cleared the dishes, and everyone lay down around the fire.

I couldn't sleep, though, and after a while, I came up here to my room, carrying two candles. I began to write this.

I know Lord Stephen and Lady Judith honoured me this evening, but I feel so sad. Holt's not my true home. Neither is Caldicot, and I wish it were. It's where I grew up, and I miss everyone, even Serle. It's weeks and weeks already since I saw Gatty, and I don't even know when I'll see her again.

To serve as a squire: that's like being a false-son. It lasts for a while, but then it comes to an end. And when it does, where will I belong?

Everything Touches

Written by ROGER MCGOUGH
Illustrated by SARA FANELLI

A version of this poem was written in response to a request from the BBC to write a hymn for a *Songs of Praise* programme to be recorded in Liverpool. Willy Russell set the words to music and it was sung by a huge choir of children at Everton's football ground, Goodison Park.

I remember running out onto the hallowed turf, imagining that a boyhood dream had come true, and that I was about to play my first game for the Blues. Of course it was to remain a dream, but when the band struck up and the choir began to sing, the blues vanished.

Roger McGough

287

EVERYTHING TOUCHES

EVERYTHING touches, LIFE interweaves
STARLIGHT and WOODSMOKE, ashes AND LEAVES
BIRDSONG and THUNDER, ACID and RAIN
Everything TOUCHES, UNBROKEN chain

RAINSTORM and RAINBOW, warrior AND PRIEST
stingray AND DOLPHIN, beauty AND beast
Heartbeat and HIGH TIDE, EBB TIDE and flow
The UNIVERSE in a CRYSTAL of SNOW

Snowdrop and DEATHCAP, HANGMAN and CLOWN
WALLS that DIVIDE come TUMBLING down
SEEN through the NIGHT, the glimmer of DAY
LIGHT is BUT DARKNESS WORN away

BLACKNESS and WHITENESS, sunset AND dawn
Those GONE before, THOSE yet to BE BORN
PAST and FUTURE, DISTANCE and TIME
ATOM to ATOM, WATER to WINE

LOOK all around AND WHAT do you see?
Everything TOUCHES, you're TOUCHING ME
LOOK ALL AROUND and what do YOU SEE?
EVERYTHING TOUCHES, YOU'RE touching ME.

SARA FANELLI

The Forest Again

From *Harry Potter and the Deathly Hallows*

Written by J. K. ROWLING
Illustrated by QUENTIN BLAKE

I admit that, at first glance, the following might not seem particularly celebratory, given that it has for its subject my hero walking to what he believes will be certain death. But when Harry takes his last, long walk into the heart of the dark Forest, he is choosing to accept a burden that fell on him when still a tiny child, in spite of the fact that he never sought the role for which he has been cast, never wanted the scar with which he has been marked. As his mentor, Albus Dumbledore, has tried to make clear to Harry, he could have refused to follow the path marked out for him. In spite of the weight of opinion and expectation that singles him out as the 'Chosen One', it is Harry's own will that takes him into the Forest to meet Voldemort, prepared to suffer the fate that he escaped sixteen years before.

The destinies of wizards and princes might seem more certain than those carved out for the rest of us, yet we all have to choose the manner in which we meet life: whether to live up (or down) to the expectations placed upon us; whether to act selfishly, or for the common good; whether to steer the course of our lives ourselves, or to allow ourselves to be buffeted around by chance and circumstance. Birthdays are often moments for reflection, moments when we pause, look around, and take stock of where we are; children gleefully contemplate how far they have come, whereas adults look forwards into the trees, wondering how much further they have to go. This extract from *Harry Potter and the Deathly Hallows* is my favourite part of the seventh book; it might even be my favourite part of the entire series, and in it, Harry demonstrates his truly heroic nature, because he overcomes his own terror to protect the people he loves from death, and the whole of his society from tyranny.

J. K. Rowling

The Forest Again

Finally, the truth. Lying with his face pressed into the dusty carpet of the office where he had once thought he was learning the secrets of victory, Harry understood at last that he was not supposed to survive. His job was to walk calmly into Death's welcoming arms. Along the way, he was to dispose of Voldemort's remaining links to life, so that when at last he flung himself across Voldemort's path, and did not raise a wand to defend himself, the end would be clean, and the job that ought to have been done in Godric's Hollow would be finished: neither would live, neither could survive.

He felt his heart pounding fiercely in his chest. How strange that in his dread of death, it pumped all the harder, valiantly keeping him alive. But it would have to stop, and soon. Its beats were numbered. How many would there be time for, as he rose and walked through the castle for the last time, out into the grounds and into the Forest?

Terror washed over him as he lay on the floor, with that funeral drum pounding inside him. Would it hurt to die? All those times he had thought that it was about to happen and escaped, he had never really thought of the thing itself: his will to live had always been so much stronger than his fear of death. Yet it did not occur to him now to try to escape, to outrun Voldemort. It was over, he knew it, and all that was left was the thing itself: dying.

If he could only have died on that summer's night when he had left number four, Privet Drive for the last time, when the noble phoenix feather wand had saved him! If he could only have died like Hedwig, so quickly he would not have known it had happened! Or if he could have launched himself in front of a wand to save someone he loved . . . he envied even his parents' deaths now. This cold-blooded walk to his own destruction would require a different kind of bravery. He felt his fingers trembling slightly and made an effort to control them, although no one could see him; the portraits on the walls were all empty.

Slowly, very slowly, he sat up, and as he did so he felt more alive, and more aware of his own living body than ever before. Why had he never appreciated what a miracle he was, brain and nerve and bounding heart? It would all be gone . . . or at least, he would be gone from it. His breath came slow and deep, and his mouth and throat were completely dry, but so were his eyes.

Dumbledore's betrayal was almost nothing. Of course there had been a bigger plan; Harry had simply been too foolish to see it, he realised that now. He had never questioned his own assumption that Dumbledore wanted him alive. Now he saw that his lifespan had always been determined by how long it took to eliminate all the Horcruxes. Dumbledore had passed the job of destroying them to him, and obediently he had continued to chip away at the bonds tying not only Voldemort, but himself, to life! How neat, how elegant, not to waste any more lives, but to give the dangerous task to the boy who had already been marked for slaughter, and whose death would not be a calamity, but another blow against Voldemort.

And Dumbledore had known that Harry would not duck out, that he would keep going to the end, even though it was *his* end, because he had taken trouble to get to know him, hadn't he? Dumbledore knew, as Voldemort knew, that Harry would not let anyone else die for him now that he had discovered it was in his power to stop it. The images of Fred, Lupin and Tonks lying dead in the Great Hall forced their way back into his mind's eye, and for a moment he could hardly breathe: Death was impatient . . .

But Dumbledore had overestimated him. He had failed: the snake survived. One Horcrux remained to bind Voldemort to the earth, even after Harry had been killed. True, that would mean an easier job for somebody. He wondered who would do it . . . Ron and Hermione would know what needed to be done, of course . . . that would have been why Dumbledore wanted him to confide in two others . . . so that if he fulfilled his true destiny a little early, they could carry on . . .

Like rain on a cold window, these thoughts pattered against the hard surface of the incontrovertible truth, which was that he must die. *I must die.* It must end.

Ron and Hermione seemed a long way away, in a far-off country; he felt as though he had parted from them long ago. There would be no goodbyes and no explanations, he was determined of that. This was a journey they could not take together, and the attempts they would make to stop him would waste valuable time. He looked down at the battered gold watch he had received on his seventeenth birthday. Nearly half of the hour allotted by Voldemort for his surrender had elapsed.

He stood up. His heart was leaping against his ribs like a frantic bird. Perhaps it knew it had little time left, perhaps it was determined to fulfil a lifetime's beats before the end. He did not look back as he closed the office door.

The castle was empty. He felt ghostly striding through it alone, as if he had already died. The portrait people were still missing from their frames; the whole place was eerily still, as if all its remaining lifeblood were concentrated in the Great Hall, where the dead and the mourners were crammed.

Harry pulled the Invisibility Cloak over himself and descended through the floors, at last walking down the marble staircase into the Entrance Hall. Perhaps some tiny part of him hoped to be sensed, to be seen, to be stopped, but the Cloak was, as ever, impenetrable, perfect, and he reached the front doors easily.

Then Neville nearly walked into him. He was one half of a pair that was carrying a body in from the grounds. Harry glanced down, and felt another dull blow to his stomach: Colin Creevey, though under-age, must have sneaked back just as Malfoy, Crabbe and Goyle had done. He was tiny in death.

'You know what? I can manage him alone, Neville,' said Oliver Wood, and he heaved Colin over his shoulder in a fireman's lift and carried him into the Great Hall.

Neville leaned against the doorframe for a moment and wiped his forehead with the back of his hand. He looked like an old man.

Then he set off down the steps again into the darkness to recover more bodies.

Harry took one glance back at the entrance of the Great Hall. People were moving around, trying to comfort each other, drinking, kneeling beside the dead, but he could not see any of the people he loved, no hint of Hermione, Ron, Ginny or any of the other Weasleys, no Luna. He felt he would have given all the time remaining to him for just one last look at them; but then, would he ever have had the strength to stop looking? It was better like this.

He moved down the steps and out into the darkness. It was nearly four in the morning and the deathly stillness of the grounds felt as though they were holding their breath, waiting to see whether he could do what he must.

Harry moved towards Neville, who was bending over another body.

'Neville.'

'Blimey, Harry, you nearly gave me heart failure!'

Harry had pulled off the Cloak: the idea had come to him out of nowhere, born out of a desire to make absolutely sure.

'Where are you going, alone?' Neville asked suspiciously.

'It's all part of the plan,' said Harry. 'There's something I've got to do. Listen – Neville—'

'Harry!' Neville looked suddenly scared. 'Harry, you're not thinking of handing yourself over?'

'No,' Harry lied easily. ''Course not . . . this is something else. But I might be out of sight for a while. You know Voldemort's snake, Neville? He's got a huge snake . . . calls it Nagini . . .'

'I've heard, yeah . . . what about it?'

'It's got to be killed. Ron and Hermione know that, but just in case they—'

The awfulness of that possibility smothered him for a moment, made it impossible to keep talking. But he pulled himself together again: this was crucial, he must be like Dumbledore, keep a cool head, make sure there were back-ups, others to carry on. Dumbledore had died knowing that three people still knew about the Horcruxes; now Neville would take Harry's place: there would still be three in the secret.

'Just in case they're – busy – and you get the chance—'

'Kill the snake?'

'Kill the snake,' Harry repeated.

'All right, Harry. You're OK, are you?'

'I'm fine. Thanks, Neville.'

But Neville seized his wrist as Harry made to move on.

'We're all going to keep fighting, Harry. You know that?'

'Yeah, I—'

The suffocating feeling extinguished the end of the sentence, he could not go on. Neville did not seem to find it strange. He patted Harry on the shoulder, released him, and walked away to look for more bodies.

Harry swung the Cloak back over himself and walked on. Someone else was moving not far away, stooping over another prone figure on the ground. He was feet away from her when he realised it was Ginny.

He stopped in his tracks. She was crouching over a girl who was whispering for her mother.

'It's all right,' Ginny was saying. 'It's OK. We're going to get you inside.'

'But I want to go *home*,' whispered the girl. 'I don't want to fight any more!'

'I know,' said Ginny, and her voice broke. 'It's going to be all right.'

Ripples of cold undulated over Harry's skin. He wanted to shout out to the night, he wanted Ginny to know that he was there, he wanted her to know where he was going. He wanted to be stopped, to be dragged back, to be sent back home . . .

But he *was* home. Hogwarts was the first and best home he had known. He and Voldemort and Snape, the abandoned boys, had all found home here . . .

Ginny was kneeling beside the injured girl now, holding her hand. With a huge effort, Harry forced himself on. He thought he saw Ginny look round as he passed and wondered whether she had sensed someone walking nearby, but he did not speak, and he did not look back.

Hagrid's hut loomed out of the darkness. There were no lights, no sound of Fang scrabbling at the door, his bark booming in welcome. All those visits to Hagrid, and the gleam of the copper kettle on the fire, and rock cakes and giant grubs, and his great, bearded face, and Ron vomiting slugs, and Hermione helping him save Norbert . . .

He moved on, and now he reached the edge of the Forest, and he stopped.

A swarm of Dementors was gliding amongst the trees; he could feel their chill, and he was not sure he would be able to pass safely through it. He had no strength left for a Patronus. He could no longer control his own trembling. It was not, after all, so easy to die. Every second he breathed, the smell of the grass, the cool air on his face, was so precious: to think that people had years and years, time to waste, so much time it dragged, and he was clinging to each second. At the same time he thought that he would not be able to go on, and knew that he must. The long game was ended, the Snitch had been caught, it was time to leave the air . . .

The Snitch. His nerveless fingers fumbled for a moment with the pouch at his neck and he pulled it out.

I open at the close.

Breathing fast and hard, he stared down at it. Now that he wanted time to move as slowly as possible, it seemed to have sped up, and understanding was coming so fast it seemed to have bypassed thought. This was the close. This was the moment.

He pressed the golden metal to his lips and whispered, 'I am about to die.'

The metal shell broke open. He lowered his shaking hand, raised Draco's wand beneath the Cloak and murmured, '*Lumos.*'

The black stone with its jagged crack running down the centre sat in the two halves of the Snitch. The Resurrection Stone had cracked down the vertical line representing the Elder Wand. The triangle and circle representing the Cloak and the stone were still discernible.

And again, Harry understood, without having to think. It did not matter about bringing them back, for he was about to join them. He was not really fetching them: they were fetching him.

He closed his eyes, and turned the stone over in his hand, three times.

He knew it had happened, because he heard slight movements around him that suggested frail bodies shifting their footing on the earthy, twig-strewn ground that marked the outer edge of the Forest. He opened his eyes and looked around.

They were neither ghost nor truly flesh, he could see that. They resembled most closely the Riddle that had escaped from the diary, so long ago, and he had been memory made nearly solid. Less substantial than living bodies, but much more than ghosts, they moved towards him, and on each face there was the same loving smile.

James was exactly the same height as Harry. He was wearing the clothes in which he had died, and his hair was untidy and ruffled, and his glasses were a little lopsided, like Mr Weasley's.

Sirius was tall and handsome, and younger by far than Harry had seen him in life. He loped with an easy grace, his hands in his pockets and a grin on his face.

Lupin was younger too, and much less shabby, and his hair was thicker and darker. He looked happy to be back in this familiar place, scene of so many adolescent wanderings.

Lily's smile was widest of all. She pushed her long hair back as she drew close to him, and her green eyes, so like his, searched his face hungrily as though she would never be able to look at him enough.

'You've been so brave.'

He could not speak. His eyes feasted on her, and he thought that he would like to stand and look at her forever, and that would be enough.

'You are nearly there,' said James. 'Very close. We are . . . so proud of you.'

'Does it hurt?'

The childish question had fallen from Harry's lips before he could stop it.

'Dying? Not at all,' said Sirius. 'Quicker and easier than falling asleep.'

'And he will want it to be quick. He wants it over,' said Lupin.

'I didn't want you to die,' Harry said. These words came without his volition. 'Any of you. I'm sorry—'

He addressed Lupin more than any of them, beseeching him.

'– right after you'd had your son . . . Remus, I'm sorry—'

'I am sorry too,' said Lupin. 'Sorry I will never know him . . . but he will know why I died and I hope he will understand. I was trying to make a world in which he could live a happier life.'

A chilly breeze that seemed to emanate from the heart of the Forest lifted the hair at Harry's brow. He knew that they would not tell him to go, that it would have to be his decision.

'You'll stay with me?'

'Until the very end,' said James.

'They won't be able to see you?' asked Harry.

'We are part of you,' said Sirius. 'Invisible to anyone else.'

Harry looked at his mother.

'Stay close to me,' he said quietly.

And he set off. The Dementors' chill did not overcome him; he passed through it with his companions, and they acted like Patronuses to him, and together they marched through the old trees that grew closely together, their branches tangled, their roots gnarled and twisted underfoot. Harry clutched the Cloak tightly around him in the darkness, travelling deeper and deeper into the Forest, with no idea where exactly Voldemort was, but sure that he would find him. Beside him, making scarcely a sound, walked James, Sirius, Lupin and Lily, and their presence was his courage, and the reason he was able to keep putting one foot in front of the other.

His body and mind felt oddly disconnected now, his limbs working without conscious instruction, as if he were passenger, not driver, in the body he was about to leave. The dead who walked beside him through the Forest were much more real to him now than the living back at the castle: Ron, Hermione, Ginny and all the others were the ones who felt like ghosts as he stumbled and slipped towards the end of his life, towards Voldemort . . .

A thud and a whisper: some other living creature had stirred close by. Harry stopped under the Cloak, peering around, listening, and his mother and father, Lupin and Sirius stopped too.

'Someone there,' came a rough whisper close at hand. 'He's got an Invisibility Cloak. Could it be—?'

Two figures emerged from behind a nearby tree: their wands flared, and Harry saw Yaxley and Dolohov peering into the darkness, directly at the place Harry, his mother and father and Sirius and Lupin stood. Apparently they could not see anything.

'Definitely heard something,' said Yaxley. 'Animal, d'you reckon?'

'That headcase Hagrid kept a whole bunch of stuff in here,' said Dolohov, glancing over his shoulder.

Yaxley looked down at his watch.

'Time's nearly up. Potter's had his hour. He's not coming.'

'And he was sure he'd come! He won't be happy.'

'Better go back,' said Yaxley. 'Find out what the plan is now.'

He and Dolohov turned and walked deeper into the Forest. Harry followed them, knowing that they would lead him exactly where he wanted to go. He glanced sideways, and his mother smiled at him, and his father nodded encouragement.

They had travelled on mere minutes when Harry saw light ahead, and Yaxley and Dolohov stepped out into a clearing that Harry knew had been the place where the monstrous Aragog had once lived. The remnants of his vast web were there still, but the swarm of descendants he had spawned had been driven out by the Death Eaters, to fight for their cause.

A fire burned in the middle of the clearing, and its flickering light fell over a crowd of completely silent, watchful Death Eaters. Some of them were still masked and hooded, others showed their faces. Two giants sat on the outskirts of the group, casting massive shadows over the scene, their faces cruel, rough-hewn like rock. Harry saw Fenrir, skulking, chewing his long nails; the great, blond Rowle was dabbing at his bleeding lip. He saw Lucius Malfoy, who looked defeated and terrified, and Narcissa, whose eyes were sunken and full of apprehension.

Every eye was fixed upon Voldemort, who stood with his head bowed, and his white hands folded over the Elder Wand in front of him. He might have been praying, or else counting silently in his mind, and Harry, standing still on the edge of the scene, thought absurdly of a child counting in a game of hide-and-seek. Behind his head, still swirling and coiling, the great snake Nagini floated in her glittering, charmed cage, like a monstrous halo.

When Dolohov and Yaxley rejoined the circle, Voldemort looked up.

'No sign of him, my Lord,' said Dolohov.

Voldemort's expression did not change. The red eyes seemed to burn in the firelight. Slowly, he drew the Elder Wand between his long fingers.

'My Lord—'

Bellatrix had spoken: she sat closest to Voldemort, dishevelled, her face a little bloody but otherwise unharmed.

Voldemort raised his hand to silence her, and she did not speak another word, but eyed him in worshipful fascination.

'I thought he would come,' said Voldemort in his high, clear voice, his eyes on the leaping flames. 'I expected him to come.'

Nobody spoke. They seemed as scared as Harry, whose heart was now throwing itself against his ribs as though determined to escape the body he was about to cast aside. His hands were sweating as he pulled off the Invisibility Cloak and stuffed it beneath his robes, with his wand. He did not want to be tempted to fight.

'I was, it seems . . . mistaken,' said Voldemort.

'You weren't.'

Harry said it as loudly as he could, with all the force he could muster: he did not want to sound afraid. The Resurrection Stone slipped from between his numb fingers and out of the corner of his eyes he saw his parents, Sirius and Lupin vanish as he stepped forwards into the firelight. At that moment he felt that nobody mattered but Voldemort. It was just the two of them.

The illusion was gone as soon as it had come. The giants roared as the Death Eaters rose together, and there were many cries, gasps, even laughter. Voldemort had frozen where he stood, but his red eyes had found Harry, and he stared as Harry moved towards him, with nothing but the fire between them.

Then a voice yelled –

'HARRY! NO!'

He turned: Hagrid was bound and trussed, tied to a tree nearby. His massive body shook the branches overhead as he struggled, desperate.

'NO! NO! HARRY, WHAT'RE YEH—?'

'QUIET!' shouted Rowle, and with a flick of his wand Hagrid was silenced.

Bellatrix, who had leapt to her feet, was looking eagerly from Voldemort to Harry, her breast heaving. The only things that moved were the flames and the snake, coiling and uncoiling in the glittering cage behind Voldemort's head.

Harry could feel his wand against his chest, but he made no attempt to draw it. He knew that the snake was too well protected, knew that if he managed to point the wand at Nagini, fifty curses would hit him first. And still, Voldemort and Harry looked at each other, and now Voldemort tilted his head a little to the side, considering the boy standing before him, and a singularly mirthless smile curled the lipless mouth.

'Harry Potter,' he said, very softly. His voice might have been part of the spitting fire. 'The boy who lived.'

None of the Death Eaters moved. They were waiting: everything was waiting. Hagrid was struggling, and Bellatrix was panting, and Harry thought inexplicably of Ginny, and her blazing look, and the feel of her lips on his—

Voldemort had raised his wand. His head was still tilted to one side, like a curious child, wondering what would happen if he proceeded. Harry looked back into the red eyes, and wanted it to happen now, quickly, while he could still stand, before he lost control, before he betrayed fear—

He saw the mouth move and a flash of green light, and everything was gone.

The Secret Sovereign

Written by EOIN COLFER
Illustrated by JOEL STEWART

My books are usually packed with leprechauns, magic, exploding stuff and one-liners, so when I write a short story I like to take a break from the crash-bang and write about little incidents in the real world. Not a leprechaun in sight.

I first had the idea for 'The Secret Sovereign' years ago when I worked as a primary teacher. Almost every week we would have a birthday in the class and it was nice to make the birthday boy or girl feel special in a small way. Usually it was homework off and we would all sing 'Happy Birthday' at home-time. Most children enjoyed the attention, but some didn't, and these were often the kids who were missing a special person on the day, be it a brother, sister, mother or father.

I remember one boy saying that his fifty-two-year-old dad wouldn't be at the party because he was having a trial for Manchester United that day. I realized the boy was trying to show us how important he was to his father, and only the most urgent business could keep Daddy away.

I began to think, what would be the ultimate reason for a parent to miss a birthday, and I came up with a secret spy mission. Surely no one could complain if Dad was a spy and could not make it home for the party. Even the most cynical classmate would have to nod and say 'Fair enough'. And so 'The Secret Sovereign' began to take shape . . .

Eoin Colfer

The Secret Sovereign

Everyone in the whole planet Ireland is afraid of English Ned Bolger. He walks around with his bike and his goat, doing terrible stuff to children. Stuff like giving them mean looks and bad dreams. He'd give you a chase too, if you tease him about his tyres being full of grass.

I always cross over the road if I see him wheeling his old bike and talking to the air. But here I am running home from the church wearing my lovely Communion dress, and bump I'm after smacking into English Ned. The bump is not the bad thing. The bad thing is the smell. Ned's old face is full of creases and the creases are full of mud. He must wash his face in puddles. He's no bike or goat with him today. That means both hands are free.

– Howye, English Ned.

– Hello, Angel.

Ned has a lovely voice when he's not shouting. The way he says hello, and not howye. Like that fellow on Sky News with the brown fingers.

– Are you here for me, Angel?

– I'm not an angel at all, Ned. I'm dressed like this because I'm just after making my Communion. And it's my birthday, two special days in one, so it should be twice as long but it's feeling twice as short.

Ned starts crying then. I dunno why he starts crying after talking to me. I'm not that bad. Maybe he's jealous about my two special days.

– Ah go on, Ned. Don't be crying.

Now I'm getting sad. The poor fella looks like he needs a nice bag of chips. The tears are after making a clean spot on the end of his nose.

– I thought it was time . . .

– Time for what, Ned?

– Time to go . . .

Mammy says English Ned is loopy and never to talk to him. But I can't help feeling sorry for the old chap.

– Are you hungry, Ned?

– Hungry, Angel?

I take the fiver Mammy gave me for my birthday out of my pocket, even though my hand doesn't want me to do it.

– I can give you the price of a bag of chips, if you have four fifty change.

I'm very good at subtraction when it's money.

– I knew you were an angel . . .

– I only look like an angel. That's because of the dress.

– Ah, an angel or maybe a princess.

– Stop it, will you. Sure I'm only an eight-year-old girl. You're just talking dopey. No wonder everyone thinks you're an eej— a bit soft. Now, have you change or not?

English Ned stops crying and gives a big smile. That's nearly worse than the smell, because of his yellow teeth.

– Oh, Mary Leary. You are the only honest person in the world.

– How do you know my name, Ned? Am I famous like you? D'you know the way you're famous for being a crazy old tramp? What am I famous for?

Now Ned is laughing, and his whole face is nearly clean from the tears.

– I know you, and your charming mother, and that boisterous little brother of yours.

– Do you know my dad? Do you know why he went away? Do you know, is he on a secret mission or something?

I ask everyone stuff about my dad. If I ask everyone then someone has to know where he is. I used to think Daddy was lost in the estates, but whenever I ask Mammy about it she has to go outside for a cigarette. This is probably because the whole thing is a secret. My daddy must be a spy.

English Ned wipes a glove across his nose – now he's filthy again. His eyes are gone all clingfilmy too, like he's only after waking up. Or maybe the smell has crept into his eyes and made them water.

– I do know your father, Mary. And he's sorry he couldn't come home for your doubly special day, but he said to give you this present . . .

Ned pulls something out of the middle of an old hanky.

– Give me what?

Then Ned spits on the thing and gives it a rub with the hanky. That's disgusting and I probably wouldn't even take the thing, whatever it is, if Daddy hadn't sent it for me.

– Here.

The thing is a coin. A big round gold one, like you sometimes get made outta chocolate. This one isn't chocolate though. It's gold. The bit I can see through the dirt is anyway.

– See that gentleman there, young Mary?

There's a knight on the sovereign, fighting a dragon.

– Yeah.

– That's Saint George.

English Ned leans down like he's got a huge secret.

– Your father's boss, on the mission.

I knew it! My daddy didn't just run off like Majella Barnes says, he's a secret agent on a mission. Off in English Ned-land killing dragons what are going around flaming innocent haystacks.

– Saint George pays his agents in coin of the realm. George gave your father this sovereign for being so brave. And your father told me to give it to you for your birthday.

He puts the coin into my hand. And I get a big surprise because it's heavy like a bag of sugar. Well, maybe a bag of sugar with seven spoons gone out of it.

– Thanks, Ned.

– Perfectly all right, my dear. Just doing my job.

– Are you a spy too?

But he doesn't answer. Instead he just bends down even lower, so I can smell the old cigarettes in his beard, and says:

– Shhhhh.

Before I can ask him again, English Ned's gone running after a fly that buzzed past his nose.

The coin is so big that I can't hide it in my hand. Your man, the king, keeps looking out through my fingers.

– Howye, King?

He says nothing.

– Ah . . . Hello, Your Majesty.

– Mary, please! says Robinson's voice in my head. Robinson is my doll and best friend. We talk all the time.

Today we have been mostly talking about how I popped her head off her body, so I could take her to the church with me. Robinson was upset about leaving her body behind, but that was the only way to fit her in the bag.

I give my handbag a smack.

– Watch it, you.

– Stop talking to that old coin then. It's only metal, you know.

– It's from my daddy.

Robinson says nothing, because she's sulking. Robinson thinks I like the coin more than her, and now she's having a big whinge.

– Here you are, Robinson.

I put the coin into my handbag.

– Look after that, will you? Because you're the only one I trust to look after it.

– All right then. Give it a wash though later. It smells like English Ned.

I have a little secret smile. Robinson would be disgusted if she knew I had tricked her out of a sulk.

– And, Robinson?

– What?

– This is our secret between two best friends. Don't even tell my mammy. She'd just be crying and smoking fags.

– Right so.

– Good.

I've always wanted a secret. When you've a secret, you can walk around with a big I've-got-a-secret face on you, and everybody'd be dying to know what it is. But I won't tell anyone, not even Holy God in my prayers, because if I do, my secret might disappear.

I walk home through the estates trying not to make the other kids jealous with my gorgeousness. I have a lovely white dress and half a tin of salon-standard mousse in my hair and white shoes that shine like door paint. In my bag I can hear Robinson talking to someone.

I lift the bag up to my ear and listen. Robinson is talking to Saint George. And Saint George is talking back.

I press my ear to the leather. Saint George's voice sounds just like Daddy's.

Afterword

We often give books as birthday presents to our friends – a habit most authors and illustrators would like to encourage, we think! But choosing the right book may not be easy. In this case we have had the rare and wonderful opportunity of actually making a book, a book to celebrate the sixtieth birthday of HRH The Prince of Wales.

Part of the aim of The Prince's Foundation for Children & the Arts has been to bring the enjoyment of stories and poems to as many young children as possible, so we have gathered together the work of some of our very best writers and poets.

Some of them have written a story specially for this book, while others have allowed us to reproduce something that has already been published. Many have also written an introduction to explain why they have made this choice. We are hugely grateful to them all. We also couldn't resist including some extracts from our favourite classic children's books, and thanks are due to those who have introduced them.

All these stories and poems have been specially illustrated for this book by a large and various band of artists who found time to get this work into their busy schedules. Like our authors, all of them gave their services free. So tremendous thanks to each of them.

We'd like to thank Random House Children's Books, the publishers, too, especially Helen Mackenzie Smith, Charlie Sheppard, Sophie Nelson, Andrea MacDonald, Claire Jones, Margaret Hope and Jane Seery for all they have done to make the book possible.

We hope you will enjoy reading it as much as we've loved putting it together.

Michael Morpurgo
Quentin Blake

The Prince's Foundation for **Children & the Arts**

We are hugely grateful to you for owning this book. Please read it, enjoy it – and then make sure that all your friends and family have copies too!

We are equally grateful to everyone who has made this book come to life: first and foremost to the authors and illustrators who have contributed their work; many have been helping us with our work since the charity first began – thank you. Thank you in particular to our wonderful co-editors, Quentin Blake and Michael Morpurgo, without whom none of this could have happened. We would also like to thank Helen Mackenzie Smith, the team at Random House Children's Books and Liz Sich of Children & the Arts' media board, all of whom have worked so hard to make this dream become a reality.

HRH The Prince of Wales created his Foundation for Children & the Arts because thousands of children across the UK have little or no access to the arts. We are now a national children's educational charity that helps children experience the very best of the arts. Through our work, we bring together local and national arts organizations with primary and secondary schools, helping the children who can benefit most.

Thanks to funding and practical support from the Foundation, children are given the opportunity to see at least two professional performances, exhibitions or concerts. Tours and workshops, both at the venue and at their school, further enhance the experience.

We believe that without access to the arts, children may miss out on the enormous benefits that our shared cultural heritage can bring. The arts can play a unique role in the development of a child.

Since Children & the Arts became one of The Prince's Charities in January 2006, we have helped many thousands of children and their teachers. Their feedback is incredibly positive, and probably the best way to sum up the impact we are having is by passing on to you some of the things they have said to us:

'The experiences you have provided through this project cannot be underestimated and will remain with the children for life' – teacher

'This is a day I will always remember because I had so much fun'
– Cara, aged 10

'The sense of awe and wonder experienced by the children was priceless'
– head teacher

'I didn't know that I was good at anything until I did this'
– Frank, aged 9

*'Many of my classes come from homes where classical music is not normally played
and giving them the means to appreciate it has built up an enthusiasm for music
that I would not have believed possible in school'* – teacher

*'They enjoy it because it is something at which they can all achieve.
They have found that they enjoy and are good at things they didn't
even know they could do'* – teacher

We believe in the power of the arts to inspire children. We hope that the words and the pictures collected together in *The Birthday Book* will inspire you – and will inspire you to keep on supporting The Prince's Foundation for Children & the Arts, and its aims. If you want to make a donation directly to the charity, or to find out more about our work, visit www.childrenandarts.org.uk.

And if you visit a museum or an art gallery or a theatre one day in the next few months and there is a group of children and teachers there, and they clearly know the place inside out, why don't you ask them if they have been working with The Prince's Foundation for Children & the Arts . . .

Rebecca Eastmond
Director, The Prince's Foundation for Children & the Arts

Acknowledgements

The publishers thank the contributors listed below
for permission to include the following material:

'ALL RIGHT'
by Anne Fine, from *Crummy Mummy and Me* (Marilyn Malin Books
in association with André Deutsch Ltd, 1988; Puffin Books, 1989), copyright © Anne Fine,
1988; reprinted by permission of David Higham Associates on behalf of the author.
Introduction copyright © Anne Fine, 2008
Illustrations copyright © Mick Manning & Brita Granström, 2008

AUGUST
by Noel Streatfeild, from *Ballet Shoes* (Dent, 1936), copyright © Noel Streatfeild,
1936; text revisions copyright © Noel Streatfeild, 1959; reproduced by kind
permission of the author's Estate and The Orion Publishing Group Ltd
Introduction copyright © Victoria Wood, 2008
Illustration copyright © Alexis Deacon, 2008

THE BIRTHDAY PARTY
by Arthur Ransome, from *Swallows and Amazons* (Jonathan Cape, 1930),
copyright © Arthur Ransome, 1930; reprinted by permission
of the author's Estate.
Introduction copyright © Bear Grylls, 2008
Illustrations copyright © John Lawrence, 2008

BLAME THE MOUSE!
by Malorie Blackman, from *Jack Sweettooth* (Viking, 1995; Young Corgi, 2008),
copyright © Malorie Oneta Blackman, 1995; reprinted by permission of
Random House Children's Books on behalf of the author.
Introduction copyright © Malorie Oneta Blackman, 2008
Illustrations copyright © Emily Gravett, 2008

BOBBY BAILEY'S BROWN BREAD BIRTHDAY
by Eleanor Updale, copyright © Eleanor Updale, 2008
Introduction copyright © Eleanor Updale, 2008
Illustrations copyright © Posy Simmonds, 2008

CHARLIE'S BIRTHDAY
by Roald Dahl, from *Charlie and the Chocolate Factory* (first published in the USA, 1964; published
in Great Britain by George Allen & Unwin, 1967; Puffin, 1973), copyright © Roald Dahl, 1964;
reprinted by permission of David Higham Associates on behalf of the author's Estate.
Introduction copyright © Johnny Depp, 2008
Illustrations copyright © Quentin Blake, 2008

THE GRAIL FEAST
by Catherine Fisher, from *Corbenic* (Red Fox, 2002), copyright © Catherine Fisher, 2002;
reprinted by permission of Random House Children's Books on behalf of the author.
Introduction copyright © Catherine Fisher, 2008
Illustrations copyright © Peter Bailey, 2008

HUMPTY DUMPTY
by Lewis Carroll, from *Through the Looking-Glass*.
Introduction copyright © Kate Mosse, 2008
Illustrations copyright © Nicola Bayley, 2008

IN THE LAND OF THE FLIBBERTIGIBBETS
by John Foster, from *The Poetry Chest* (Oxford University Press, 2007),
copyright © John Foster, 2007; reprinted by permission of the author.
Introduction copyright © John Foster, 2008
Illustrations copyright © Emma Chichester Clark, 2008

A LETTER FROM TIM DIAMOND
by Anthony Horowitz, copyright © Anthony Horowitz, 2008

MIDWINTER'S EVE
by Susan Cooper, from *The Dark Is Rising* (Chatto and Windus, 1973), copyright © Susan Cooper,
1973; reprinted by permission of Random House Children's Books on behalf of the author.
Introduction copyright © Susan Cooper, 2008
Illustrations copyright © Quentin Blake, 2008

MRS FLITTERSNOOP'S BIRTHDAY PRESENT
by Norman Hunter, from *Professor Branestawm's Great Revolution* (The Bodley Head, 1974),
copyright © Norman Hunter, 1974; reprinted by permission of the author's Estate.
Introduction copyright © Charlie Higson, 2008
Illustrations copyright © Bruce Ingman, 2008

MY BIRTHDAY
by Kevin Crossley-Holland, from *At the Crossing-Places* (The Orion Publishing Group Ltd, 2001),
copyright © Kevin Crossley-Holland, 2001; reprinted by permission of The Orion Publishing
Group Ltd on behalf of the author.
Introduction copyright © Kevin Crossley-Holland, 2008
Illustrations copyright © Chris Wormell, 2008

MY FATHER IS A POLAR BEAR
by Michael Morpurgo, from *From Hereabout Hill* (Egmont Books, 2000), copyright © Michael
Morpurgo, 2000; reprinted by permission of Egmont UK Limited on behalf of the author.
Introduction copyright © Michael Morpurgo, 2008
Illustrations copyright © Michael Foreman, 2008